I ♥ Cole!

COLE

a
BACHELORS OF THE RIDGE
novel

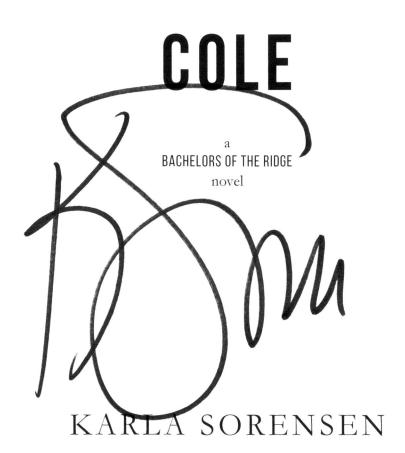

KARLA SORENSEN

COLE

© 2017 by Karla Sorensen

To Whitney,

I almost don't dare dedicate this book to you, because you'll never let me forget that I did something so publicly nice. But... Cole and Julia's history wouldn't be what it is without you. Neither would I.

I want to tell you
about the longing in my bones.
The way it whimpers in the night.
The way it keeps me up,
whispering for you.

There is a reaching
that races
beneath my skin,
when the world quiets,
when the sun is in slumber.

I try to keep up
with the river there.
I try to devour the air that
hasn't touched your skin in years.
I try to ride the current
that doesn't feel like
your current, your touch.

I want to tell you
about the longing
in my veins.

I want to tell you.
Come back to me so that I can tell you.

- JR Rogue

CHAPTER ONE

COLE

I woke up on a choking gasp, hand clutching at the clammy skin over my thundering heart. *I'm sorry, you can't have it back. It's mine, Cole.* Her words rattled through my sleep-sluggish brain while I tried to slow my breathing. The dream always ended that way. Like it was some tease that Julia's voice in my subconscious was the only way I could still hear her. It had been almost seven years since she walked out the door. Five since her lawyer served me divorce papers in an unassuming manila envelope. It was impossible to consider torturing myself with wedding videos or pictures of us that were left on my old cell phone that sat in the bottom drawer of my dresser. But the dream haunted me. Glimpses of her hair over her shoulders, the peek of dimple on her left cheek and the flash of her hazel eyes before she started crying. I didn't have to endure it much, maybe a handful of times a year.

Lately though, the dream had been slamming into my sleep at least three times a week. Because she was here. She was back in Denver. My heart had finally slowed into a normal rhythm when my new, tempting, taunting reality crept into my brain. For the first time in almost a decade, I knew Julia was in the same city as me. Around every corner, I looked for her. At every gas station and every restaurant. For over a month now, my eyes burned from the desire to make her appear. Like from the sheer force of my will, I could give her the power of sublimation. That her body would slide through whatever barrier separated us and she'd be in front of me again.

But she hadn't.

I blew out a hard breath and sat up in bed. Patience was never my strong suit, especially when it came to her. But the years of silence had taught me one thing; that even if I never saw her again, not a single glimpse, I'd love Julia with a wasted heart for the rest of my life.

When my phone let out a harsh vibration on the bedside table next to me, I picked it up quickly. After so many years, I was more than accustomed to the odd hours of being a realtor. So even though the clock still read in the six o'clock hour and the sun was just rising over the Rocky Mountains to the west of my house, I knew my work day had begun.

Three clients had emailed me while I slept, with links of houses that they wanted to check out and a new lead had been sent to me as she'd asked for me by name. Still sitting in bed with my back braced against the cold wooden headboard, I emailed all of them, looking through a few different things. The first couple had a budget that did not match their tastes, large though that budget was. But they weren't from Colorado, so they were in for a shock as far as what the market was doing right now. I sent the wife a few more modest options, gently letting her know that unless they were willing to increase their budget by about fifty to seventy thousand, we weren't likely to find the kind of older craftsman home in Washington Park like they wanted.

I was fortunate. I'd developed a nice niche with upper middle class families that could afford the more expensive homes, all the way up to a few incredibly wealthy clients who'd found me through word of mouth. That's why my latest referral was an oddity for me. Her email into the main office said she was a single mom expecting her first child and she wanted a home in a safe neighborhood with families and a good school district, a fenced-in backyard and at least two full bathrooms. Her budget was modest, but workable.

With narrowed eyes, I ran my thumb over her name, like it was jiggling something in my mind. Brooke Camden. When I couldn't immediately place it, I did a quick initial search and found a large number of homes that might work for her. I emailed her back saying that I'd be thrilled to find her first home for her and her child and asked when we could meet to talk and go over a few things. It could've been handled by email or a phone call, but I liked to put eyeballs on my clients right away. Seeing their faces when they talked about what they needed in a home was one of my favorite parts of the process, outside of handing them the keys once we found it and the closing papers were signed.

Twenty minutes later, I was showered and dressed, tightening the knot on my tie before getting into my car to meet a client at the next house on her never-ending list of options. By the time I pulled into the driveway, I knew it would be another bust. Ashton was adamant about a few things, and neighbors too close to her house was one of them. The brick houses on either side would never fly. But I got out anyway, tapping the code into the lock box on the door while I waited for her to show up.

My knuckles rapped on the granite counters when I heard her car purr into the driveway. Ashton was a few years older than me, divorced as well, although the ink was barely dry on her settlement with her former-NFL player husband. It gave us an, ahem, healthy budget to work with, but she had so many demands on that budget that I was starting to think we'd never find a home for her.

"Cole?" her voice called from the sprawling foyer.

"Take a right past the stairs," I said. "I'm in the kitchen."

"Neighbors are way too close," she told me as soon as she cleared the arched opening to where I was standing.

I smiled politely even though I wanted to laugh. "I thought you might think so. Do you still want to look around? Backyard is great. It's got the mature landscaping you've been wanting."

She flipped her long blonde hair over one shoulder and gave my body a slow, obvious look. Whatever perfume she was wearing hit me with the subtlety of a semi carrying a load of bricks. Inwardly, I sighed. More often than not, my single (and sometimes married) female clients undressed me with their eyes so often that I occasionally questioned whether I'd forgotten to zip my fly.

I cleared my throat and she blinked up to my face with an unrepentant curve of her lips. Lips that were just a tad too puffed up to be natural.

"Sure, why not?" she finally answered, leaning her hands on the kitchen island that separated us, causing the tasteful V of her black dress to gape in a way that was absolutely not accidental. Was I tempted to look?

Hell no.

Most men might think I was lying. Completely full of shit. That an obviously beautiful, if overdone, woman was all but offering me her cleavage with a lit-up road map and I wasn't tempted to drop my eyes past her chin. But I wasn't.

I wished that I was. I wished that I was tempted by someone like Ashton. She was single. She was beautiful. She'd probably kick me out of the house before my pants were zipped up. For some men, I'm sure she seemed perfect.

But her hair was too light. Too obviously fake. Her nose was too small. Her laugh was too loud, too harsh. She was too short. Though considering that I was almost six five, most women were too short for me.

She wasn't Julia. None of them were Julia. So I wasn't tempted. Not once.

When I turned and started talking about the flow between rooms and what they might point out in an inspection, I heard Ashton sigh, but she followed me anyway.

By the time we finished wandering around and heard the final tally of why this house wouldn't work either, I had a headache creeping up the base of my neck. It was moments like the one earlier with Ashton where I felt defective. Like something vital had broken inside of me when Julia divorced me.

Not so much when she left, because I carried almost a sick level of hope that despite her silence, she'd just show up one day and say she was ready to talk again. When she didn't, when the silence stretched out from weeks into months into two years, something cracked and moved. Like when the tectonic plates shifted and triggered the slow rolling of the earth, triggering unimaginable destruction, unfixable changes in the structure of an entire place.

Oddly enough though, it didn't make me feel like less of a man. Not in the way that society might have told me that I was, because only one woman stoked the fire inside of me. It just made me feel empty and aching without her.

Just like she always told me in my dream ... my nightmare, rather.

She had reached into my chest and ripped out my heart. It was hers, and I'd never get it back.

My house was dark when I walked through the garage door into the kitchen that evening. I could have worked here for the last few hours of the day, but sometimes being in the space by myself was too much to bear. Nothing echoed off the walls except the noises that I made. The click of my glass onto the coffee table or when I walked down the hardwood floor to the master bedroom didn't make me feel better, feel less alone. Almost like I walked quietly so as not to make any noise. Reminders that I lived alone were better off ignored.

The first thing I did was change into drawstring pajama pants and a t-shirt so I could drink a beer on the couch comfortably. I'd just sat down with an IPA when my phone buzzed with a text from my friend Garrett. I took a deep breath before looking at it. He and his girlfriend Rory were the reason I knew Julia was back in town. A few weeks earlier Rory had let it slip that she was interviewing Julia for a position at the financial firm that she and Garrett ran together, not knowing that I had any connection to her, let alone that I'd been married to her years earlier.

Making a generalization, I didn't handle it well when I thought they might not hire Julia. Being specific, I lost my damn mind. Last week, maybe a little bit longer, I called and harassed him at work to hire Julia, and for the first time in our six-year long friendship, we'd fought.

Garrett and I hadn't spoken since, and I almost caused the end of his relationship with Rory. It wasn't their fault that hearing Julia's name made me completely unable to stay at the emotional capacity of a normal, sane person. The guilt of what I'd said to Garrett gnawed at me, but I'd avoided him because close behind the guilt was an overwhelming shame at how I'd treated my friend.

I'd never spoken to my friends about what happened between me and Julia. Apologizing to Garrett, something that I knew that I needed to do, felt like I was opening Pandora's Box when it came to Julia. And I still wasn't sure I was ready to do that. A pathetic excuse for why I hadn't done it yet, but it was still true.

But that didn't change the fact that I'd been a capital A Asshole. *Demanding* was a tepid word for how I'd last spoken to him. I'd disrespected him, and worse, I'd disrespected Rory by demanding that Garrett hire Julia without Rory's knowledge, without her consent.

After taking a weighted breath, I swiped open the text.

Garrett: You home?

Me: Yeah, come on over.

Garrett, just like our three other friends, Dylan, Michael and Tristan, lived in the same neighborhood that I did, The Ridge at Alta Vista, so it only took a few minutes to hear a soft knock on the front door. My brows lifted in surprise when he didn't barge in like usual, so I went to open the door. When I was met by Rory instead of Garrett, I let out an extremely intelligent, "Umm, hi?"

Rory was beautiful. Striking and tall, with long blonde hair and unusually blue eyes that missed nothing. Her sharp features were trained on me without so much as a smile on her face. She arched one brow when I didn't move out of the doorway. Then she lifted a six-pack of beer. "I was told to bring these for entrance."

"Right." I backed up a step and motioned for her to come in. This was the first time I'd ever been around just Rory, and I felt a pinch of awkwardness that I wasn't accustomed to. "Sorry, I was expecting Garrett."

Her heels sounded foreign on the floor, a sound I wasn't accustomed to in my home given that Julia had never lived here. After she set the beer down on the counter, she made a sharp turn to face me. "I know. He told me he was coming over and I changed his mind."

I smiled a little, scratching the side of my face. "Wish I could have seen that."

"Well," she said with a tiny smile of her own, "I decided to give you an opportunity to apologize to my face for being an asshole."

Ball-buster. I believe that was the appropriate adjective for Rory in that moment. The woman had no fear on her face and not even the slightest appearance of apprehension at talking to me like that, even though she didn't really know me. Then I laughed, because it was so obvious why she was good for Garrett. Dude needed someone like her to keep him in check.

Rory arched that brow again when I laughed, so I gestured at the family room. "Care to sit?"

She nodded and took a seat in the closest chair to the kitchen, giving me an expectant look while I took one opposite of her. Having her in front of me, perched primly on the black patterned chair made me feel like I was sitting in front of the principal or something. In truth, I think I felt nervous because Rory was my link. My only real link to Julia's unexpected presence in Colorado. She'd sat in the same room as her. Had spoken to her. Heard her voice.

Even though it killed me not to, I didn't ask about Julia. I rubbed my hands along the tops of my thighs before meeting Rory's implacable face. Even though I hadn't been expecting her, the days since my argument with Garrett had given me plenty of time to think about what I would say to him when I got the chance. Rory too.

"Rory, I am sorry for a lot of things. I'm sorry that I made you come here when it was long overdue that I seek you and Garrett out. I'm sorry that I lost my temper on Garrett when it has nothing to do with him, and I'm truly, deeply sorry that I spoke about you in a way that was completely unacceptable. I hope you can forgive me."

Her eyes searched my face, like any kernel of dishonesty would seep through my skin, but she must have been satisfied with what she saw because after a few long moments, she nodded. "Apology accepted."

"Thank you," I said on an exhale. If someone had spoken about Julia the way I had about Rory, I would have gone homicidal. I couldn't help but respect Garrett for knowing she was capable of fighting her own battles.

"Don't do it again though," she warned with slightly narrowed eyes. "I don't care how you much you loved her. Love doesn't give you leave to treat people like shit."

"Love," I corrected gently. At her confused expression, I said it again. "Love. Not *loved*. I still love her."

Rory's face softened, but only a tiny bit. "Okay. Same principle applies. Garrett is your friend, which means you four giant bundles of testosterone are a package deal because I love him. And if you're my friend now too, that means I'll speak to you honestly. I don't know what happened to end your marriage, it's not important that I do."

I nodded, gritting my teeth against the influx of emotions that were packed into words like *what happened to end your marriage.* As if it could be contained into six simple words. Years of heartache and tears and disappointed hopes that continually got jammed into a powder keg with a hair trigger ready for one massive explosion.

Rory gently touched my knee and I looked back up at her, trying to push past the things filtering through my head. "But what *is* important is that you know I respect you enough to be honest with you."

"Thank you," I told her in a gruff voice. Rory was only the third woman that I could consider a friend since Julia left. Garrett's sister Anna was one, and Kat, Dylan's girlfriend, was the other. Rory was an interesting addition, with a clear steel backbone and bracing honesty. But I liked it. I liked her.

When she cleared her throat, I realized that she wasn't finished. "In the vein of honesty, I'll put you out of your misery and tell you that I'm going to offer Julia the job."

My breath left me so quickly and so heavily that I felt a wave of light-headedness. Like my ribs were too big for my skin, fairly bursting at the edges of my body in an attempt to corral my heart. "Thank you."

Apparently, it was the only thing I was capable of saying to her now.

"Garrett didn't want to. Mainly because of your history with her." She held my eyes and dared me to argue. I swallowed everything back, determined not to meet her low expectations of my ability to deal with all things Julia. I couldn't blame her for them. "But I'm ignoring that because she's the best for the job."

I nodded, breathing through the swell of nerves skittering over my skin.

"However," Rory said softly, "I will be telling her that you're Garrett's friend when I offer her the job. I won't let her walk into that kind of situation blindly."

And just like that, I was screwed. Julia all but vanished in front of me, her fingers outstretched in a thin film of smoke that would dissipate the second I tried to touch her.

I pinched the bridge of my nose until my eyes burned. When I dropped my hand, Rory was watching me patiently.

"You're doing the right thing," I told her after another few seconds of silence. Another tiny corner of my heart shriveled up into a thick, dark, viscous thing, just like it always did when I realized just how far away Julia was from me. She could have been sitting right next to me, and she'd be a continent away. Eventually, I'd be like the Grinch, a heart that was three sizes too small in the massive cavity of my chest.

"I know I am." Rory smiled, but it was sad. "I'm sorry, Cole. This can't be easy for you."

When she stood, I did the same. She paused before walking out the door and I gave her the most honest answer I could. "It never gets easier."

CHAPTER TWO

JULIA

Through the bustle of Union Station, I took a deep breath from the mug parked under my nose. French Roast, or anything other than the lightest of roasts loaded down with cream, wasn't my typical choice. But I was tired. Like I could fit four small children into the bags under my eyes because they were so big.

Before I saw her, I heard Aurora (I'd heard her colleagues call her Rory, but I didn't feel like I was at nickname status yet. Potential boss and all) approach by the fast click of her heels on the marble floor. I smiled, because she walked with so much purpose, you'd think she was about to start a war council, not meet little ol' me for coffee.

We'd only met in person once before, when I interviewed for the director of marketing position at Calder Financial Services a couple weeks prior. Our phone calls had always been pleasant, a warmth coming through in her voice that didn't match her uber-collected, icy blonde exterior the first time she shook my hand across the conference room table.

"Sorry I'm late," she said with a hint of a smile, belying the fact that she knew she wasn't actually late but was being polite anyway.

I waved her off. "You're not. *This*," I gestured to the sprawling open area of the main terminal of Union Station, the arched windows and sharp marble floors that I'd already fallen in love with, "wasn't even a thing the last time I was in Denver, so I wanted to check it out before you got here. I can see why you wanted to meet here."

While she shrugged her purse onto the table in between us, she narrowed her eyes in my direction. "I can't remember. How many years were you away?"

Six years, four months and five days. Give or take a handful of hours.

"Half a dozen or so," was the answer I gave instead. Must not look like a psycho in front of the nice woman who would possibly offer me the job I so desperately wanted. I didn't need the job, I could admit that much. My savings were padded quite nicely after the sale of my house in Connecticut three months earlier, but idle hands and me did not mix. What was that saying? They were the devil's playground? Something like that.

I could feel the restlessness trickling into my veins. I needed something to do every day besides wait on my sister Brooke, who was bedridden by doctor's orders.

"Do you want some coffee?" I asked Aurora when I realized she was still watching me with a thoughtful look on her face instead of responding to what I'd said.

She shook her head, crossed one long leg over the other and settled more fully into the dark leather chair across from me. "I'd like to offer you the job at CFS."

A sharp breath pushed out of my lungs, heavy with relief. When I set a hand to my chest, I laughed at Aurora. "Goodness, you had me nervous for a minute. That's wonderful, thank you."

But instead of smiling back, she lifted a finger like, *well, just wait a hot second before you go cashing your first check*. If a finger could say all of that, at least. "We had a couple really good candidates. But you're the best for the job. We want to grow, and I think you'd fit perfectly with the vision that Garrett and I have for the company."

I nodded. I hadn't met Garrett Calder, but I knew he was the CEO. Young, from what I could see on the company's website. Young and handsome, but that was neither here nor there. I'd worked for good looking men back east, and I had no problem slipping on the hot man blinders when I was at the office.

"He's my boyfriend," she said next and I blinked. Okay. Maybe Aurora didn't have those blinders. "Feels ridiculous to use that word over the age of thirty, but anything else sounds silly. He's my significant other, and fortunately we've been able to find a balance of work and our personal life."

"Oh," I replied slowly, trying to figure out why she was telling me as part of my job offer. "Congratulations?"

She laughed under her breath, pulled the end of her sleek blond ponytail over one shoulder, the light color a jarring contrast with the black blazer she wore. "There's a point, I promise."

Quite belatedly, I realized that Aurora's movements betrayed just a hint of nerves. Nerves and offering someone a job didn't usually go together, especially with someone like her; the gorgeous, smart, Amazon woman who looked like she could run with the world with one hand tied behind her back. Okay, I was just as tall as Aurora, I guess it was horribly hypocritical for me to call her Amazon woman when I'd had nicknames like that my entire life.

"You sure you don't want a coffee?" I asked her gently, wanting her to feel at ease. If we were going to work together, her being my boss and all, I wanted to start this relationship off on the right foot. "We've got time."

Then she met my eyes with a startling directness. "The reason I wanted to meet with you to give you the job offer is because there's something I want to tell you before you decide whether you're going to accept it or not."

Decide whether I was going to accept it? I didn't think my tongue would be able to form the words *fast* enough to accept it, but I swallowed the words back and let her finish. Something uncomfortable niggled at my stomach, a tiny worm of doubt that threatened whatever excitement had sprouted there first. When Aurora took a deep breath, the worm grew bigger, the excitement just a little bit smaller.

"I thought you deserved to know that Garrett is good friends with Cole."

Wham. A rock against my temple, an anvil to the gut, maybe even a steel pipe sliding through my heart would have surprised me less. I sat forward, balancing my elbows on my thighs and covering my mouth with both hands, actively using my nose to pull in the slowest breath in the history of breaths. I counted to ten before looking at her again. Then once more. I might have made it to forty before I felt like I could uncover my mouth without puking my coffee up.

"W-what?" I whispered shakily, rubbing at my temple like it would center my racing thoughts. Cole. Oh, *Cole.* How did he always find himself right back into the foundation of my world when I wasn't paying attention? I couldn't say anything other than that, my heart thundering in my chest and my ribs threatening to break under the weight of the galloping rhythm.

Cole.

Cole.

Cole.

I'd shoved him so far down into the darkest corners of my memories, of my heart, because I couldn't bear to pull him any higher. I couldn't for fear that thinking about him too much would send me straight back to the place I'd been when I'd left him. Even moving back here to the city that we'd lived when we were married, I didn't unchain him from the safe place I'd locked him up. Denial, stupid, simple denial that had worked pretty damn well until Aurora said his name.

Somewhere in between my fuzzy, jumbled, stupefied thoughts, I noticed that Aurora had moved into the chair next to me and laid her hand on my back. The small circles that she rubbed between my shoulder blades gradually slowed my breathing from panic-attack levels.

"Here, have some water," she said quietly, handing me an unopened bottle that she fished from her purse. I couldn't refuse, didn't even really particularly want to, so I did as she said, taking a few long sips of the tepid, room temperature water.

"I'm so sorry," I croaked, attempting a smile in her direction, but it probably looked as pained as it felt. "I just ... didn't expect you to say that."

"I know. And maybe I should have had you come into the office. Given us some privacy."

She glanced around, but nothing registered on her face, so maybe no one noticed my little (big) freak-out.

After another round of deep breaths did little to calm the waves of unexpected chaos in my head, I sat back and tilted my chin up to the ceiling. I didn't want to ask Aurora anything, but I didn't think I *couldn't*. So without risking a glance at her, I went ahead and asked, "What did he tell you?"

"Cole?"

I nodded.

"About your relationship?"

I nodded again, belly quivering at what she might say.

"Barely anything. Honestly, I don't know Cole all that well. When I mentioned your name in casual conversation, no clue what I was stepping into, it was only the second time I'd ever met him."

A hysterical laugh bubbled up my throat, but it was preferable to breaking down in spine-cracking sobs, which was the only other alternative. Imagining the look on his face when he heard my name, the shock that must have stamped over his strong, handsome face, I felt the burn press against my vocal chords. An unsteady stuttering of my heart made me look over at Aurora. Her blue eyes held so much sympathy that I wanted to bolt. Wanted to run so fast and so far.

But that was always my problem, wasn't it? I knew Cole would agree to that. That when all that big emotion pressed up against me, I ran from it, ran from the things that I struggled to put a name to, that struggled to swallow me whole. Staying in the same place with him every time we had a pregnancy test come back with a negative instead of a positive, after all the hormones and the acupuncture and the nasty teas, every time he found me curled up in a ball in our bed and sobbing quietly into my pillow so he might not hear me, had taken every shred of my strength for years. Until one day all the shreds were gone. Until they were frayed and fragile and couldn't hold me up anymore.

So I ran.

I ran from a man who loved me with every fiber of his being.

And in that moment with Aurora, I wanted to run again. Instead, I took a slow sip of my lukewarm coffee and pulled a leg up into the chair so I could face her more fully. When I tucked my foot under, the sharp press of the heel served as a strangely grounding sensation.

"I bet that went over well." When Aurora looked confused for a second, I knew I'd been quiet much longer than I realized. "When you said my name," I clarified.

She chuckled, lifting her eyebrows briefly. "Honestly? He kissed me when I explained that I was interviewing you. Garrett hadn't even heard your name before that, so he and the guys were pretty shocked."

Aurora kept talking like she hadn't said Cole kissed her. Like my brain wouldn't throw up some massive iron brakes at the thought. "He ... he kissed you?"

"Yeah. Garrett about ripped his arm out of the socket yanking him off me." Even though the words came out with a slightly annoyed edge, there was a satisfactory smirk on her face that told me she loved it. She glanced at me again. "Look, I won't say anything else if you're not ready to hear about it."

Feeling the chains of the last few years press against my shoulders, I rubbed at a random spot on my forehead. "It's not about being ready. Sometimes I don't think I'd ever be ready to hear about him again."

"Your divorce was that ugly?" she asked quietly.

A hot brick of tears lodged in my stomach, threatening to push its way up my unwilling throat. "I didn't give it the chance to be ugly. If I'd seen him one more time, one single time, I wouldn't have been able to leave him."

With all the people milling around us, completely oblivious to my world imploding, Aurora couldn't possibly know that I'd never admitted that out loud before. Not to Brooke, not anyone. At my disposal, I had a convenient list of reasons why I'd left. Why I'd frozen him out so completely. We'd had years of arguments and tension harbored by disappointed hopes and an unwillingness to see where the other person was coming from. The only other people who could truly understand were other couples who fought the same battle we had for the majority of our marriage. Some had worked it out, others hadn't. If I'd actually spoken to a counselor, or a support group, I'm sure they wouldn't have blamed me for being too exhausted to keep trying. But in the same part of my heart that I'd locked Cole, I knew that he could've convinced me to stay if I'd had the courage to face him again. It wouldn't have been hard for him to, either.

"Well, shit. That's ... really depressing, Julia."

My answering laugh was thick with emotion and I managed a genuine smile. "Agreed."

Aurora clapped her hands together before she stood and made her way back to her chair across from me. "Okay. Moving on. Now that you're not going to lose it in the middle of this very nice building and you know the big thing that I was nervous to tell you, are you going to come and work with me?"

I dropped my head in my hands and laughed. When I looked back up at her, I slicked my hair back from my face and took about two seconds to make my decision. "I can't. I'm sorry."

"To my knowledge, Cole has never randomly stopped by the office," she said. "If that helps."

"Doesn't matter," I told her honestly. "He would if he knew I worked there." Unthinkingly, my hands curled into a fist and I pressed it over my heart. "I can't do it, Aurora."

"Rory," she said with a smile. "My friends call me Rory."

"Are we friends?"

She shrugged one shoulder. "I'd like to be. I don't have many girlfriends, Julia. I don't make that offer lightly."

"So I'd be like, part of a VIP club?"

Her smile was part amused, part self-deprecating. "Sure. If you want to think of it that way. It's more like I've never cared to try before Garrett." She rolled her eyes. "He's social. I'm trying to break from my complete introvert lifestyle, but it's still a work in progress."

The overwhelming desire to ask how long Garrett had been friends with Cole, or where they met, if she knew how he was doing, took me by surprise. Naturally, I sank my teeth into my tongue so that I didn't act on it. Having a friend in Denver besides Brooke would be nice.

"I'd be happy to help then," I said honestly. Rory looked intimidating at first glance, but sometimes I felt like that was a tall girl curse. One that I knew well, even though I didn't have the striking beauty that she did. I was more girl-next-door than model beautiful. "Any chance you'd keep that from Garrett?" I risked asking.

"No," she answered with a smile. "I won't lie to him. But don't worry. He's such a *guy*, he won't think to pass along to Cole if you and I meet for sangria some night."

Rory's easy refusal to keep something from her significant other pricked at me, not in a painful way. It fell somewhere more along the lines of envy. But then again, I'd probably felt like that at one time too. When I was twenty and newly married to a handsome man who made me feel like a queen, who I wanted to love and take care of and grow old with and start a family with ... immediately.

That train of thought would get me nowhere fast, so I blinked out of it while Rory stood to give me a quick hug. "I have to get back to the office."

"Of course." I picked up my purse. "I appreciate you telling me,

Rory. That couldn't have been easy."

"It wasn't," she said. "Selfishly, I wanted to keep that from you until the ink was dry on your employment contract, but then the angel on my shoulder slapped the hell out of me."

I laughed and shook my head. "I'm glad it did."

Rory eyed me for a second. "Can I be honest?"

"Of course."

"Obviously, I don't know you very well, but it seems to me that your past will keep messing up your present unless you face it head on." She smiled gently and slipped her messenger bag over her shoulder before I could react to what she'd said. "If you change your mind about the job, let me know."

I smiled at her and she walked away, but I felt frozen in my seat. Facing my past head-on felt like sitting on a roller coaster with no option for a seat belt. Insane, terrifying, unthinkable. Unthinkable because of how wide the chasm was, how deep the emotional wounds were.

Eventually, I stood from my chair and wandered through downtown Denver, not stopping in any shops or even seeing what was in the windows. By the time I made it back to my car, the sun was starting to fall behind the mountains, the vivid orange and pink clinging to the tips of the jagged peaks.

There was so much rolling through my head, the things Rory had told me and the fact that I just turned down a job that I'd been genuinely excited about, thoughts of Cole that I hadn't entertained in so long that I couldn't even turn the key and start the car. Maybe that should have concerned me, but the only thing it did was make me sad.

If I thought I was capable of sitting down with Cole and facing our past, the way Rory said, like it was the most obvious thing in the world, I would have done it. Just the thought made my chest seize, my stomach bottom out. The worst possible version of myself was what waited for me if that situation ever happened. The part of me that was weak and selfish, that ran away from a man who loved me, who I had loved completely. That's what waited for me in revisiting my past. The Julia that I hated, that I actively ignored.

My brain and heart were so full of emotions, things that I couldn't even define, that I realized why it all felt so different.

I'd spent six years, four months and a handful of days emptying those emotions out for my sanity. Feeding the weakest parts of me by shoving them all away. And apparently, the other parts of me, the parts that still had the invisible string connecting me to my old life, to Cole, weren't having it anymore.

Awesome.

With a deep, cleansing breath, I started my car and drove back to my sister's apartment.

CHAPTER THREE

JULIA

"Honey, I'm home," I called out when I shoved through the heavy metal door of Brooke's one bedroom apartment. Since it was all of eight hundred square feet, I could hear her snicker from where she was propped up on her bed. My drive from downtown back out into the suburbs outside of Denver gave me plenty of time to stem the tide of crazy that Rory unknowingly triggered.

Which was a good thing, because by the time I dropped my purse onto the floor and turned the corner into Brooke's bedroom, I needed to be steady. After so many years of never feeling the roll of a child in my belly, I'd perfected *steady* every time I saw someone rub slow circles over their own. And seeing my little sister do it? Especially since she hadn't meant to get pregnant meant that steady was necessary.

I loved Brooke. I'd step in front of a moving car for Brooke. But I couldn't stop the dull ache in my heart when I saw her experiencing something that Cole and I would have given anything to go through. Especially considering that my complete and utter inability to let go of that dream was the catalyst for me leaving.

Brooke smiled at me from her new prison, as she called it, considering she'd been placed on bed rest two weeks earlier than her doctor expected to avoid going into preterm labor with the twins that currently fought for space in her formerly thin torso. "So? Did you get the job?"

Explaining what had taken place with Rory sounded about as fun as an appendectomy without anesthesia. Especially because Brooke had always been Team Cole. She'd taken the reins as Queen of all things guilt-trip after I left him and then our subsequent divorce. If I told her about Rory's little nugget of information, she'd break her bed rest mandate and drive me over to CFS to sign the paperwork before the day's end. More than that, she'd probably start combing the streets of the greater Denver area in hopes of a Cole sighting.

"No," I told her with a smile that hopefully looked disappointed. "It wasn't a good fit, I guess."

"Whores. Should we egg their cars?"

I laughed while I sat on the edge of her bed and reached out to tweak the end of her dark hair. "Probably not."

Brooke dropped her head back onto her pillow. "Damn. That would have been something fun for me to look forward to."

"You're not supposed to get out of bed. How exactly would you be able to egg someone's car?"

Her smile was easy and it helped chase away some of the dark circles under her eyes. "I'd manage the project. You could push me around in a wheelchair and I'd hand over the perfect eggs."

The big sister in me wanted to smooth over those dark circles with my thumb, try to see if I could erase them. Of course, it wasn't that simple. So instead, I laid my hand over her swollen belly and felt for some gently rolling body parts. When an elbow or foot pressed back against my hand, I smiled. "How are my favorite niece and nephew?"

"Rude. They keep shoving down on my bladder."

"What little jerks. Almost like they have nowhere else to go, huh?"

Brooke grunted and shifted onto her hip. "How am I going to survive the next twelve weeks in this freaking bed? I think I'll die of boredom before I give birth."

"Good thing you're not being dramatic about it all. It's only twelve weeks if you make it to forty."

She narrowed her eyes over the rim of her hot pink water jug. Then she set it back down on her bedside table. "You know, if you hadn't just uprooted your entire life in order to help me because my ex is a giant douchebag with no balls *or* sense of responsibility, I'd really give you shit for that comment."

I stood with a laugh. "Glad I'm safe for the moment. What'd you do while I was gone?"

Her arms spread out in a magnanimous gesture. "Why, I made sure that this bed stayed in one spot by weighing it down with my giant ass."

Before leaving the room, I gave the top of her head a patronizing pat that I knew she'd hate. "Well done. Did your realtor get back to you with some options?"

Brooke hummed in agreement. "Sure did. He sent me four places I'm really excited about. I was just about to email him that you'd be meeting him in my place."

"Good. Because taking those babies home to this place would be a wee bit cramped."

We both looked around and started laughing. Brooke had shared the small apartment with her ball-less, devoid of responsibility ex-boyfriend for the last two years of their unfortunately long relationship, and for *them* it had been too small. Now that I was bunked on the couch in the space that might be referred to as a family room, if it wasn't so tiny, and two little babies with an arrival date only a couple months out, she needed a house like yesterday. Focusing on that was good for me. Taking care of my sister when she needed me, needed family was my priority, not worrying about someone who wasn't part of my life anymore.

It was probably for the best that the job at CFS hadn't worked out anyway. Sure, it was perfect for me and I'd loved the idea of working with Rory, but my move back to Denver wasn't just about me. The last thing I needed was to be gone forty plus hours a week right now. Yes, I'd been getting bored the last couple weeks, but once we found a house for her, that would change. Packing and moving, prepping a house for the babies would keep me nice and busy. Brooke's cell phone beeped with a FaceTime request and we both groaned.

"Why did we show Mom how to use that again?" she asked from behind her hands.

With my eyes closed from the impending exhaustion I was about to feel, I shook my head. "No freaking idea. We have to tell her that there's a data limit or something. Maybe they'll stop."

Brooke accepted the call and we pasted matching smiles on our faces and looked into the screen. My mom's forehead was centered in the screen, waaaaay closer than it needed to be. So all we could see was her silvery hairline, wrinkle-free forehead and her eyebrows.

"Mom," Brooke said, "pull the phone back a little bit. We can't see your face."

She did. "Well, I'm just trying to get a good look at you two. You look haggard, Brooke. Didn't you shower today?"

"Nope. I'm making Julia give me sponge baths now. She loves it."

I rolled my eyes. "Hi, Mom. You guys having fun, fun, fun in Italy?"

"It's so cold. Holy Mother of Mary, I told your father we should have come in the spring again, but he insisted."

If we weren't looking directly into a camera where she could judge our every move, Brooke and I would have shared a look. A *so why are you spending four months there* kind of look. As much as it bugged me that they hadn't changed their plans to help with Brooke, it was nice to not have them breathing down our necks all the time. Overbearing expectations and passive aggressive guilt trips were created and perfected by Catalina and Marcus Rossi.

"So why are you spending four months there?" Brooke asked flatly.

I smothered my laugh by turning it into a cough.

Mom arched a perfectly shaped eyebrow. "Because we always come to Italy for four months a year. It wouldn't do if we stopped the tradition now."

The fact that my sister and I hadn't stayed in the quasi-Italian, quasi-WASPy mold that we'd been brought up in never failed to bug the hell out of our parents. Given that I was thirty-four, divorced and childless was a massive blight on their record. Brooke might have been pregnant, which brought no end of joy to my dad, but she hadn't been married and would now be a single mother.

Our dad's face popped over Mom's shoulder and he looked over both of us with pursed lips.

"Hi, Dad," we said in unison.

"How are the babies?" he asked before we even finished.

"Still camping out comfortably in my uterus, thank you for asking."

"You sure it's a boy and girl?" He squinted down at the bottom of the camera like he'd be able to see them. "You sure the ultrasound wasn't wrong?"

I shook my head and rubbed a hand up Brooke's back.

"No, Dad," she responded with a blithe smile. "Still just one boy, one girl. Sorry to disappoint you."

His answering grunt had me looking away from the camera, fighting a roll of nausea.

How can you let their ridiculous demands weigh on you so much, Julia? They don't own you, they don't own our relationship. We can have a family any damn way we want to.

Cole's voice whispered through my head, triggered by that underwhelmed grunt from my father. I'd heard it so many times. Every time another calendar year flipped over without me adding to the family tree. Everything that I'd managed to hold at bay since I walked back into the apartment crashed over me again. Brooke's jokes and light-hearted abilities weren't a match for my parents' steadfast disappointment at my inability to conceive, at the press of Cole's memory pushing at the limits of my heart. The thick walls of skin around that life-giving organ had held him just fine until a couple hours ago.

Now they felt thin and unstable, like the slightest push of the wrong memory would make them collapse completely. Brooke grabbed my hand and squeezed, almost as if she could sense my impending breakdown. Even though she had no idea what I'd learned from Rory, the way my parents badgered me about my infertility was no secret. It was shoved under a harsh spotlight now that Brooke was pregnant. The fact that she was unmarried was one ding against her in my parents' eyes. The fact that the baby daddy had run as far and as fast as he could was another, but even with those things against her, she'd been given a *Get out of Jail Free* card because of it, unable to do any wrong now that she was adding a male to the Rossi family tree.

Something I'd been completely, heart-breakingly, soul-suckingly incapable of doing.

I extracted my hand from hers and stood, ignoring my mom's inquiries as to what was wrong with me, ignoring my dad talking about whether Brooke would name the boy after him, making him Marcus Leonardo Rossi the third. Somehow, I managed not to slam the bathroom door shut behind me, closing it quietly instead. Their voices were muffled, but I could still hear my dad rambling about something while I braced my hands on the cold porcelain sink. My reflection was fuzzy through the tears that gathered in my eyes.

They didn't fall though. I breathed steadily until they were gone. One hand went to my stomach and I pressed against it, pressed against the empty cavity that sometimes felt too big for my body to contain. The emptiness in me felt too big, the walls of the bathroom too small, too close. The edges of my vision wavered, and I knew I was one beat away from a panic attack.

Two in one day. Hashtag winning.

But it was unavoidable. Nothing made you feel more defective, more of a failure than the vicious cycle of being infertile. When the only thing your soul cries out for is the feeling, the fullness of your body, the kicks and pushes from something growing inside of you, the weight of them in your arms after so many months of loving them. When you can't do that, when you face the monthly realization that you've failed … again, the last thing you need is your family to remind you of that failure.

Yeah, panic attacks seemed pretty rational given my already shitty day. My eyes dried out and my heart slowed down after a few long minutes. My hair hung around my face, so I fished a hair tie out of my front pocket and wrapped it all up into a heavy, messy bun on the top of my head. They were still on the phone, which meant I had to be somewhere else.

Anywhere else.

When I left the bathroom, I mouthed *grocery store* at Brooke and got a sad smile in return. The pity stamped all over her face made me want to claw my skin off. Being single for so many years had tempered people's pity a bit. Tempered the way people tiptoed around announcing their pregnancy in front of me, or the looks they gave me at baby showers while people cooed over onesies and impossibly small shoes. Like the fact that I didn't have Cole anymore had lessened my desire to hold my own child in my arms.

My shaking hands gripped the railing of the stairs when I walked back down to the parking lot. On auto-pilot, I drove to the King Soopers down the street, passing a couple subdivisions on the way, places I didn't recognize. So much was new since I'd moved away from Denver. In some ways, it helped.

If everything had stayed frozen the way I remembered it with Cole, it might have been harder to return. Been harder to slip back into day-to-day life there. When I pulled into a parking space toward the front of the lot, I took a few minutes to steady myself again.

Then I laughed, dropping my forehead to the steering wheel. This day was one for the freaking books. Maybe they sold Xanax at the grocery store now, and I could chase away the crawling sensation of being crazy. I guess wine would have to do for the time being. So I marched for that aisle first, snatching a basket and avoiding eye contact with the woman who was giving me a strange look.

Three bottles clanked together in the bottom of the basket when I hooked it on my arm and walked slowly back down the aisle. Honestly, I didn't even know what kind they were. The bottles were at eye level and filled with wine. Good enough for me.

Instead of checking out and cracking one of them in the parking lot, I figured it was prudent to grab a few things that weren't alcohol-based in nature. Aimlessly, I wandered, grabbing a few boxes of crackers and some cookies. My small basket was packed full and I paused before going down the next row, trying to decide if I needed a cart. I could add more wine that way.

In the second I paused to think about it, my eyes lifted up to the end of the aisle, blinking at the tall, broad-shouldered man that stood at the opposite side.

And my heart exploded in my chest, a messy, visceral explosion, when I saw his profile.

Cole.

I yanked back behind the end cap and peeked over a row of pasta sauce jars to make sure I hadn't lost my damn mind. That I wasn't imagining him standing there because of how my day had played out.

Nope. No. Oh holy shit, no, he was not a specter sent to haunt me.

His dark hair was shorter than the last time I'd seen him, his frame larger. My stomach turned in on itself at the insane moment. The tears I'd pushed down in Brooke's bathroom spilled over my cheeks while I stared at him. His arm reached out to pluck a box of pasta from the shelf, and the way his forehead furrowed while he read the label made me back up a step so I couldn't see him for a beat. Like I was capable of not looking again. Ha.

The universe hated me.

A hysterical giggle lodged in my throat when I considered that the entire freaking cosmos was playing a joke on me, that I might have been living so close to Cole that we shared a grocery store for the last month. And no matter how much I wanted that wine, my feet had already angled toward the exit. When he started to turn in my direction, I didn't think, didn't question.

I shoved my basket onto an empty bottom shelf and turned to leave, plowing into the chest of a store employee carrying an armful of canned vegetables, which hit the ground with awkward, loud bounces.

Go! I screamed in my head. But my head lifted instead.

His eyes locked on mine, widening in the next heartbeat.

"Julia," he called out, the hoarse crack in his deep voice opening a chasm in between my ribs.

And I was gone, fleeing the store without a backwards glance.

CHAPTER FOUR

COLE

I shoved my cart away from me and took off, making a fast sidestep to avoid the employee on the floor who was gathering the fallen cans. Someone shouted at me to watch where I was going, but I couldn't even stop to apologize. My heart thundered in my ears as I cleared the doors of the store and looked around the parking lot frantically to see if I could spot Julia.

Julia.

"Oh God," I breathed, not sure if it was a prayer or a curse. Both of my hands gripped the sides of my head, trying to contain the frantic racing of my brain. It was her, I knew it was her. She wasn't as thin as before, her hair darker, but it was her.

To my right there was a loud slamming of a car door and I jogged toward the noise, and there she was. Slumped into the driver's seat, with her head in her hands. Her shoulders were shaking. She was crying, I knew it like I knew my name.

In one breath, I knew I couldn't go after her. If I became that man, pounding on the car window, trying to open a locked door, I'd push her away forever. She'd close in on herself, stiffen her spine and convince herself that I was insane, that what I felt for her was too much. Maybe it was, but fate or destiny, God or whatever the hell she wanted to call it, had handed her back into my life. Had handed me back into hers.

So I stood there and just looked, took the greediest, most selfish moment I could remember and just stared at her. Her back expanded on a deep breath. Her hair, a darker shade of brown than when I last saw her, was piled on her head in a messy bun, which was very unlike her. Unlike the Julia that I used to know.

I wanted to know *this* Julia. Wanted to sit and watch her for hours, let her show me this new version of her that had formed over the past handful of years.

When she dropped her hands and wiped at her cheeks, I felt the gut punch of seeing her face so fully for the first time, now that the searing moment of shock was gone. The slope of her nose that had the slightest bump at the bridge, breaking up the perfection of her features. The bow of her lips when she blew out a breath. I was far enough away that I couldn't see the dark sweep of her lashes, but I knew how they curved, how they framed her hazel eyes.

There were a million things that I loved about her face, but her eyes topped the list. I'd never seen eyes like Julia's, streaks of brown and gold and green that showed every single thing she was thinking.

I swiped a hand over my mouth when she turned the key in the ignition, fighting against the screaming instinct to go after her. Every shred of me that was pragmatic and rational, weighing all of my options carefully before deciding on a course of action, was completely silent, completely still.

Probably because there was absolutely nothing rational about how I felt about her. It's why I hadn't touched another woman since the day she walked out, why my wasted heart still ached for her after years of silence. But despite those things, I stood there in the parking lot and watched her drive away.

Numbly, and after she'd been out of sight for at least five minutes, I walked back into the store and paid for my abandoned groceries. I drove back home, finding myself watching for her modest gray car as I did. If she was at my usual store, it probably meant she was staying somewhere close. That made me smile a little as I put the food away into cupboards and the fridge.

The rest of the evening passed in a blur, and I stared blankly at the screen of my laptop while I pretended to work. Memories of Julia from before mixed with the new glimpses of Julia today on repeat, sapping any focus I might have had. It felt like destiny. It felt like we'd never reach a point in our lives where we'd truly be free of each other.

With a rough laugh, I realized it was exactly like when we'd met, the long fingers of fate reaching in to rearrange our lives so that we were pointed in each other's direction. At nineteen, you don't assume you'll meet the woman who'll own your soul, but that's exactly how it played out.

I curled my fingers around the cold neck of a bottle of beer and thought about it again, one of the memories that I replayed often when I felt low. I'd picked up my dry cleaning at the cheapest place close to campus, not looking underneath the white plastic sleeve that was supposed to hold my suit for a winter formal that weekend. When I got back to my dorm room, uncovering a scarlet red dress was not what I was expecting. There was no name attached to the bag, but I took a second to look at the really, really hot dress before covering it back up and heading back to the dry cleaner. The tiny woman behind the counter was ancient and didn't speak a word of English, unlike the guy who had helped me earlier in the day. I'd uncovered the dress gave her a look like, isn't it obvious what my problem is?

She'd only laughed, saying something that I couldn't understand and pointing at the short dress that I held in my hands. Behind us, the door had swung open and someone delicately cleared their throat.

"It's definitely not your color, so I don't dare ask what you're doing with my dress."

When I turned and saw her, saw Julia, I stopped breathing.

It was all of her, the smile, the tiny dimple, the amused glint in her incredible eyes, the impossibly long legs that I knew would be showing underneath the small dress I was still in possession of. Every piece of her took my breath away.

I felt like an oaf, a huge, lumbering oaf standing there and gaping at her. She'd lifted an eyebrow and her smile widened. "Are you going to give it back? Because if not, I'll need a new dress for Saturday and I already blew my budget on that one. Of course, my roommate had to make it worse when she spilled her Boone's Farm on it before I could even hang it in the closet."

"Sorry," I said, shoving it back at her with absolutely no finesse. She only laughed and I'd felt my face heat. Women, I was not a natural with women. I always felt too tall, too big, too awkward. And now there was this beautiful creature looking at me. Words, gone. Face, probably bright red. "I didn't ... it wasn't like that." When I gestured at the woman behind the counter, she was watching us with a giant smile on her weathered face. "It was a mistake. That's supposed to be my suit, I didn't know it was wrong until I got back to my room. I'm sorry. I didn't do anything weird to it, I promise."

"Well, that's a relief," she'd answered, those lips still curved up into a smile. A lot of women might have huffed and snarled at me for being the weird asshole holding their dress, but she hadn't been like that. She smiled, she laughed, she was so ... so light. I'd wanted to move closer, wanted to be in her gravity, just to see if I could feel that lightness too.

When she looked down to pull her wallet out of her purse, I reached out and stilled her hand. Her eyes whipped up to mine, widening in surprise. And me, I couldn't move again, couldn't breathe again, at how her hand felt under mine. She was taller than most women I knew, and there was an insane moment where I realized that it would be so easy to kiss her. All she'd have to do was tilt up her chin, and we'd be so close.

"I already paid for it," I'd told her in a rough voice, pulling my hand back even though I did not want to. "Please, let me. For all the confusion."

She was still staring up at me, and she finally nodded. The little old woman broke the moment by chattering away, handing a plastic covered hanger over the counter at me. When I didn't reach for it, she lifted up the plastic to show my suit.

"Cole?" she asked in a heavily accented voice, pointing at the suit with a gnarled, arthritic finger.

"Yeah, that's me." I took the bag and reached for my wallet, but she waved me away with a wink, then lifted her chin behind me. The door swung shut again, and when I looked over my shoulder, the girl was gone. Not questioning why, I'd ran out the door and called out to her.

"Wait, please."

She stopped, her long hair swinging like a dark gold-colored curtain when she glanced back at me.

"Are you going to the formal this weekend?"

Her eyes searched my face before she answered, and I knew I'd do anything to be able to see her again. This was lightning in my veins, electricity in my heart, something I'd never, ever felt before.

"I am," she answered, offering nothing else.

For a few charged seconds, we stared at each other. I cleared my throat and shuffled my feet. "I'm Cole."

Her smile spread across her face. "Julia."

"Will you save a dance for me this weekend?"

Julia nodded, a shy smile on her face. I was grinning when I walked away. My mom died when I was in high school, and even sick and exhausted from chemo, she'd joked that my future wife would have to be the kind of woman who knocked me on my ass the moment I met her otherwise I'd never pay attention.

How right she was. When I got back to my dorm room, I tapped the edge of the framed picture of my parents and grinned at my mom's face.

A year later, exactly one year later, we got married at the courthouse downtown in front of my dad and her sister. Her parents thought we were insane and refused to attend. She wore the red dress and I wore my cheap suit and it was perfect.

With a long swallow, I finished my beer and stood from my chair with a sigh. Even when I missed Julia with an ache that was embedded into the marrow of my bones, when it felt impossible that I could ever move on from her, there was an inescapableness to us, to what we were together. It's why I hadn't chased after her, why I felt so certain that I'd find her again, that she'd find me somehow, when she was ready.

When I fell into my bed, when my eyes drifted shut and my brain slowed from the events of the day, I knew that I would dream of her. With my arms curled around my pillow and face pressed into it, I prayed for sleep to come quickly, no matter how my dreams of Julia gutted me, just so I could get back to her.

"Just drop it, Cole," Julia ground out, showing me her back again. I stood a few feet away from her and fisted my hands at my sides so I didn't reach out to shake her. Then I tried, thinking that maybe if I shook her that she'd hear me, that she'd actually listen to what I was saying, that she'd see how much this hurt me too.

But my hands didn't work, they were shackled to my sides with thick, heavy black chains. Helpless. Unable to reach out to her. Unable to do a single thing to make it better for her.

"I get a say in this too, you know," I snapped back, frustrated by my powerlessness. *"This isn't just about you."*

Julia whipped around, her eyes shining with tears. I hated her tears. Hated how they ripped at my skin and clawed at my heart. *"I know that. You think I don't know that? I'm not a completely selfish person."*

When I didn't agree with her, didn't verbally back that up, she gasped *and stepped back like I'd told her she was. My mouth was zipped shut, and not because I was trying to speak, but because I'd thought it. I'd thought it more than once over the last four years of trying and failing to conceive.*

A tear hit her cheek and I swore under my breath. "I didn't say you were selfish. Don't put words in my mouth. You always put words in my mouth."

"I don't have to. You're screaming it at me right now," she said, her eyes full of naked hurt, full of betrayal. "Without saying a word, you're screaming it at me."

My arms lifted out to the side. "But you refuse to even consider *adoption. And you won't tell me why. Every time I want to talk about it with you, you completely shut me out, act like I'm betraying you."*

"I am exhausted, Cole. I can't keep talking about it with you because you refuse to understand how hard it is for me!"

"Understand? I have been there every step of the way with you for years. I waited to bring this up until six months ago because I hate watching you hurt so much. Nice to know my thoughtfulness is being rewarded like this."

Julia grew in size, her anger making her tower over me. I shrank, feeling like the tiniest version of myself, like the tiniest version of a man. "Don't you get it? It feels like a betrayal when you refuse to acknowledge how important it is for me to carry my own child."

"Our child," I said in a warning tone. I pointed a shaking finger at her. My rage equaled out our sizes again. "Our child. You always do that. You say your child, your body, your opinion, what your family whispers in your ear and poisons you with. Because it's all about what you want. You don't give one shit about what I want."

"Original." She shook her head, her hair starting to lick with flames. I reached out to smother them out, to keep them from engulfing her completely but she swatted my hand away. "Blame my family for this. There is nothing wrong with the fact that they're supporting me in how I want to do this."

The look I gave her was full of dry disbelief, because it was the only shield that I had from releasing the ugly spew of words that I kept reserved for her parents, especially her father. "Don't be that person, Julia. You are smart enough to know the difference between support and manipulation."

"So now I'm stupid."

"I never said that," I yelled.

"Oh, I'm smart enough *to read between the lines. Your problem is that you care more about whether you're doing the right thing. Your entire world is so black and white, full of Cole's rules for how things should be done. And I'm just supposed to toe the line, regardless of how," she swallowed, clutching a fist over her heart, "of how much my entire soul longs to do it a different way. It's hard enough to get the pitying looks from everyone else, to have people tiptoe around me when they send me shower invites or birth announcements, when they tell me they're pregnant. But if you start looking at me differently, I won't be able to do it, Cole."*

A heavy wave of exhaustion cloaked me, hard iron wrapped around my shoulders. The same words on a different day, more harshly spoken than the last time we'd had this fight. Julia's eyes were dark and lifeless, the spark that I'd loved so much when we first met completely extinguished. I was tired, but she was sleep-walking, only coming back to me in brief, bright moments of time.

"No, baby," I groaned, clasping the sides of her face and trying to kiss her. But she was mist, gone the second before my mouth touched hers. When I wheeled around, she was holding her stomach and weeping. I dropped to my knees and pressed my forehead to her middle. "You'll never have to do this and feel alone."

Her hands touched the back of my head, raking through my hair and her nails turned into knives. With a hiss, I pulled back and stared up at her. Her eyes were black as coal and she was crying fire. "There's nothing there, Cole. Why isn't there anything there?"

I could fix it. I had to be able to fix this for her. Months and months of nothing but disappointment, of wiping tears from her face, of short tempers, of laying in bed and pretending that I didn't know she was crying quietly into her pillow because I knew she didn't want to have me hear, I had to be able to fix it. Fix her.

Still on my knees in front of her, like a supplicant praying before a deity,

COLE

I laid my hands on her stomach and pushed in. She wailed, but I pressed in further only to have her turn into a foggy apparition. The more I tried to dig for something, the wispier she became. My fingers touched air, only cold tendrils over my skin and I started crying.

Why couldn't I find anything?

Why couldn't I give her what she wanted?

Failure coated me in a thick dark sludge that I couldn't wipe off of me, off of my soul. Because I didn't understand. I didn't understand my wife, the woman who I loved more than my own life. What did that say about me?

I staggered back to my feet and stammered an apology when she curled into herself and wept. She was getting further and further away. Then I looked down and touched the spot over my heart, felt the fog. My hand felt as far into my chest as possible and there was nothing there. My whole body stretched thin, my skin unable to contain me anymore.

"Julia?" I asked frantically. She was in front of me again, holding my beating heart in her hands. Her fingers were coated in dark blood and I lurched forward, tried to take it back.

But she shook her head, gave me a strange look, unable to figure out what I was doing. "I'm sorry, but you can't have this back. It's mine now, Cole. It's always been mine."

I woke with a choked gasp, hand clasped over the skin of my chest and I pinched my eyes back shut.

"Son of a bitch," I whispered.

My phone went off, a lifeline that pulled me from the sickening emptiness that always ended the dream. I grasped it eagerly, taking the reprieve even though I knew I'd relive my nightmare again soon.

CHAPTER FIVE

COLE

The dream had been even more vivid this time. Julia looked the way she had earlier at the store, not like when we'd had that fight. Her hair was shorter back then, lighter than it was now. And the fight itself, the way it had actually played out, had been much worse than the way it cycled through my tortured subconscious.

She'd called me a self-righteous, stubborn prick.

I'd called her selfish. Called her a coward for not standing up to her family.

The word had barely left my lips before she'd stormed out, slamming the door so hard that it rattled the entire room. Her bag was packed within fifteen minutes, despite my pleading apologies, her car left the driveway shortly after. Three days later, her sister Brooke had showed up with a sad smile on her face and told me she was there to get more stuff. When Brooke's SUV was filled with boxes, I knew I was in the deepest kind of shit that a man could find himself in with the woman he loved.

I sat up and scrubbed at my face, then leaned over to grab my phone when it went off again. I'd only been asleep for an hour.

Garrett: Get your ass over here. I'm sick of pretending like we're still in a fight.

It was so Garrett. He, like Michael and Tristan, was one of my oldest friends. They were from the post-Julia phase of my life, as was Dylan, who moved to Colorado a bit over a year ago and also lived in our same neighborhood. Nobody doubted that my stubbornness would likely have outlasted Garrett's in this particular instance, even though I was the one who owed him an apology. Making amends with Rory was one thing, but Garrett was still one of the people I was closest to, which was the only reason I got my ass out of bed and threw some clothes on.

It was still warm that evening, with November right around the corner. Heading into the busy-ness of the holidays meant a rare lull in my workload. As much as I loved my job, and I did, I always welcomed a couple months of extra free time. People didn't want to list their homes during the holidays if it was at all possible, nor did people relish the thought of moving in the winter in Colorado.

Before I could text Garrett back, my phone chimed with a new email. Unread notifications made me twitchy, so I clicked over to it to see if it could wait until the next morning. Even though it was a Friday evening, that didn't mean anything when you worked in real estate. My hours were odd, never the same from week to week. It had been the biggest source of comfort after I signed the divorce papers.

Facing an empty house every night and weekend would have driven me into a padded cell after a few short months. Throwing myself into work, taking every client sent my way and working my ass off is why I was even still standing. The only mistress I could handle was my job.

The email waiting for me was from my new client Brooke Camden, whom I'd sent some initial options just two days prior. I scrubbed my face again, because it had felt like weeks since I'd emailed her.

Hey Cole,

Thank you so much for getting back to me so quickly. I love, love, love all of those options! In my email to your assistant, I mentioned that I'm expecting in a few months. I'm pregnant with twins, and my doctor placed me on bed rest for the remainder of my pregnancy,(I have not gone stir crazy yet, which is a miracle in and of itself, believe me) which makes it all but impossible for me to physically look at the houses with you. My sister is staying with me in my cramped one-bedroom apartment, so she's equally motivated for me to find a bigger place to welcome my new brood home to. I'll be sending her in my place to see those first four options. I hope that's okay. Thank you SO MUCH. You have no idea how much I'm looking forward to working with you. Seriously.

Brooke

She included her cell phone, which I quickly saved into my contacts. When I read through her email again, I got that same nagging sensation that she was someone I knew, especially given how she ended it. But Brooke was a common enough name, so I shot her a succinct reply that meeting with her sister would be fine with me and that I'd let her know when I had the first showing set up, along with my cell number, saying that if texting was easier for her, it worked for me as well.

I threw on some jeans and pulled a sweatshirt over my chest before grabbing a six pack of beer from the fridge. The walk over to Garrett's place was quick and I pulled in a deep breath of night air, looking up at star-speckled sky before I turned up his driveway. Before I even opened his front door, I heard a burst of laughter. I'd avoided all of them a bit in the past few weeks, after my argument with Garrett, and hearing them laugh made me really, really glad I'd decided to go.

Hiding was easy. Unfortunately, it had become second nature for me after Julia. None of the guys knew what happened with her, why we got divorced. All they knew was that I was the chump who still pined for his ex-wife after almost seven years.

When I walked into the house, Michael choked on his beer. His brother Tristan, gave him a dry look and thumped him on the back. "Don't die, man. It's just Cole."

Dylan smiled and shook my hand. "Good to see you."

Kat, Dylan's pint-sized girlfriend who unashamedly crashed our guy time, pinched me in the stomach. "Are you eating? You look like you're wasting away."

"Why?" I swatted her hand away when she actually twisted skin. "You gonna cook for me?"

She smiled sweetly, batting her eyelashes. "No, I don't even cook for him," she said, jerking a thumb at Dylan. "I'm just asking because it feels like the polite thing to do. We'll consider it my charitable contribution to society."

"You've got yourself a special one," I whispered over Kat's head to Dylan, who laughed.

Garrett was in the kitchen tapping a mini-keg and just grinned at me. "'Bout time, asshole. You thought you could avoid me forever?"

"I certainly hoped so," I said easily, nodding my chin at Tristan. "Sending Rory after me was a nice touch. I can see why you have a hard time saying no to her."

Garrett's chest puffed up with pride, his smile unrepentant. "She's incredible, right? We had a meeting with a lawyer yesterday over some new contracts and Rory damn near made him cry. It was beautiful."

The guys laughed, as did I, but I still felt a dull ache behind my ribs. I used to do that with Julia, too. Brag about her to my buddies. I had different friends then, most of them fell out of touch with me because their wives were still Team Julia, so to speak. I couldn't even blame them, honestly. So when I moved into my place, and connected easily with Garrett, Michael and Tristan, it was a welcome relief for me. To have friends that made me laugh, that cared about my life and made time for each other, it saved me as much as work had.

While conversation flowed around me, I felt an easing of the tightness in my shoulders and neck after my dream. Honestly, I couldn't figure out why I kept thinking of it as a dream. It was a nightmare. Sometimes I caught myself labeling it appropriately, but for the most part, I think it was because even seeing Julia in my sleep, reliving the thing that splintered her from me, was something that I viewed as a positive.

Sick, I know. A shrink would probably have a field day with me.

I tapped Garrett's arm and nodded for him to follow me out to his backyard. He did, taking a seat on a lounge chair that was new since the last time I was at his place.

"Obviously I apologized to Rory the other day, but I still owe you one." I held his eyes, even though I wanted to focus on anything else around us. Thinking back on the things I said to him, driven by the intense, searing desire to know something, anything about Julia, swamped me with shame.

He stared back, not reacting for a second, but then he nodded slowly. "She told me. Sounds like you won her over."

"I wouldn't blame her if I hadn't." I rubbed at the back of my neck self-consciously. Obviously he wasn't going to make this too easy on me, despite his olive branch in inviting me over. "I know I screwed up. It's not an excuse, but this Julia thing threw me way more than I expected it to. Knowing she's here. Knowing she's just around any corner I turn, it messed up my head." Then I met his eyes again to make sure he knew that I meant what I was about to say. "I took it out on you, and I'm sorry. The way I spoke to you, the way I goaded you into blowing up so someone could feel the same level of helplessness that I did, I hate that I treated you that way. I hate how I spoke about Rory. It was unacceptable. You have every right to not forgive me, but I'll ask for it anyway."

Garrett didn't even hesitate, holding out his hand to me. "And I'll give it. That's what friends do."

We shook, did the guy thing and stood to thump each other's backs in a pseudo-hug. "Thanks, man."

He nodded and took a sip of his beer. "You okay with everything else?"

"I saw her today." When Garrett's eyes widened, I sighed. "At the grocery store. She ran out like I was freaking Stalin or something."

"Damn," he said under his breath, giving me a concerned look. "You okay?"

My answering laugh was strained. "No. I'm not."

"You ready to talk about it with us?"

I weighed that before answering. "No, I'm not."

"Well. Best get more beer in you then."

So we did. Even though I felt marginally better than when I'd left my house, there was still a lingering strain behind my eyes that I couldn't blink away. Back at the dining room table, everyone was laughing at something Kat was saying. Well, Tristan wasn't laughing, but he was smiling, which was his equivalent.

"I'm serious!" Kat protested on a laugh. "I'm really good at it."

Michael rolled his eyes as Garrett and I sat. "You spend all day around dogs, you're just picking random things and assuming we won't know the difference."

"So what are we doing here?" Garrett asked.

Kat eyed Michael, the mock glare almost looking ridiculous on her pixie face. "I told them that one of my secret talents is that I can liken every person I meet to which dog breed they're most similar to with like ninety-nine percent accuracy."

"Pray tell," Garrett said, "upon which scale do you gauge the accuracy of such a secret talent?"

"Anyway," Kat drawled, shoving a palm on Garrett's face. "Watch. I'll do you guys."

There was a beat of silence before Michael snickered. Kat blushed and we all laughed. Dylan took pity on her and hooked a hand around her neck, drawing her close for a kiss. It had taken almost six months for Kat to be comfortable with displays of affection around us, but she still gave us an embarrassed smile when she pulled back.

"So. I'll work clockwise, so nobody thinks I'm playing favorites."

"I'm your favorite," Dylan said.

"Obvs." She turned to him. "You, my love, are a German Shepherd."

"I like this game," Dylan said instantly. "Tell me more."

She held up her hands like she was Vanna White and Dylan was on display. "You're strong, athletic and handsome." Garrett made a gagging sound and Kat ignored him. "You're smart and loyal, and a good leader. People respect you, might be intimidated when they first see you, but quickly realize that you'd do anything for the people you take care of."

"That could be forty-seven different kinds of dog breeds," Michael interjected.

"Garrett's turn," Kat kept on, nonplussed. "Garrett is a Border Collie."

"Because he's high maintenance and destructive when bored?" Michael asked with a wide smile.

"I'm going to tell Rory you said that," Garrett mumbled. Michael's eyes widened in genuine fear.

But Kat laughed. "Because he's smart, and people love him instantly because of how entertaining he is. Your antics can hide how loyal and devoted you are. And yes, destructive when bored or not worked to your full potential."

I lifted my eyebrows and Garrett shifted in his seat. Last year, Garrett was pretty much forced to take over his late father's company, something he never thought he wanted, until he actually did it. Now he loved it, and was doing a damn fine job, too.

Michael clapped his hands. "I lied. This is fun. Because that shit is the truth, right there." He elbowed his brother next to him. "Tristan's turn. Make sure it's a breed that has the same pretty hair that he does. Is there a dog with a man bun?"

Tristan took a deep breath, but looked over at Kat with the mildest spark of amusement that he allowed on his stony features. Kat smiled at him. "Tristan is an easy one. He's an Akita."

"An a-what-a?" Garrett asked. I couldn't believe it, but Kat had the entire table rapt with her little game. Even me, which was a feat considering my day.

"Akita," she explained. Tristan's dark brows lowered, but he didn't say anything. "Akitas are aloof, especially with people they don't know. They're fierce guard dogs and will do anything to protect the people they love, which is usually a select few. They're careful, cautious, and can be stubborn and willful unless handled correctly, by the exact right person. But for that person, they'll be loyal forever."

And then miracle of all miracles, a slow smile bloomed on Tristan's face. He even laughed under his breath, one slow puff of sound. He tipped his chin at Kat while we all gaped at this magnitude of expression from the normally stoic Tristan. "Pretty good, kid." Then he nodded at his little brother. "What about Dumbass over here?"

"Easy," Kat said sweetly. "Michael is the mutt who whores himself around the neighborhood but can't be caught or castrated, despite many, *many* attempts."

We all laughed, but Michael glared at Kat after taking an exaggerated sip of his beer. When she blew him a kiss, he rolled his eyes, but smiled at her. "It is kinda true," he conceded when we quieted down. "*So* many attempts."

"Dare I ask?" I said to Kat.

She reached over and patted the space over my heart, which still felt a bit pinched and empty after the dream, after seeing Julia.

"Cole, you're like ... you're the perfect mix of a Lab and Great Dane."

Michael slugged me. "Hey! You're a mutt just like me."

But Kat shook her head. "No, he's just so strongly both. Your size makes people watch you, they can't help it. Your size makes you impressive, sure. So does your intelligence, your kindness. But at the heart of both breeds isn't size or intelligence, it's their loyalty. What they want more than anything is to just be with their people. Forever."

I took a deep breath and let it out, glancing at my friends' faces before reaching to tweak the end of Kat's messy blonde hair. "Tristan's right. That's pretty good, kid."

Everyone moved on, but I mulled over Kat's words for the rest of the night. I started laughing to myself when I pictured laying down at Julia's feet and hoping she'd scratch behind my ears, but I couldn't deny that I'd do it, given the chance. Kat wasn't wrong, about any of us, really. And even though our circumstances were different, Kat had been a foster kid, and I lost my parents years apart from sickness, she and I both knew the value of the group of friends that we shared. It was a family, one that we'd created. Currently the only one I had, which is why smoothing things over with Garrett would probably help me sleep better that night.

But Julia had been my family before them, and at some point, I needed to be able to trust them with the weight of what I carried with me every single day. Let them be able to help me with it, not by removing it from my shoulders, but by propping me up if I needed it.

Before I went to bed, I sent Brooke Camden a text telling her that I'd meet her sister at the first of the houses the next afternoon, and drifted off to sleep without a single nightmare to chase me.

CHAPTER SIX

JULIA

"I still can't get over it," Brooke said around a mouthful of biscuits dipped in ranch. Gross, but apparently the one major craving she couldn't let go of. "He was right there, Jules. I cannot believe you ran."

From where I stood in front of the mirror in her bedroom, she saw me roll my eyes and threw a balled up napkin at me, but it fell ineffectually to the floor just past her bed.

I smoothed the cotton blouse over my stomach, my oddly flippy stomach. All morning I'd had a strange, gnawing pit of nerves that I couldn't shake. "As opposed to what? Have a happy, awkward, terrible reunion in the middle of the pasta aisle?"

"Yes," Brooke drawled, pinning me with a serious look that I couldn't avoid in the reflection of the mirror. "Who says it'd be awkward and terrible? You're assuming because you've spent so long avoiding him." She licked some ranch off her hand and then pointed at me. "And don't even get me started on *that*."

The rush of defensiveness that accompanied the subject of Cole pricked along my skin, just like it always did when Brooke brought him up. In the early months and years following our divorce, she did it a lot more often. Brooke was so Team Cole it was ridiculous. When my parents simply sniffed and said I could do better than someone who didn't respect my opinion, Brooke would always shake her head, set her jaw and give me a look that I roughly interpreted as *I cannot believe you're letting them in your head.*

I had let them in my head. And I was far enough removed from the situation now that I firmly understood that when my parents referenced Cole not supporting my opinion, they really meant that Cole didn't support *their* opinion. Both of my parents came from established east coast families, my father's rich with a long Italian bloodline and my mother's with one that supposedly came across on the Mayflower. I'd never seen proof of that, but it also didn't interest me.

Brooke sighed, snapping me out of my head.

"In the beginning, I'll admit that I avoided Cole. Before I moved and before I decided to divorce him."

My sister's voice was gentle when she responded. Gentle, but also *I know you well enough to know your bullshit* firm. "You decided the day you left him."

"That's not true." I brushed my hair out, doing a spectacular job of avoiding her eyes in the mirror.

"Yes, it is. I saw it in your eyes when you showed up that night. You just," she shook her head, "you looked so detached."

I couldn't help the laugh that came out. What Brooke clearly didn't know, because I hadn't told her, was that I'd sat in my car for two hours after walking out the door and sobbed into the steering wheel, much like I had yesterday at the grocery store, the sheer magnitude of everything Cole was capable of making me feel pouring down my face in salty lines. Back then it was because of the things he'd said to me, the things I'd said to him, the way it felt so final and so impossible to overcome. Yesterday it was because just the sight of him turned my heart inside out, set my skin on fire.

It was the worst possible reaction. If I'd seen him and felt nothing, felt the cool stretch of distance between us, then I could have walked up to him and said hello, asked him how he'd been in the time since we'd seen each other. Maybe I could have asked him if he'd remarried, started a family.

When my skin flushed, my heart thrashed against my ribs, I looked down and saw that my hands had curled into fists. The thought of Cole as a husband to someone else, as a father to a little boy who had his dark eyes and square jaw made me feel physically ill. Made me want to smash my fist into the mirror in front of me, and I had no right. I had absolutely zero right to feel that way, but there it was. Seeing him again, hearing him say my name sent me spinning so badly that I'd had no choice but to run home and sob onto the bed so Brooke could comfort me and tell me it was okay to drown my sorrows in alcohol, which I had.

"When I left Cole," I started, choosing my words very carefully, "there was a lot more going on than I'd ever explained to you. I *had* to be detached to be able to move on."

"Well that's stupid."

I whipped around, lifting my eyebrows at her. "Excuse me?"

With her back propped up against her headboard, the soft roundness of her belly against the pillows next to her body more pronounced than it had even looked yesterday, I lost a bit of my fire. Brooke loved me, and even though this constant, unwavering support of Cole got tedious, I knew it was based on what she thought would make me happy. Because she was five years younger than me, she'd still been in college when I left Cole. She'd never had a serious boyfriend, so delving into my marital issues with my little sister hadn't been high on my priority list. The soft, sympathetic look on her face now made me realize that if I had talked to her about it, as opposed to my parents, maybe my path would have unfolded a little differently.

What if I'd had someone reminding me that Cole brought out the best sides of me, who pushed me to be better, who never looked down on my ambitions. What if those had been the whispered conversations, instead of the litany of reasons why he wasn't good for me, why he didn't respect our family, which meant he didn't respect me.

"I don't mean you're stupid," Brooke clarified, oblivious to my pointless ruminations. I hadn't talked to her about it back then, so to wonder what would have happened if I did would get me nowhere fast, except wanting to dive into another bottle of wine. "Why don't you wear that purple shirt you got at Cherry Creek last week?"

Her change of topic made me blink. "What?"

The unimpressed look that she gave my cream top said it all. "That's just a little ... boring."

"Thanks," I said dryly, but turned to look in the mirror again. The scoop neck and three quarter length sleeves didn't exactly make me feel amazing, but it wasn't like I was impressing anyone. All that was necessary for me was to look at the houses, not look like I was about to walk into a club. The shirt I was wearing was perfectly *fine*.

Okay. It looked like something our mother would wear. With a huff, I ripped the shirt over my head and yanked the purple top from inside Brooke's closet. It was silk, with a deep V and gorgeous draping that made my torso look long, my waist small. "I guess if you don't think it's too much just to look at a house."

"Nope. I love it." She nodded at the closet. "And you can wear those nude heels that don't fit my stupid puffy feet anymore."

"Now that's too much. I am *not* wearing stilettos."

"But they make your legs look so stupid long." She huffed before settling further into her nest of pillows. "It's not fair, really. You're all Julia Roberts leggy and I got my little stumps."

I laughed and slid my feet into the much more sedate booties. "You're five seven, that's hardly short."

"For the rest of the world, sure. But I have an amazon for a sister. You make me feel like a midget." Then she blinked, a comically innocent portrait. "That's why Cole was so perfect for you. He's even more of a giant than you are."

All I could do was sigh. She'd really never quit, now that she knew I'd seen him, that he probably lived within a fifteen-minute radius from her apartment. Or at least, until she moved. There was no sweeping rush of relief at the thought, not like I expected, just that same uncomfortable pit that had been in my stomach all day. Weird.

"You're sure you don't want to wear the heels?" she asked when I ignored her comment about Cole's height. I couldn't even argue that one. He was the only man I'd dated who was so much taller than me. He made me feel safe. Protected. When he tucked my head under his chin, wrapped his arms around my back, I'd felt so small within his embrace. "Just remember that they do phenomenal things to your ass."

"Goodbye, Brooke," I called while I walked out the bedroom door and pulled my purse over my shoulder.

She let out a dramatic sigh. "Fine, be that way. You have the address?"

"Yes, Mom."

"And you remember how much I love you, right?"

I pulled up short, my hand resting on the doorknob. "What's that about?"

From the open doorway into her bedroom, I could see her perfectly. She wasn't looking at me, her eyes trained on her fingers where she worried the edge of the purple velvet pillow that she favored for propping up her belly. When she spoke again, her voice was serious, so I stepped away from the door.

"Nothing, I just ... I know I hassle you about Cole a lot. But I love you, and that's why I do it. I just want you to be happy."

My steps were slow when I walked back into her room and sat on the edge of the bed. "I love you too. I'll forgive you hassling me about him, if you forgive me ignoring everything you say."

She laughed under her breath, but her face was still serious. "Deal."

The pit in my stomach didn't fade when I plugged the address of the house into my GPS, but it didn't grow either. The drive took less time than I thought, into one of the older neighborhoods in Aurora, one with a great school district. The mature trees lining the street made me smile, and there were boys riding bikes down the sidewalks. I found the right house, a split level with black shutters and a nice front porch. There was no other car in the driveway, so I took a few moments to flip through my phone after I'd parked next to the curb. I snapped a picture and sent it to Brooke.

Me: I can see us enjoying some drinks on the front porch.

Brooke: Obviously the realtor isn't there yet?

Me: Nope. Didn't take as long as I thought to get here. I love the outside. Great curb appeal.

Brooke: I do like the porch. Take lots of pictures of the backyard, there weren't many online, which probably means it sucks.
Brooke: Also, I love you.

Me: I love you too, even though you're a total weirdo. Try not to pass that along to your innocent children.

She was acting so odd. When I didn't see the little dancing dots of her typing a reply, I tucked my phone into my purse and decided to walk around a little without someone following my every move. The driveway had some pretty major cracks, but nothing that needed to be redone immediately, and the siding was aluminum, but looked freshly painted. I took the curved walkway up to the porch and ran my hand along the white-painted railing. It looked solidly built, nothing that was recently redone. When I heard the sound of a car pulling into the driveway, I was smiling at the two rocking chairs sitting in the corner of the porch, imagining me and Brooke each rocking a baby while we watched kids riding their bikes. If I couldn't have kids of my own, I'd be the best damn aunt that ever existed.

When the car turned off and I didn't hear the sound of a door closing right away, I walked down the steps of the porch with the smile still on my face.

Until I saw who had just stood up from the driver's seat with a look on his handsome face that said he was just as surprised to see me as I was to see him. I blew out a slow breath and stared at my ex-husband, filtering through the million and one ways that I would murder my sister when I got back to her apartment.

CHAPTER SEVEN

COLE

"Hi, Julia," I said by way of greeting. Original, I know, and not the most gripping thing I could've said. But it was my Plan B. Plan A, which I'd concocted the instant I saw her car by the curb, complete with a U Conn bumper sticker on it just like the other day, had involved falling to my knees in front of her, begging for her to give me the smallest scrap of time to lay out all the reasons why we should never be apart again.

Plan A got scrapped for obvious reasons, the inevitable, and rightfully deserved, kick in the balls that I'd receive in answer dissuaded me from opening that way. Plan B involved me playing it cool, taking her lead, not smothering her with the intensity that coursed hot and thick through my veins at being so close to her. At being able to see her after so long. Really see her, not the quick, unplanned, greedy glimpse that I'd gotten at the grocery store.

My heart was hammering in my chest so hard that I was starting to lose feeling in my hands, an unplanned byproduct of having an anxiety-induced heart attack at the age of thirty-four. Brooke, oh that genius Brooke, I'd owe her for eternity. But a little heads-up *might* have been nice.

"How are you?" I asked quietly, a stark contradiction to the riot inside my body at being so close to her.

She hadn't run, that was an important first step. But she hadn't answered me yet either. Julia just stood there, her hands gripping the strap of her purse, her hazel eyes wary, hot and bright with the sheen of tears, of anger, hopefully at me and Brooke in equal measure, and her sweet, pink lips were pressed into a thin line.

It almost seemed impossible that we were so close, that I could see every detail of her face after so many years. Her hair was longer, swinging well past her shoulders in a sleek curtain. Her face hadn't really aged, and she was wearing minimal makeup, which I loved. She'd never needed it. I used to trace the lines of her face while we laid in bed, the tiny imperfection on the bridge of her nose that she hated was one of my favorite spots to kiss. It kept her from being too perfect, I used to tell her. Gave her beauty a character that other women could only dream of.

"From the look on your face, you had no idea about this either."

Her voice. My knees almost buckled at the sound of it. I had to take a second, close my eyes and clench my jaw, at the sheer magnitude of what her voice did to me. The hair lifted on the back of my neck, and I felt the low, soft tone wrap around my spine and flow through my bones.

But if I was going to do this, be around her and not scare her off, I had to pull my shit together. No Plan A, no Plan B or Plan C. *Get your shit together, Cole, show her you can do this.* So I opened my eyes and met her gaze full-on. "I didn't know Brooke was *your* Brooke until I recognized your car from the other night. Her email had a different last name."

Julia took in a shaky breath, eyes darting to the offending vehicle, and I braced for her to bolt again. "Of course it did." She gave me a tight smile. "Clearly, my sister put a lot of thought into this."

"Clearly." My voice trailed off by the end of the word, the awkwardness so thick around us, I felt like I might choke at any second.

"Well," she rubbed at her arms even though the air felt warm from the bright sun in a cloudless sky, "we're here. I might as well look at the house."

Okay. In the thirty seconds that I took in the car to try and process what was about to happen, there'd been a list of how she might react and they filtered through my head like a revolving door of awfulness. Avoidance, escape, anger, sadness, disgust. There were varying degrees to which I could handle all of those options. Escape was what I expected. Disgust or anger would have made me want to tear my heart out. Avoidance wasn't preferable, because it meant she'd stay and still work with me.

Sadness was what I hoped for, honestly. Because if sadness was her immediate, unfiltered reaction, that meant she had the same ache working through her that I'd lived with for the past handful of years. Sadness meant that her anguish possibly matched mine. It was hard to imagine that hers was bigger, because I was the one left behind, but even if hers came close, I had hope.

But it looked like avoidance was the way we'd be playing this. Escape might not have been the choice that she made, probably out of love for her sister, but I knew stubborn Julia. I'd been faced with her more times than I cared to count, and if she planned on slipping into professional and polite, then I could do the same. I took a ragged breath, thinking about being polite with her. But I could do it.

At least for a while. I could play the avoidance game with her until she gave me an opening. It didn't have to be a big one, it could be a sliver, just the tiniest crack to let me see the light shining through. But if she showed it to me, I'd walk through in a heartbeat. I'd let her see everything in my heart, every untouched piece of emotion that I kept only for her.

I could do this. So I pulled in another deep breath and nodded, then gestured toward the front door. She gave me one long look before turning and walking back up the front steps. Julia moved to the side so I could key in the lock box code and take out the house key.

I wasn't too macho to admit that my fingers shook while I tried the code the first time, and messed it up. But I could smell her next to me, just a hint of vanilla and oranges, and it was wreaking absolute havoc on me.

"The house matches up with comps in the area," I told her while I finally punched in the code successfully and extracted the key. "They priced it fairly, given what I know about it from the listing agent."

"That's ... good."

I smiled a little at her hesitancy, meeting her eyes over my shoulder while I unlocked the door. But my smile fell at the blank look on her face. Her eyes were trained on the house, completely avoiding my face. It would take time. The tiniest steps in the world up a freaking mountain felt like the most appropriate description to dealing with Julia in a way that wouldn't set us backward.

At my sigh, her eyes flicked to me, and the uncertainty I saw there gave me a swift balloon of hope. She didn't how to navigate this any better than I did.

"After you." I pushed open the door and moved back so she could enter without risking us accidentally touching. Julia swallowed audibly and went in. We were silent as we moved through a nice hallway entry with a dining room off to the side. The house was empty, and I liked how the dining room opened into the bright, updated kitchen through a custom archway.

Julia trailed her fingers along the large island in the center of the kitchen, her eyes looking at the cherry cabinets and tiled backsplash.

"I like this room." She shot me a quick look over her shoulder, almost like she hadn't meant to engage with me.

Keep it cool. Keep it professional. "They updated the kitchen a couple years ago. It's on the high end of your sister's budget, but it hits all the things on her list and I don't think there's much she'd have to update, beyond cosmetic stuff. The backyard is completely fenced in, which I know was a big deal to her, but it does need a lot of work."

She took that in and nodded, showing me her back when she crossed into the large sunken family room that had the slider which led into the backyard. When Julia took the two steps down into the family room, she looked back at me. "Not sure about these though."

"The steps?"

Her eyes moved away to the slider. "With the babies, especially when they're younger."

A thin, hot knife of pain slipped in between my ribs and slowly drained the air out of my lungs. "Right."

At the rough texture of my voice, the things loaded into one word, Julia's eyes closed for a few seconds. Then she sniffed and blinked herself into being composed again. "I'm going to go look at the backyard."

Translation from someone who'd been married to the woman: *don't you dare even dream about following me.* A second later, she was out on the deck and I sagged against the wall next to me, feeling very much like I'd just gone three rounds with Ronda Rousey and she'd had her merry way with me. The temptation to go to the slider or the window in the kitchen to see what Julia was doing was almost too much for me to bear, but I resisted. I couldn't shake the feeling that if I saw her sadness again like I had in the store parking lot, I could handle this better. Not because I reveled in her sadness. On the contrary, when Julia cried, it was as if she had an iron-wrapped line to my soul, as if her tears had an unfailing ability to make me feel like the most awful person in the world because I'd caused her pain.

No, I wanted to see it because I had an almost sick desire to know whether she was still enslaved to us in the way that I still was. I scrubbed at my face with rough hands and struggled to pull it together. It was so much harder than I thought, trying to keep it together around her when all I wanted to do was pull her in my arms and let us comfort each other. Remind myself that there was hope for me, for us, because the universe had shoved us back together.

The slider opened slowly, and when Julia walked back in, she kept her face down at first. When she passed me, I saw the redness in the whites of her eyes. It was the sign that she was fighting tears, that she hadn't succumbed to them yet. To keep from reaching out to her, I clenched my teeth together so tightly my jaw burned.

"The backyard does need work," she said while I followed her down the hallway and up the stairs that led to the three bedrooms. "I took a couple pictures, but I think it's more than we can handle with the babies coming."

Her sister being pregnant, being alone, couldn't be easy for Julia. I'd held her on countless occasions when someone announced their pregnancy and she caved to the emotions of inadequacy, of envy, of desire and sadness. But now wasn't the time to ask her about it. So I let her walk in front of me in silence while we ascended the stairs.

The reason I knew that my emotional state was at risk of drowning me was that I didn't even have to struggle not to check out her ass while we walked up the stairs. I was too afraid that she'd look back and catch me, shove me backwards down the flight of stairs so hard that I'd probably crack my head open and die or something. We cleared the landing and Julia looked at the linen closet that held the washer and dryer, then turned into the full bath.

"Shower's a little small," she commented after sliding the door open and peering inside.

"Gives me claustrophobia just looking at it," I said honestly. To my surprise, Julia laughed under her breath and turned her head away like she might be hiding it from me. When we'd been looking for a house to buy, the forever home we always wanted, finding a shower big enough for me was an issue, became a running joke with every place we looked at. Most of the places we saw, I would have had to crouch like six inches down just to get my head wet. "But then again, Brooke is normal people size."

Julia's lips curved up, just slightly, and I wanted to crow in triumph. "She said something to me before I left about that. That she feels short because she has an amazon for a sister."

"She is short." I shrugged when Julia looked back at me with lifted eyebrows. "Well, she is. She's a foot shorter than me."

"Unless you grew two inches in the last few years, she is *not* a foot shorter than you," she said, oblivious to the fact that her gentle teasing was doing apoplectic things to my heart. "You just always wished you could say that to her and it would be true."

I grinned, like I wasn't one teasing word away from weeping tears of happiness, and walked out of the bathroom, gestured for her to go down the hallway and check out the master bedroom across the hall. "She always did hate that."

Julia stared at me for a beat, her eyes heavy with questions and with confusion. The ease of which we flipped from her gathering herself in the backyard to trading stories about how I loved teasing her sister didn't look as comfortable for her as it was for me. Or maybe it wasn't comfortable. That wasn't the right word. But it was welcome. It was so, so welcome. It wasn't the opening I was looking for, but it was something.

After that long moment of her studying me, she pulled back again, visibly shored up her defenses. While she was looking through the master, she snapped a few pictures on her phone, probably to show Brooke. To get a better shot of the walk-in closet, she leaned back and I stared, unabashedly. The long, lean lines of her body looked almost exactly the same. Her curves, just as perfect as they had been the day I met her. Her legs were so long it was almost criminal. They gave her this loose-hipped walk that made me lose my mind.

"Cole?"

I blinked at her, snapped out of my perusal by the abject torture of hearing her say my name for the first time since the night of our fight. My breath thundered in and out of my lungs and I stammered an apology before letting her pass by me. Julia was looking down at her phone when she walked into the next bedroom. It barely registered which room she was going in because I was still so discombobulated from hearing her say that, just four letters that defined me, but hearing them from her made me want to weep, made me want to fall to my knees in thanks. But I heard her soft, "Oh" and I looked up. She was standing in the doorway of the room that was beautifully decorated as a nursery. The white crib in the corner was ornate, and her hand reached out to follow the curved line of the edges. From where I stood in the hallway, I could see the slight tremble of her long fingers.

"Shit," I muttered under my breath, unprepared for the sight of her in the pink and white room. "Are you okay?" She was completely silent, completely still at first. But then her shoulders shook slightly, her breath sawed in and out of her lungs.

"Why?" She whispered.

God, I wanted to reach for her. "Why what?" I rasped out, my throat thick with emotion.

"Why did I think I could do this with you? I can't *do* this, Cole." She turned and brushed past me, and I caught sight of a tear on her face. Julia all but flew down the stairs before I could even breathe again. I only took one second to try and steady myself before I ran after her.

CHAPTER EIGHT

JULIA

The doorknob under my palm zapped me with an electric shock when I yanked on it and wrenched the door open. By the time the outside air hit my heated skin, I heard Cole shout my name and thunder down the stairs.

"Julia, please! *Please* wait."

A sob lodged in my throat at the pain in his voice, the desperation. But it was enough to stop me, even though my legs fairly itched to keep going, to run until I was locked safe in my car. Tears dripped down my chin, and I did nothing to stop them, the cold splash of them down my neck felt like the only thing grounding me. My lungs stretched with a deep breath when I heard him come to a stop behind me. Cole didn't touch me, and in the moments that we stood there, my back to him, my face wet with tears, I was surprised.

How long had it been since I'd been surprised by any of his reactions? I knew him, or at least I used to. Before he'd open his mouth to speak, I could pinpoint exactly what he'd say. Knew that if we fought over something, he'd be so quick to kiss me, to run his hands over me in a way that was soothing and arousing, completely distracting. But the fact that Cole didn't reach for me now, didn't try to turn me to face him, I couldn't process that.

"Julia, please don't cry," he whispered brokenly. "It kills me when you cry."

Finally I turned, keeping my shoulder against the inside door, a flimsy barrier between us. His eyes were so dark on my face, so deep that I knew they could inhale me, swallow me whole if I let them. They'd always seen straight through into every piece of me, even when I didn't want them to. And now, now I didn't want them to, because I was afraid of what he'd see.

"How can you do this?" I sobbed. "How is it that you can stand up there and talk about closets and showers and counters?"

Cole speared his hands through his hair and stared at me helplessly. "Because I was trying to do what I had to, trying to keep you from running."

I blinked rapidly, swiping a hand over my face to stem the wetness, to no avail, of course. I was past calming myself. Everything swelled and rolled inside of me, the torture on his face enough to crack me in two. When I fisted my hand over my stomach and swallowed another sob, his broad shoulders shifted, he teeth clenched. His desire to reach out to me, to gather me in his arms was a tangible thing wrapped around me. Because it was something he did so easily.

"So acting like nothing is wrong, acting like I'm some stranger, you thought that would help?"

"I didn't *know*, Julia. The last time I saw you, you bolted before I could say *anything*. Do you think it doesn't gut me to be standing so close to you?" Cole's eyes glossed over and I sobbed again. He lifted a hand and pressed it over his stomach, mirroring what I'd just done. "You ran. So easily. Don't you know how much that kills me?"

"How could I?" I whispered in a watery voice, hating the quaver that was so obvious. "For all I know you hate me, Cole. And then you're *here*, I have no idea how and no clue to be prepared for it. And you're so … polite. Like it's so easy for you to act like I'm nobody."

"*Easy?*" His voice was incredulous, heavy with a dark-edged confusion and my tears started again. "You thought this was easy for me? What the *hell*, Julia? I haven't changed that much since you walked out."

God, my heart. It caved in on me, making my knees weak and my stomach pitch in revolt. It was too much. Standing there with him within reaching distance, but so damn far away that I felt like I'd never reach him, even if I was strong enough to try. I covered my mouth when he took a step, felt the tears run underneath my fingers.

We were so close, he was so close, but he wasn't close enough, and I hated myself for thinking it. But I didn't know how much longer I could stand there with my soul cracking at the edges. Seeing that nursery may have lit the match, seeing a tiny piece of the future he and I had imploded over, but this, this was setting bombs off inside of me with every word out of his mouth. Because I deserved his anger, I deserved his pain. Even if it crushed me, destroyed me from the inside out, I deserved every shred of it.

"This isn't easy for me," he went on. "Because for the last two thousand, three hundred and seventy-two days, I have missed you. Every single day I wake up and I miss you, Julia." Cries wracked my frame, but I held them in with my hand, holding his eyes because I owed him that. "The last time I kissed you was the day before we fought and you were wearing vanilla lip balm. I can't smell vanilla without wanting to *break* something, because I miss you so damn much." Cole shook his head and took a deep breath, giving me the first look of frustration in his eyes, like my tears shifted his frustration, his hurt, into something else. "No, Julia, this isn't easy for me, because I love you. I have never stopped loving you, and you disappeared." His voice cracked on the last word, and I lost the tenuous hold that I had on my tears.

My arms wrapped around my middle and I sank against the door, unable to stop the ugly sobs from escaping. My cowardly exit from his life, my empty life without him, and now this, it was too much. My body couldn't contain it, couldn't function with so much black emotion filtering through my veins. His hand landed on my shoulder, smoothed a small circle. I didn't shrug away, didn't back up, so he took another step toward me. I couldn't let go of myself, but I didn't fight him when he pulled me into his arms.

I didn't fight when he held me tightly against him, let me cry into his impossibly broad, impossibly strong chest. Didn't fight him when he sighed into the top of my head, and ran a hand up and down my spine in a gesture so comforting that it made me hate myself even more. The selfish desire to stay there, to let him hold me up, make me feel better about the greatest shame of my life was so strong that I let myself indulge in it for a few more minutes while my tears quieted and slowed.

Before leaving Cole, I never knew it was possible to hate yourself so fully, so deeply without actually labeling it. But it was, because that loathing drove every decision I'd made since the day I walked out, even if I was fooling myself into thinking that it was some sense of benevolence or desire to be a better person.

It was my penance, my atonement for breaking the heart of a man who loved me. Even uprooting my life for Brooke wasn't completely selfless, wasn't completely driven by love for my sister. Because seeing her pregnant, knowing she hadn't even tried, it tore at my soul. And feeling those pinches of pain were welcome, something to add to my penitence. So I cried for him, for what I'd done to him, and how far I'd let myself fall into the rabbit hole of denial. And I cried for me, because I knew I didn't deserve his love, but he'd give it to me anyway.

That was the reason why I didn't reach around him and press myself even closer, because it would mean something to him. It would mean something to me too, but the last thing I would do is give Cole hope if I wasn't sure I could follow through. But for those minutes, eternally long and soul-warming minutes, I let myself be held by him.

How long had it been since someone had wrapped themselves around me like they wanted to take away my pain? Years. The crispness of his shirt against my face, rich with his warm, spicy scent slipped under my skin, it was too much in the best possible way. I sniffed, let myself press my forehead over his heart and feel the steady thumping from underneath his skin. It was so deep and sure, unchanging in its rhythm, which was so appropriate for Cole. He was the most loyal person I'd ever known, which is why he was holding me in my grief and not shoving past me and leaving me to deal with it on my own, like he had every right to do.

He wasn't yelling at me about our last fight, demanding to know the reason why. Why I'd left, why I'd left him in silence and confusion. He had every right to pull those answers from me, and I knew in that moment, that I'd have to look him in the eye at some point and explain. Some day. But not today. Everything was too fresh, too tenuous, and I didn't have enough of a grip on my sanity to try.

I straightened to my full height and backed away from him, his arms loosened because he didn't have a choice. They fell to his sides, and I mourned the loss of his warmth immediately. When he pulled in a slow breath through his nose, I dared a glance to his face. I don't know what I expected, but the implacable mask wasn't it. The only hint to the depth of his feeling was in his eyes. And they burned.

With love. With regret. And most of all, with pain.

"I have to go," I told him when I was sure I could speak calmly again. I held his eyes. "I'm not running, but I do have to go."

A muscle popped in his jaw while he stared at me. I let him take a good long look at my face, which was probably puffy, red, and splotchy. Some women were pretty criers. I was not one of them, which Cole knew. Finally, he nodded slowly and relaxed his jaw. He didn't stop me when I turned and walked down the steps, down the driveway and into my car. When I pulled away from the house, he was still in the doorway watching me.

When I couldn't see him anymore, couldn't see the house in my rear view mirror, I took a deep, cleansing breath and tried to sort through what the hell even happened. But the thing I kept getting stuck on, more than the way he'd looked in the driveway in his slate gray suit, staring at me with that quiet intensity that did strange things to my belly, is what he'd said about the last day he kissed me.

I knew exactly what he was talking about, because I'd replayed it in my head more than I cared to admit. The night before our final, awful fight, he'd received a call from a particularly finicky client about going to see a house, even though it was after eight at night, and Cole was usually done working by that point. Everything had been tense between us since he'd brought up the adoption thing, and I'd refused to consider it.

"Can't you just tell him that you'll take him through the house tomorrow morning?" I'd asked. "It's not like it's going anywhere."

His hands, big and capable, with callouses on the palms that caught on my skin in a way that I loved, straightened the knot on his tie while he looked at me in the mirror of our apartment bathroom. "I work for him, Julia. The commission that I'll get from him will be more than any deal I've done before. Can you imagine what that money could do for us?"

An annoying drum beat at the back of my head, because I damn well knew what he meant. It could be a huge stepping stone for buying a bigger house. Or funding an adoption.

"Yes, I'm aware," I told him calmly, instead of sniping, *I'm not an idiot,* like I wanted to. The way he patronized me sometimes made me want to smother him with a pillow. That's why marriage was so weird. You could plot their death when they snored and kept you awake, but nights like that one, when all I wanted to do was be with him, curl up on the couch with him wrapped behind me, the thought of him walking away made me want to cry. The tension that followed us like a cloud for the previous six months was cumbersome, and for one night, I wanted to pretend like it wasn't there. If I'd asked him, would he have stayed back? If I'd told him just how important it was to try and be

Cole and Julia again, would he have stayed?

I'd never know, because I hadn't asked him. I sat back while he got ready to leave, watched him gather papers and slip on his suit jacket, tie the laces on his black dress shoes and stewed, felt the dark, bubbling annoyance brew in my blood.

Cole caught my eye while he tucked his cell phone into the clip on his belt. "You know I have to go, Julia."

The fact that I didn't answer made him sigh deeply, the sound so rife with *everything* that I closed my eyes, walked to him and wrapped my arms around his waist.

Only one of his arms came around me, absently stroking the spot between my shoulder blades, but not fully engulfing me the way that I loved. Foreboding snaked down my spine, sending a blast of ice through my bones so strongly that I shivered. I wrapped my hand around his tie when I leaned back, trying to see if he was feeling the same premonition that I was. But he was looking at the clock over my shoulder.

Ass.

His eyes snapped to mine when I yanked on his tie. "Don't start ignoring me before you've even walked out the door."

"I'm not ignor-"

Because I didn't want to hear it, couldn't hear it when I was already pissed he was leaving, I leaned up on the balls of my feet and gave him a soft kiss, just a glimpse of our lips. For a second, we hovered there, and I desperately hoped he'd deepen the kiss, spare a moment for me. For us.

A sound escaped my lips on a wispy puff of air, something unconscious that must have given me away, because Cole's eyes heated and his hand moved up under my hair to grip it tightly. He tilted his head and dove in for a kiss so hot, so deep, so searching that I moaned. His tongue slid against mine and I tasted his toothpaste. When my fingers curved around the back of his skull and held him to me, Cole stepped forward and pressed me up against the kitchen table. Two seconds, it only took us two seconds of kissing to turn incendiary.

But that was never our problem. It was so easy to mask our discomfort, our disagreements, our fundamental differences in how we wanted the rest of our life to play out, in bed. Maybe that's why I pushed him before he walked out the door, because it was the easiest step to take, the easiest way to bridge the gap when I couldn't just open my damn mouth and tell him I didn't want him to ignore me.

It was that insecurity, that manipulation, that cowardly refusal to be honest with him that haunted me so many years later. Two thousand, six hundred and seventy-two days, apparently.

The fact that he knew how many days it had been since I left made me hate myself all over again as I pulled back into the parking lot at Brooke's apartment building. When I'd lived back east, I never explained Cole, explained my divorce, because I knew that putting it into words would make me look insane.

How could you leave that kind of man? That's what they would have asked.

"I don't know," I whispered into the interior of my car. Even now, my excuses felt whisper-thin, so unstable that I couldn't hold a feather with them. Tears pricked at my eyes again and I willed them back down. It was useless to cry about it now, to let the guilt eat at me when there was nothing I could do about it. Cole was back in my life, at least temporarily.

Yeah. And whose fault was that?

My eyes zeroed in on the window of Brooke's bedroom. And then I was pissed, irritation spurring me out of my car in jerky movements. But instead of stomping up the stairs and slamming the door open, I unlocked it calmly, set my purse down on the small table right next to it and took a deep breath before walking into Brooke's room.

As she normally was, Brooke was in her nest of pillows and watching *Gilmore Girls* on Netflix. Rapid-fire banter came from the TV while Brooke ignored me as I stared at her with my hands perched on my hips. It was no mystery how this would play out. We were both capable of Olympic-level stubbornness, courtesy of our mother, so I'd have to either wait until her bladder exploded or I was too tired to stand there anymore.

"Care to share anything with me?" I asked quietly.

"You know," Brooke said, keeping her eyes glued to the screen, "the old Julia would have come in here with scary bullet eyes, throwing all the swear words at me for what I did." She finally looked at me, completely unrepentant. Typical fricken younger sister. "This," she gestured at me, "is freaking me out."

"So you admit to doing something wrong? It's a miracle. Shall I call Mom and Dad to note the momentous occasion? They'll probably be thrilled with your meddling."

Brooke snorted. "Like I care. Look, it's never been a secret that I thought you made a huge mistake by leaving him, by refusing to even speak with him again because our parents were shouting in your ear that you shouldn't." Then she shrugged. "This was my way of forcing the issue since you're back here for good. Or at least for the next couple years." I opened my mouth, feeling those obscenities crawl their way up my throat when she lifted a hand to stop me. "You *never* would have sought him out, Julia. Because you're a chicken-shit when it comes to him."

"You have no right to butt your nose into my business, Brooke," I yelled, stepping into her room and pointing a finger at her.

"Yes I do, because you are a shell of yourself without him. It would be one thing if you were all, yay woman power! I don't need no stinkin' man, but you're not. He has your heart. Don't even deny it."

Every word hit me with perfect accuracy, worming into me so deeply that I wish I could have yanked them back out. "So what exactly do you expect from me now? Huh? Go find your dream home with my ex-husband and pretend like it's okay?"

"Yes," she said. Her chin was lifted and her eyes hard as stone.

The anger that swamped me was instant, hot, and overwhelming. "I get that you're bored as hell because you're stuck in bed for twelve weeks, but do not *ever* ambush me with something like that again. I've already got one set of overbearing parents, I don't need a meddlesome little brat stepping in and making my life worse, got it?"

Brooke blinked, hurt covering her face, causing me to let out a heavy breath as I rubbed my forehead. A headache started blooming at the base of my skull, partly from the insane amount of tears that I'd expelled today, and partly from the anger that I rarely let loose on Brooke.

"I'm sorry," she said quietly.

"I'm sorry, too. I shouldn't have called you a brat." I looked up. "But you were meddlesome."

She smiled at me. "I expected much worse than brat, actually." She lifted her hand, a business card wedged between her fingers. Then she tossed it at me. It landed on the floor and when I leaned down to grab it, I saw Cole's name. "I can find a new realtor if you really can't do it. But I know you're strong enough to just talk to him. That's all I'm asking. Just to talk to him."

I traced the edge of his card, the heavy material feeling like an anchor in my hands, threatening to pull me under. Brooke sounded so sincere, but it wasn't a promise I could make to her in that moment, not with the intensity of what I'd just been through with him.

But she didn't need the promise, because when I tucked the card into my pocket, I caught her smile before I turned and walked away.

CHAPTER NINE

COLE

That entryway, that simple doorway, tilted my entire universe on its axis. Even ten minutes after Julia drove away, I stood there, my arms tingling and my throat raw from holding in the roar that wanted to escape from within me. If I let it out, if I gave voice to the whipping maelstrom inside of me; grief, rage, elation and confusion, I'd topple the house on top of me from the sheer force of what I was feeling. The walls weren't strong enough to withstand it, probably wouldn't have been unless they were ten solid feet of concrete.

When I rubbed my hand over my mouth, still completely unable to process what had just happened, I had to pinch my eyes shut, because I could smell her on my skin. Just from holding her in my arms.

"Holy hell," I said on a gasp, and stumbled back until I sank down on the landing of the stairs behind me. Holding my head up was impossible, so I gripped the sides with my hands and balanced my elbows on my knees. Normally, I could be counted on to be the steady one, to keep my cool in any situation. But not when it came to Julia.

It turned me into this knot of emotions so tangled up that there was no way I could ever smooth them into a straight, understandable line.

But still, after all these years, all the distance and silence between us, she wrecked me. She fit in my arms so perfectly, after all the years and distance and silence, allowing me to comfort her when part of me wanted to shake her, yell at her and demand answers for why I'd had to live in purgatory all these years.

The thing that made me the biggest chump of all though was that those moments of holding her, feeling her up against me, being able to feel the cool, smooth strands of her hair against my face would probably be enough to sustain me through another year of silence, if that's what she deemed necessary.

I'd hate it. But I'd lived through worse.

My phone vibrated angrily, and I ignored it, content to wallow in what had just happened between us.

I'm not running, but I do have to go.

And what the hell was I supposed to assume that meant? Given our history, I had no reason to think she wouldn't run from this again. And I'd be powerless to stop her, because she'd simply disappear.

The vibrating started again, and I yanked my phone out, practically snarling at the screen when I saw it was Ashton. I'd sent her four more houses to look at over the last forty-eight hours, and apparently she wanted to see them all.

Ashton Mason-Fourtier: I love the options you sent, Cole. Go ahead and schedule something at all four places, I'm completely flexible when it comes to you.

My fingers tightened around my phone, and for a brief second, I wondered what it might feel like to squeeze so tightly that the plastic would break. How hard would I have to work to crack the screen, right through her words that made me feel disgusting after what had just happened with Julia. Holding Julia in my arms while she wept meant more to me than sleeping with a thousand beautiful women like Ashton. There was enough emptiness in the way the world interacted now, hiding behind computers and phones, letting blatant innuendo in a few typed out words replace her coming up to me and saying, Hey, Cole. I'm attracted to you. Would you like to go out sometime?

I'd have said no, of course. But her insinuations and over-sexualized flirting felt cheap and disgusting now, instead of vaguely annoying like it used to be. So I did something that I'd never done before. I lied to her and pawned her off on another agent. After sending a quick text to Mark, who was happily married and had referred clients to me when his workload was too full, I sent another to Ashton.

Me: Glad you like the houses, Ashton. I've had a personal emergency come up, so I've passed all of your information on to one of my colleagues, Mark, and he's looking forward to setting up viewings of all four houses. Best of luck.

Without waiting for a response, and feeling a thousand pounds lighter, I locked up the house and walked back to my car. The drive back to my house went fast, and even though there was a still a lot of day left, I knew I couldn't handle being at the office in my current frame of mind. At least at home, I'd be able to obsess about, dissect and break apart every minute of my interactions with Julia.

Like I'd be doing until I saw her again. *If* I saw her again. But I shook that aside when I pulled into the garage of my place and unlocked the door before heading in. I was just rifling through my mail when there was a knock on the front door. It was instinctive to feel a rush of happiness that it might be Julia, but then I remembered she couldn't possibly know where I lived. The office would never give out my home address to a client, so I swallowed back my disappointment and opened the door.

Dylan was holding up a propane tank with a sheepish smile on his face.

"Hey, man," I said, holding the door open for him, feeling only the slightest pinch of irritation at having to be sociable in a moment where all I wanted to do was be alone.

"Sorry it took me so long to replace the one I borrowed from you." When I didn't respond right away, he shifted the tank in his hands. "Where do you want me to set this?"

I blinked, mentally slapping myself. Don't be an asshole needed to be my new mantra with my friends after what had happened with Garrett, especially since none of them had a single idea of what had happened with Julia. They had no reason to cut me any slack, and it was my own fault. "Come on in, I'll stick it in the garage." While I took it from him, I jerked my chin toward the kitchen. "Grab a beer if you'd like."

Dylan laughed. "If I didn't have to close at the bar tonight, I would, trust me."

"They still working you too much?"

"I'm a manager. Comes with the territory." Dylan smiled when I walked back into the kitchen. "You know how it is. You've got the same crazy hours that I do."

I lifted my eyebrows in concession. "Well, I don't go 'til two a.m. last I checked, but yeah, I'm hardly working a nine to five. I like it that way though. Keeps me from getting bored."

We lapsed into silence, and I felt Dylan staring at me like he wanted to say something. Since he'd moved here, he fit into our group seamlessly, but I still hadn't spent a whole lot of time with just him, not like the other three. Suddenly, I wished I could blurt out everything that had happened in the last couple days. Tell someone that I was freaking the hell out, that I didn't even know how I felt about everything that was happening.

"You okay, Cole?" Dylan asked quietly.

"I don't know," I answered him honestly. I caught his eyes before looking back down at the granite counter where I had my elbows braced. "Garrett tell you that I saw Julia? My ex-wife," I clarified.

Dylan rubbed at his jaw, trying to hide a smile. "Yeah. I know who she is. And yeah, he mentioned it after you left the other night."

"He's worse than my grandmother at spreading gossip, I swear."

We laughed, because Garrett really was. How Rory put up with him was a miracle.

"Wanna talk about it?"

Briefly, I closed my eyes, pinched the bridge of my nose while I thought about that. I did. And I didn't. Starting from scratch and trying to encapsulate the demise of a marriage to someone I still loved to this day was beyond daunting. Impossible. Heart-breaking, to relive at least.

"I've never tried," I admitted after a beat. Dylan's eyes widened and I couldn't help but smile. "Crazy, right?"

"What about your family? I mean, I know you met the guys right after you two got divorced. But what about before? You had no one to talk to?"

Whether Dylan was drinking or not, I stood from the bar stool and grabbed a beer from the fridge, cracking it open and taking my time pouring it into a pint glass before I sat again. "My mom died from cancer when I was a freshman in college." He made a sympathetic noise. "My dad passed about two years after Julia and I got married."

"Holy shit, Cole. I'm so sorry. And, it's just you, right? No siblings?"

I nodded, keeping my eyes trained on the slow path of bubbles that flowed from the bottom of the glass up to the foamy top. "Just me. That's why Julia and I wanted to start a family even though we were so young. It meant a lot to me, to her, too. And that," I swallowed roughly, "that's what went wrong."

Obviously, Dylan wasn't going to interrupt, so I rolled my neck, felt the satisfying pop before I spoke again.

"The short version is that we ... disagreed how to make that family. And four years of infertility, of tests showing that there wasn't anything clearly wrong with either us, and when you can't agree on the next steps was the hardest fucking thing I've ever gone through. You're helpless. Every single month. And her parents, Dylan, I can easily admit it now because they're not my in-laws anymore, but I hated that her parents had so much sway with her." I laughed under my breath, a harsh puff of sound. "More than me, in the end."

I took another sip of my beer, promised myself that I wouldn't second guess my words to him, wouldn't filter anything about how I was feeling. "We had an awful fight. She walked out, and I can't even really blame her after what I said. But, when she left, I had no clue that she wouldn't come back. When I was at work about a week later, she came and packed up her stuff, sent her sister later for more. I *know* it's because her parents convinced her not to come back to me, convinced her to just walk away, even though we both loved each other. I didn't see her for over seven years."

"Until last week."

"Until last week."

Dylan let out a low whistle. "I can't even imagine, man. I don't know if I'm ... allowed to ask this, I guess, but any miscarriages?"

I felt a dull ache beneath my ribs, but I shook my head. "We tried IUI a few times, but ... no, never got that far."

"So now what? You ran into her at the store, and that's been it? I know Garrett said she turned down the job working for him."

"About that..." While I filled him in on what had happened with Brooke, Dylan actually started laughing.

"She's got some balls to pull that off."

"Yeah, Brooke does have those."

The humor of it, the complete insanity of what Brooke had done honestly hadn't hit me until Dylan laughed about it. But my smile was real, for the first time all day, I felt a strange sense of comfort. Brooke obviously wanted Julia to deal with me, one way or the other, and I'd told a friend the soap-opera level ending to my marriage, and he hadn't so much as blinked. Leaning on other people with shit like this, it didn't come naturally to me. And more than once, sitting around a table playing poker with the guys, it struck me that the reason adoption had been a viable option for me was because I knew that family wasn't just blood. It didn't matter that I'd never share DNA with Garrett or Michael or Tristan, even Dylan now, they were brothers to me.

Julia had been my family too, and I didn't care if the baby came from Guatemala or Africa or from someone down the street, we'd have loved that baby and made it the center of our world. DNA didn't change that. It was something that Julia's parents, with their long bloodlines, massive family trees, and old money, just didn't understand. And to add to my list of things I didn't know was whether Julia still felt that way too. It came right under whether she hated me on that list.

"I just don't know whether Julia will go along with working with me." I fisted my hand and tapped it on the counter, a fraction of the roiling frustration still trapped in me. "And as well as I know her, or knew her, I don't know what the hell to do. I played it cool today, kept it professional, and that backfired on me too."

Dylan let out a deep breath. "Obviously I've never been married. But I don't think it's different from a lot of tough situations in life. There's not always an easy answer. I think this is one of those shitty things that's a razor's edge away from more than one outcome."

I thought about that for a second, knew the awful truth of it. "I'm screwed if I push too hard."

"Or if you don't show her that you still love her."

"Oh, I let that bomb slip earlier. That I still loved her."

Dylan smiled. "I said show. Not tell."

So easy, right? Show the woman who ran away from me for seven years and would avoid me as much as possible that I still loved her. I'd have better luck convincing the general population that a tarantula was a great pet to cuddle with.

"It's obvious to us that you still love her, Cole. I don't say that to be a dick, but," he paused until I looked at him again, "loving her and wanting to try again with her, those are two completely different things."

I laughed, but I didn't particularly find it funny. "Dylan, I've spent more than six years believing that those things were so tightly intertwined that I'd never be able to separate them."

Did I love Julia? Yes. Unequivocally.

And if she showed up today, showed up on my doorstep and told me she loved me too, would I want to start over again? Yes. Unequivocally. But I had to know that it might not be so clear for her, especially since she'd been the runner, not the chaser.

"Look, even if you can't separate them, just figure out a way to show her you love her without suffocating her. She ran from you once. Don't give her another reason to."

Then I did laugh. Heartily, with a slight tinge of hysteria to it. Like Dylan hadn't just summed up the impossibility of my relationship with Julia into a few sentences.

"Just like that, huh?" I asked him wearily.

Dylan clapped me on the shoulder and stood from his chair. "Just like that." He paused before opening the door and smiled. "Talk to us, man. We're here for you. Happy to remind you anytime that we're really damn glad it's not us who has to pull that off."

Even after the door shut, I was smiling, which was a welcome change to how I felt before Dylan knocked. Some of the hopelessness was still there, some of the unease at knowing that Julia could run from me again, very easily. But underneath both of those things was a steadily growing stream of hope. We'd found each other once, and I had to hold onto the belief that we could do it again.

So I grabbed my phone and sent out another text. This time to my very favorite former sister-in-law.

CHAPTER TEN

JULIA

"Oooooh yeah, baby," Brooke practically purred from the couch while I fastened the buckle around my ankles. If I hadn't been so damn nervous, I would've smirked, maybe held my leg out so she could admire the snakeskin pattern. I'd worked in marketing and advertising long enough, both on the east coast and Colorado, that I'd accumulated a helluva wardrobe for occasions such as this.

Okay. Maybe not *exactly* like this occasion. Big meetings, I was prepared for. Pitches that could ensure a promotion. Those were the occasions that this particular outfit was good for. But knowingly walking into an empty house with my ex-husband, the only man I'd ever loved, and who apparently still loved me, even after I'd left him cruelly and callously? That was an occasion that demanded the outfit and expensive lipstick. And the blowout that I'd had done at the salon that Brooke was currently on medical leave from.

"What's ironic is that two days ago, I told you that those stupid nude heels were overkill," I mumbled. Brooke all but cackled. I'd helped her move from the bed to the couch (aka *my* bed) while I got ready, because we both felt like we needed a change of scenery for my preparation to see Cole again.

Preparation. Ha. As if I could ever be fully prepared to walk right back into the same situation again. The word preparation brought to mind something that you had some modicum of control over, and other than knowing the address of the next house, and what I was wearing, there was nothing about this that felt within my control.

"That is ironic," she said in a deceptively mild tone. Deceptive because I knew her. She eyed me for a second before speaking again. "And why are we looking so hot to go see him again?"

I stared at my shoes, tried to figure out how to put it in words. "A lot of women feel better about themselves when they look their best."

Of course, she wouldn't accept a token answer. She kept right on staring at me, that pregnant little hussy. So I rolled my eyes and faced her.

"Fine. Because I've given this far more thought than I should have." I expelled a whispered curse word. "If I look like shit, he'll wonder if there's something wrong with me. Or that I don't care. And it's not that I don't care, I just ... I don't *know* what I feel right now." I lifted my shoulders helplessly. "I want to look good because it's the first time I'm knowingly facing him in a really, really long time. You've got to be able to understand that."

After a loaded silence, she finally nodded. "Yeah. I can understand that. This is something you can control."

I laughed under my breath while I turned the other direction. "Exactly."

"You still never really explained to me why you decided to go along with this. You could've refused."

Glancing over my shoulder at Brooke, I lifted an eyebrow. "Is that right? Weren't your exact words, unless you want my poor children to come home to this shoebox apartment, then you'll get your skinny ass to the next house with Cole? That was you, right?"

Brooke blew a raspberry with her lips, shifted on the couch with a wince. "At that particular moment, I was also in the midst of heartburn so bad that I felt like someone dropped me into the seventh circle of hell. Truth is, I *always* expect you to argue with me when it comes to Cole."

That was the crux of it, which Brooke had no way of knowing. The truth was that I couldn't quite explain why I decided not to put my foot down. Maybe my oh-so-pretty breakdown the first, er, second time seeing him had jarred something loose in my brain. That was the only explanation to me.

I'd *never* hated Cole, even when I was so mad at him that kicking him in the balls wasn't out of the question. And hate might have been the only thing that could have driven me to refuse Brooke in this.

No, hate was not what I felt. A lot of confusion, mixed up with uncertainty and only the tiniest splash of excitement. That tiny splash was why I draped myself in the armor of a woman who wants a man to think she's beautiful. It was stupid, really. That an almost thirty-four year old woman could feel this way about man she'd already left once.

"You get why it was so hard for me to hear you defend him, right?" I asked Brooke. "He and I had been divorced for years, and you still defended him. I felt like I had no choice but to argue."

Brooke sighed, rubbing a small circle on her belly. "And now you're free from that feeling because he's here and you're here and the universe has put you back together again."

I laughed. "*You* put us back together, Brooke. And we're not *together*, you know that."

"Mmmkay."

"Brooke," I said firmly. "This isn't a movie. It's not a neatly typed up script that always ends with the couple kissing and riding off into the sunset." Emotion lodged in my throat, thick and woolly, and I had to work to swallow it down. I'd long ago given up on Cole and I having that kind of ending, and even with this new plot twist in my life, there was nothing like that in sight for me. If there was, I sure as shit couldn't see it. "I get that you're trying to help, but ... there's just so much between us that, I don't even know. We don't need any outside hands, messing up an already messy pot."

The color was high on Brooke's cheeks while she watched me, watching my fingers fidget and my knees bounce. "I said I was sorry, right?"

I closed my eyes before standing and taking one final deep breath. Then I faced her, holding out my hand so she could take hold. "Yeah, Brooke. You did."

"'Kay, good," she said quietly.

"Want me to help you back to your room before I go? Get you anything to eat?"

She shook her head and settled back against the cushions. "I'm good. Just ... just one last thing."

"Name it."

Brooke took a deep breath and let it out slowly. "Just talk to him. Hear what he has to say, if anything. I won't ask you if you still love him, because I know you do. Not many people get a second chance, opportunity, whatever you want to call this. So just, just talk to him, okay?"

Whatever minor pinch of frustration I felt at her words, the implication that I'd *not* talk to him, was swamped by my love for my little sister. Our parents were absent at best now. It was just me and Brooke. So I walked over and planted a kiss on the top of her head, rubbed her belly before cupping the side of her face. "Okay. I love you, sister."

She grinned, looking like Brooke again. "Love you too. Now go find my dream home."

And her dream home it was. Once again, I'd beaten Cole to the location, and when I pulled my car up against the curb in front of the white ranch home, I knew that Brooke would be in love. The lawn, though dry and crunchy from the cold, would be beautiful when the weather warmed. It led up to the long white house with black shutters and a bright red door. The landscaping was neat and colorful, or would be in the spring, and the sprawling tree in the front yard had a bright blue swing hanging from a gnarled branch. The sound of kids filtered through my open window, and a young woman pushing a stroller down the sidewalk smiled at me when she passed.

My door opened with a creak, and I couldn't help but smile back at her. After waiting for a car to pass, I walked across the street and up the driveway. There was a basketball hoop mounted over the garage, and I couldn't wait to tell her how crazy that would make Dad. We'd begged for one growing up, but he said that the last thing he and Mom needed was the infernal, constant banging of the ball hitting the backboard in the background.

A gust of wind made me shiver, even though the sun was shining, causing me to pull my too-thin jacket around me for what little good it did.

The sound of his car pulling up made me turn toward the house, just to have another moment to collect my bearings. Cole cleared his throat after I heard the sound of his car door closing and I turned to face him.

Wait. That whimper, did that come from me? Dear Lord in heaven, please don't let him have heard that, because I couldn't stand being embarrassed on top of everything else.

Cole looked ... he looked like perfection in a suit. Dark blue this time, tailored impeccably around his tall, broad frame. The shirt underneath was white and crisp, and the tie. His scarlet tie was exactly the same color that he'd worn on the day we got married at the courthouse in downtown Denver, the same color as my wedding dress. I swallowed, fully aware that I was staring. But so was he.

I'd tied his tie for him the day we exchanged our simple vows in front of the judge, his father and Brooke our two witnesses. Even though we'd been living together for six months before we got married, his hands shook when he tried to get the knot exactly right.

Only twenty, neither one of us had given much thought to the traditions of not seeing each other the day of the wedding, so I'd set down my curling iron and swept his hand aside so I could do it for him. The way he'd smiled at me when I perched on the bathroom counter, still in my fluffy white robe, made my heart swoop down into my stomach.

He'd be my husband before the day was done. This handsome, strong, kind man who kissed me until my knees were weak, loved me like he'd been born to do it, would be my husband. I remember thinking it so vividly, like it had happened yesterday, not fourteen years earlier.

"What if I forget my vows?" he'd asked me, watching my face while I finished his tie.

"All you do is repeat what the judge says." I yanked the tie tighter than necessary, making him laugh in a way that raised goosebumps on my skin. "You better not."

"Anything that has to do with you, I could never forget." He was so serious, looking into me so deeply that I didn't care how young we were. Didn't care how my parents said we were ridiculous and immature, that I was throwing away my life by tethering myself to him. I held his face in both of my hands, kissed him so deeply that only three beats of my heart later, he'd opened my robe and pushed me farther back onto the counter. The tie, the crisp edges of it, the satin material, felt cool against my breasts when he whispered in my ear, "You're my soul, Julia. My *wife*. You'll never not be a part of me."

"Julia?" Cole asked and I blinked at him, still trapped in the memory, feeling the flush of mortification sweep my face. No biggie, right? I'd been staring at him, remembering when he screwed me on the bathroom counter two hours before we got married. Suddenly, I was not so cold.

"Hi," I said to him. "Sorry. Just ... gathering myself."

His face smoothed out in relief when I spoke, because he'd probably prepared himself for the worst. For more tears, for closed-off Julia, or for my anger. "It's not a problem. Ready to go in?"

The words and delivery were polite, he was gesturing for me to head to the front door, but his eyes were warmer than the last time I'd seen him. And I don't know what I expected, in truth. Cole would be polite with me, would want to do his job and treat me with respect, which is what he should do. It wasn't like I was expecting him to beg me for details on my life from when we were apart. And it certainly wasn't like I'd be begging him for details on his life.

Immediately, my eyes looked at his left hand, but it was tucked into his pants pocket. He'd told me he still loved me, but that didn't mean he wasn't capable of loving someone else, too. Irrationality wasn't a typical reaction for me, but I'd learned in the last fifteen years, that I wasn't always rational when it came to Cole.

He was speaking about the neighborhood, about the lot size in comparison to the other houses we might look at, and the low timbre of his voice calmed my racing heart. Oh, if he knew that, he'd smile. He'd be so happy. Maybe someday I'd be able to tell him that, but for now, I nodded and followed him to the front door, promising myself that this house visit would end in an entirely different way than the last one had.

Cole pulled the key out of the lock box and turned to me with a crooked smile, my very favorite of all of his smiles. "Ready?"

With a deep breath, I gave him a smile of my own. "Yeah. I think so."

And I followed him in.

CHAPTER ELEVEN

COLE

"And the great thing is that there aren't any stairs that Brooke will have to deal with on a daily basis." I pointed to the closed door in front of stairs that led to the simple, unfinished basement. "Everything is framed out down there, so if she wanted to add in another family room someday, it would be pretty easy. Lots of room to grow into for the future."

Julia nodded, sweeping her eyes over the kitchen. "It's exactly her style."

I hitched my hip on the island and watched her unabashedly. Today was different. The way she smiled at me in the driveway was shy, a little hesitant, which were words I'd never typically use to describe Julia. And the way she looked… the way she looked was as if she took a steel bat to my lungs. I didn't stand a chance with her, even if I'd had any intention of preparing myself for the way she impacted me.

"How is Brooke?"

She lifted an eyebrow, only making eye contact briefly. It still gutted me, brief though it was. "Besides pregnant and recently abandoned by the father of her unborn children?"

If her tone hadn't been light and playful, I would have felt like camping out under a rock. I laughed under my breath. "Yeah, besides that. Am I allowed to ask what happened?"

Julia took a deep breath and wandered from the kitchen to the adjoining family room. Framed on the mantle of the brick fireplace was a smiling family of four with matching blonde hair and bright blue eyes. Normally, the presence of family pictures could make it harder for the potential buyer to envision themselves in the space, but it didn't seem to bother Julia. She touched the edge of the frame, her profile to me.

"Brooke wouldn't mind if I told you," she finally said, giving me a brief smile. "Apparently she still favors you."

I tipped my chin and laughed in response. "Apparently."

She smiled in answer, but it faded pretty quickly. "She'd been with Kevin for years. They never married, much to my parents' chagrin." My teeth instantly clenched at the mention of her parents, or as I liked to refer to them, Mr. and Mrs. Lucifer. "He was okay, but I think a huge part of his appeal was how much my parents hated him."

"But they wanted Brooke to marry him?"

"Right? Don't ask me to explain my mom and dad. I think the only reason is because it sounds better that she had a husband, not a boyfriend that she'd lived with for six years but had no visible sign of commitment from. He hopped from job to job, always on the brink of something that he'd *really* love." Her brows bent in and she held my eyes for the longest all afternoon. My heart skipped in my chest, warmth spreading through my veins. "And apparently, he didn't really love the idea that he'd now have to provide for two babies that he didn't plan for or particularly want. So he moved out three weeks after she found out she was having twins."

The breath I released was a long hiss. My hands actually shook with the desire to break bones or draw blood or something equally barbaric. Still, Julia held my eyes, and I could see the same fire in her eyes that I felt in my belly. When I felt like I could speak without using a string of four letter words, I spoke in a low voice. "He doesn't deserve someone like Brooke, doesn't deserve to be able to father her children."

"Exactly. That's why I moved back. Because she's on bed rest now, because she'll need help when the babies are born, and I have this lingering fear that he'll show up on the doorstep someday to beg her forgiveness." She narrowed her eyes, and I felt a hot flush of pride at how fierce she looked. "And if I'm the one to answer the door if he does show up, I think I just might skin him alive with a butter knife."

"Well, let me know if you'd want help burying the body," I told her with a small smile, hoping that it would make me look like I was in control of my emotions, instead of the truth. The truth was that hearing Julia talk about murdering someone that hurt a loved one, even in jest, made me want her with a sharp visceral pang. There was a side to Julia, the nurturing, caring side that drew people to her, made them feel comfortable around her. And the other side was equally attractive, staggering in how it affected me. That other side was the fierce protectiveness that she had for the people she loved, for her tribe.

If Julia could read my thoughts, she didn't show it, simply laughed out a short breath. "Deal."

The moment was over and I straightened. "Want to see the basement? I think we could get the seller to move the washer and dryer up to the main floor. There's already a water hookup in the mudroom off the garage. They already plan to leave those here, so it's an easy request."

Julia didn't answer right away, and I caught her staring at my left hand. At my empty ring finger. If she'd ran into me on the street, even two years after we got divorced, she still would have seen the simple gold band that she insisted she buy me when we got married.

We walked downstairs in silence, and I had to fight not to grab her elbow while she navigated the wooden steps in her ridiculous, albeit sexy, heels. It was one of the hottest things to me about Julia. She stood almost six feet tall without shoes, but she didn't hesitate in the slightest to strap on some shoes that nudged her closer to six three.

"Watch your head," I told her before she cleared the bottom. I ducked when I passed the low hanging edge of the ceiling and caught her smiling. "What?"

But she only shook her head and walked around the large open basement, just concrete floors with framed out wood on the walls. "Could she add bedrooms down here eventually?"

"No, unfortunately. Those easement windows don't meet the fire code. But she could add a bathroom, any other kind of room as long as there's no walls enclosing something that's specifically meant to be a bedroom." I held up my hands. "So if she put a bed down here, but didn't put walls around it, my lips are sealed."

"Noted," Julia said, sounding amused. Music to my freaking ears. She moved around the space, asking good questions about the water heater and the furnace. From her facial expressions, it was obvious that she loved it. A lot. The bedroom sizes weren't huge, but according to her, they didn't need to be. There were two full bathrooms and a double lot in the backyard, so Brooke would have plenty of space for the kids to play. And the neighborhood itself was skewing younger, something I knew would appeal to her.

Then I stopped short. If this was it, if Julia told me to put in an offer on the house, what excuse would I have to see her? It was a fight to let her wander in silence around the space that really didn't have much to see, but she was studying it as if it held the answers to everything. Finally, she stopped moving and faced me, her hands clasped in front of her. The elegant lines of her collarbone disappeared under the shirt she was wearing, and I knew how the hard bone felt under my lips, how soft her skin was against the edge of my tongue when I used to trace the entire length across her chest.

"So what do you think?" I asked, aware that my question was rife with other meanings. Are you ready for this to be done? Are you ready to give some hint, some clue as to what you're thinking? I wasn't ready for her to go, even though the sky was darkening outside, the mountains would disappear from view shortly once the sun sank behind them.

Julia's chest expanded on a deep breath, her lips pursed into a tiny O when she let it out, but her eyes gave nothing away. "I think Brooke will love this house. It's perfect for her."

My heart sank. "Of course. I can call her later and talk about putting in an offer." I swallowed and held her eyes, risking the fact that she'd see how desperately I didn't want this to be done. "Unless you think she'd still want you to see the last house. I called the listing agent before I got here, it's open tonight if you want to check it out."

"It's getting late." Her eyes darted to my hand again and I couldn't help the curving of my lips. "I wouldn't want to keep you."

I shrugged. "Goes with the job. You remember that."

She peered at me from under her lashes, just for a moment. "How many hours are you working these days?"

"A lot. More than I used to."

"You must not be home much."

Searching, she was definitely searching. It wasn't hard to smother the triumphant grin that wanted to emerge, because I would do anything to keep her talking to me like this. It wasn't how we used to be, this was something different, with a veneer of politeness and tip-toeing around each other that we'd never had to deal with before. Dancing was never my forte, but if that's what I had to do with her for a while, I'd strap some damn tap shoes on right in front of her.

"Just ask me, Julia," I said quietly, the hint of a smile still on my face. Her face flushed. "You know you want to."

She cleared her throat, a crisp sound of denial that said more than any words could. "I wasn't going to ask you anything."

I smiled. "Okay. Come on, it's cold down here."

We cleared the steps and while I turned off all the lights in the kitchen, I looked at her over my shoulder. "There's no one waiting for me, if that's what you weren't going to ask me."

Her eyes narrowed at me and there was a tightening in my stomach, the really good kind. "I wasn't going to ask, Cole. It's not my business if you have someone waiting for you or not."

If she was baiting me into getting angry, to rise to the spark of challenge laden in her defensiveness, she'd be sorely disappointed. I was long past the point of assuming that I could read every thought of hers. She was far too complex, far too puzzling after so many years apart. But to see her like this, so worked up because I did nail her so clearly, was too entertaining to be something that could anger me.

"Understood," I said easily. "But just figured I'd put it out there."

The color was still high in her cheeks, and I wished I could reach out and run my thumb along the skin, see if it felt as warm as it looked. We'd get there, I knew with complete certainty. How long it would take, or how difficult the path would be, I didn't know.

If it took seven more years to get her back, I'd do it in a heartbeat. It sounded insane, and somewhere in my head, I knew that. But it still felt true down to my marrow. Which meant I wasn't ready to rush this along. So I pulled my phone out and frowned. "Actually, do you mind if we see the next house tomorrow or the next day? I forgot about something I need to do at the office tonight."

Julia looked relieved, and even if it was simply because she was still annoyed with me, I didn't really care. I'd take it. Any emotion she could throw at me, I'd accept the weight with gladness. Because it meant that some part of her still cared. To what degree, I still needed to figure out.

"That's fine." She tucked a piece of hair behind her ear. "This is my only job right now, so I can work with your schedule."

"Great. I'll let you know tomorrow morning."

A quick smile, and she was gone.

This time, quite unlike the first time, I watched her car drive away with a completely different emotion lodged in my chest.

Underneath the unpleasant knowledge that we'd eventually have to talk about everything that we were avoiding right now, there was a strong pulse of hope. And I could survive on that for a very, very long time.

COLE

The guys gathered at my place a few hours later for the Thursday night football game, Broncos versus Chargers. To be a dick, Michael came wearing Chargers colors, and we threw popcorn at his head for pretty much the entire first quarter. The distraction was nice, because too much silence meant too much time in my own head. I'd been there so much in the last seven years that I was getting sick of my own internal dialogue.

Which is why, at the commercial break before the second quarter started, I started laughing when I caught Garrett and Dylan giving me frequent, worried looks.

"Okay," I said. "How many of you know what I talked to Dylan about a couple nights ago?"

Crickets. Then Garrett raised his hand.

"I stay out of that stuff, man," Michael said when I looked at him. "Unless you want to talk about it, of course."

When I glanced at Tristan, he gave me a look like, what do *you* think? Okay, so Tristan didn't know anything. Our group of friends had an interesting dynamic. We straddled the line between the friends that only did the beer and sports thing together, discussing trades and rosters and the bare minimum of how work was going. For a lot of guys, that was sufficient. No messy talks about relationships or families, politics or religion. But we were somewhere in the middle of the two.

Occasionally, relationship stuff came up, family stuff came up, and none of them shied away from it. Garrett would say that we were worse than a pack of elderly women when it came to gossiping, but since I'd met some pretty kick-ass women in their 80s, it didn't bother me in the slightest. But through all of it, I'd never explained Julia to them, without a solid reason why.

Probably because it was too painful, too fresh, despite the years that separated me from our marriage. They didn't understand my devotion to her, that much was obvious. But how could they? I'd never told them anything.

Actually, that was a lie. Tristan got it. He was the only one who didn't rib me about it, but that's probably because he'd been in love with Garrett's little sister, Anna, for as long as I'd been separated from Julia. He was even more monk-like than me. And he'd never talked about that either, but it was obvious to anyone with eyeballs. Unless you were Anna, she was either blind, or actively ignored it. Given she was still married to someone who actively ignored her, it was probably the latter.

Either way, I had at least one person who didn't think I was batshit crazy for pining for someone I couldn't have, couldn't touch.

"But like," Michael continued, "if you wanted to explain why you're batshit crazy about this woman, I certainly wouldn't mind knowing. Because, hell, I don't get it."

Tristan's mouth curved up in a smile and Garrett coughed into his beer. They wouldn't judge me, I trusted them that much. Understanding might be different, because unless you'd experienced the vicious, exhausting, soul-draining cycle of infertility, you'd never truly understand.

But this was my family, in the truest sense of the word. They'd drop anything for me, and I'd do the same for them.

So I opened my mouth and started talking. Tristan muted the game, and not once did their attention waver. Not even Michael's, which was practically a miracle.

I talked about my parents, how their deaths spurred on an intense desire for Julia and I to start a family, even though we were practically babies ourselves. I told them about the first time Julia came home with a pregnancy test, and I was so excited that I got on my knees and kissed her stomach, prayed that there was something tiny and perfect in there, only to find there wasn't. She hadn't cried that time, and neither had I.

Those tears came later. More than I could fit into my hands, if I'd tried to catch them all for her. The death of my father—unexpected but peaceful—two years after we got married and one year into our fertility journey. How that lit a fire under me to have a family, far brighter and hotter than I could have anticipated. I told them about the tests, the procedures that yielded no results. The arguments about the next steps. How arguments dissolved into fights and bitterness, an exhaustion so deep that sometimes I still felt it weighing down my bones.

And I told them about how she walked out, how I never saw her again until last week. That like the chump I was for her, I didn't fight her on the divorce, because if it was what she truly wanted—to be away from me—I gave it to her. That was the exhaustion talking, because I didn't have it in me to keep fighting her. Probably in the same way that she didn't have it in her to keep fighting me.

About Brooke and why Julia was back here. About her damned parents and how their pernicious snobbery colored Julia's opinion. How I was given this opportunity to spend time with her again, and we kept dancing around anything substantial. How much I still loved her, was still chained to her in the most primitive way, and I had no desire to unshackle myself.

By the time I finished, my throat hurt, the words coming up dry and rough. I talked through the entire first half, into the third quarter before I stopped.

Ironically, Tristan was the first to talk. "Holy hell, Cole."

I laughed, took a sip of beer to wet my throat. "Yeah."

Dylan gave me a sympathetic smile and Garrett was fiddling with the label of his drink.

"Well you're clearly going about this the wrong way," Michael said decisively.

My head turned to him in surprise, the unapologetic bachelor, the man who was allergic to commitment, who went through women like he was a human Pez dispenser. "Come again?"

Tristan shifted in his seat to face his younger brother, the lift in his eyebrows showing his surprise too.

Michael leaned forward and balanced his elbows on his legs. "I mean, I get that it's got to seem impossible to figure out how you *show* her that you still love her, but that's not really the issue, is it?"

"How do you figure?" Dylan asked him.

"Well, Cole has this weird, intense, freaky-eye thing that he does when he talks about Julia. And he's told her he still loves her, she probably knows him well enough not to question that he means it. Isn't the most important thing right now to figure out what *she* feels about you?"

I flopped back in my chair, staring at him incredulously, feeling like there was a neon sign pointing at me. *This one is an idiot*, it read in bright red letters.

Tristan was still staring at Michael. "Who *are* you right now?"

"Yeah, I'm a little impressed too," Garrett said suspiciously.

Michael rolled his eyes. "Just because I'd rather drop dead than be in your shoes right now doesn't mean I'm an idiot. I pay attention to shit," he told me. "She's the wild card. Not you. It doesn't matter how much you love her if she's already made up her mind that you're the absolute last man she'll ever be with again. Obviously she loves her sister if she showed up again today. But that could be the extent of it."

"No," I spoke up. "She was fishing to see if I was with anyone today. Looking to find out if I was wearing a ring."

"Jealousy is great," Michael said. "But it's not love. You've got to know *that*, Cole."

I let out a low laugh, some of the pressure easing in my chest, despite the daunting challenge I had in front of me. And there was no mistake, it was daunting. Talking about our issues would come eventually, if I could read enough of Julia's signals to really see how she felt about me. Past the shock, past the feigned indifference, and past the quick flash of jealousy that I saw.

Was she capable of loving me again? Or even more, did she still love me?

Michael laughed, pointing at whatever look was on my face. "Seriously. I'd rather drop dead."

"Thanks," I said dryly. My phone vibrated with a message from the listing agent on the next house on Brooke's list that we could go look tomorrow late morning if we were still available.

Apparently I'd get my chance in less than twenty-four hours, if I could stand to wait that long.

CHAPTER TWELVE

COLE

Never in my life have I dressed up so much for work. Back when I started, suits and ties were the norm. For every showing, for every open house. Not as much the past few years, now that I had established my career more, I knew that wasn't me.

But knowing that it was Julia that I would be seeing, I wanted her to see that version of me. The version of me that would most closely resemble that man she married. It might have been considered underhanded, to have picked a bright red tie that was almost identical to the one I wore when we got married, but I wasn't too good to drop little reminders for her, see if she noticed them.

Today, it was a blue tie, the same color that I wore to the formal the weekend we met. Whether or not that was considered our first date had been a common argument between us. I said it was, because within ten minutes of walking through the front door, I found her, asked her to dance, and we barely parted for the rest of the night.

Julia claimed it didn't count because it wasn't premeditated that we ended up like that. To which I would always reply, maybe it was premeditated by someone else. She smiled, every single time I said it. The same soft, amused smile that she gave me after our first dance.

"Please tell me that's not the only dance I'll get tonight," I had whispered in her ear, taking an unabashed whiff of her sleek hair. My thumbs rubbed over her knuckles, where I held our hands over my chest. "You'll break my heart if it is."

And that smile. At the time, it made me feel like a man, not the fumbling boy that I was accustomed to feeling like.

"We wouldn't want that, would we?" she said, staring at the column of my throat before taking a small step closer to me, pressing our bodies together so fully that I had to swallow a groan. The red satin of her dress was smooth against my palm where it was pressed against her back, warmed from her body underneath. "I certainly wouldn't want to be responsible for that kind of wreckage."

The masochist in me flinched, replaying what she'd said to me that night, with no artifice or possible portent of how significant the words would be for us. Maybe it was stupid for me to wear a tie that could remind her of that night, but Michael's words kept ringing and ringing and ringing in my head. It wasn't about how I felt. I'd made certain of that by vomiting my heart out at her. But Julia's feelings, they were much less clear.

It was unseasonably warm outside, so through the screen door, I heard Julia's car pull into the driveway. When I woke this morning, I wanted to make certain that I'd arrive before her for once, so I got to the house a full twenty minutes before we scheduled to meet.

She didn't come in right away, which was fine with me. While I waited, my phone chimed. I started laughing when I read the screen.

Brooke: She'll kill me for telling you this, but she changed her shoes five times before she left. Me thinks somebody is nervous.

Me: I owe you.

Brooke: I accept payments of wine in about 4-5 months. Must be hand delivered though.

Me: You're right. She'll kill you.

Brooke: Good thing I've got you on my side then, huh?

There wasn't time for me to reply, because I heard Julia come up the steps to the front door, only hesitating a moment before she opened it. I still had a smile on my face from Brooke's text, and it softened when I saw Julia. Dressed more casually than the last time I saw her, with her hair swept up from her face, she still looked stunning.

"Nice shoes," I told her. I didn't even know what they looked like because I was incapable of moving my gaze from her face yet.

Julia narrowed her eyes at me briefly. "Thank you." Her attention dropped to my tie and held there, only the slight tightening of her lips betraying the fact that she picked up exactly what I'd wanted her to. It was a slow, suspended moment before she met my eyes again and I didn't look away. This was the kind of crack in the door I'd been looking for, because in her eyes there was nostalgia. And pain.

But that was okay to me. If she hurt in the same way that I did, thinking about that night, about the hours we danced and talked, whispered into each other's ears while a packed room moved around us, then it still meant something to her.

"Ready to look around?"

She pulled in a deep breath and nodded. "The neighborhood isn't quite as nice as the other two."

"No, it's not," I agreed. "Not quite as family-friendly either. But it hits a lot of things on her list, so I figured it was worth a look."

Julia was quiet, more quiet than usual, while we wandered the split level house. Occasionally, I'd point something out and she'd nod or make a quiet noise of acknowledgment. Through the back slider, I showed her the portion of the fencing that needed to be replaced, and she walked up next to me, but didn't look through the glass.

I turned my head, and she was watching me, thoughtful and considering.

"What is it?" I asked.

She shook her head, gave me an embarrassed half-smile. "You're just ... you're really good at your job. I thought it at the last house, when we were in the basement, and I should have told you. It's nice seeing you in your element."

A pleased smile covered my face, and when her eyes flicked to my mouth, it grew wider. "Thank you. That means a lot."

Julia turned quickly, breaking the perfectly polite moment. With anyone else, at least, it would have been. It seemed like everything we did, said, didn't say, was so loaded down with subtext that it was a miracle we could make our bodies move at all. Weeding through that subtext might not be easy, but one thing was clear to me today. She definitely didn't hate me. Maybe she didn't still love me, but the attraction was still there. It was a banked fire in her eyes, in those brief flicks to my mouth, or my hands, it flared up and blasted me with its heat.

But no matter what anyone might believe, I didn't want simply attraction. I didn't want the fire by itself. I wanted every piece of Julia, wanted her to have every piece of me.

I cleared my throat and followed her into the next room, even though I knew this wasn't the house for Brooke. Julia was clearing the step into the kitchen, with me right behind her, when her shoe caught on the lip of the hardwood floor.

"Careful," I said and grabbed her waist to steady her. We held like that, with her back to me and my hand on the curve of her waist. Oh, how I wished I could see her face. Very slowly, I removed my hand and eased her away from me, even though I very much didn't want to. But this was one place I wouldn't push her, wouldn't tread too closely to the invisible line between us.

Julia didn't move into the kitchen, neither did I.

She spoke slowly, quietly, at first. "This is ... this still feels impossible to me, Cole."

I sighed and walked around her into the kitchen, needing to see her face, which was pale. She didn't meet my eyes when she followed me into the room, but her hands were shaking.

"What does?"

"The first day was so hard, you know? Too hard. And yesterday was almost bizarre in how polite it was." She lifted her eyes, and they burned hot, bright with emotion that I couldn't place, but it made my heart race all the same. "I still don't," she swallowed, pressed her hands to her stomach, "I still don't know how to do this."

I sighed heavily, kept my eyes on her. "I don't either."

"And I get it," she said in a rush, but I still heard the thickening of emotion behind the quickly spoken words. "I get why we can't just stand in some stranger's house and rehash everything that went wrong with us, but I can't stand ignoring it either."

I rubbed at the back of my neck, weighing the truth of her words. "I know. I know, I ... I'm trying not to look at it as ignoring, I guess. I just don't know what the appropriate time is either, where we start, when we have the time to do it," I told her with as much honesty as I could. "I'm scared too. Aren't you?"

My admission hung there, something she could have probably used as a weapon against me, if she was so inclined. Julia stared down at the floor, and I hated that I couldn't see her eyes anymore.

"Yes, Cole," she whispered, and I heard the tears in her voice. "Yes, that scares me too."

Her shoulders shook, and she cried quietly, but she didn't run.

It wasn't much, but it was something.

CHAPTER THIRTEEN

JULIA

Weak. I was so weak. Not even an hour in his presence, seeing him smile, trying to make me comfortable, and I cracked. This thing hanging over was so big and so heavy, pressing against all sides of me that I couldn't push it away.

But the thought of really talking with Cole, the way Brooke had begged me to, brought the tears as quickly and as easily as breathing. And the proverbial straw that broke the camel's back was Cole's admission that he was scared. Fear was an emotion that I carried well. Too well. I'd lived with it as a companion from the time I realized I couldn't conceive easily. It served as a tight binding around the emotions that I couldn't place, held my tongue in moments where I should probably speak, and let tears loose when I wished they'd stay in. I hated it. Hated it and didn't know how to change it.

"Please don't cry," he begged as he stepped closer to me and lifted a hand to comfort me. Instead of the tentative pause the last time I lost my mind around him, this time he was sure and steady, starting at my shoulder and running his hand down my upper arm.

Like there was a string tugging me toward him, I swayed, but instead of letting the momentum take me in his direction, I straightened my spine and stayed where I was. My palm dashed away a tear while I stared up into his face. "I'm sorry. I had no intention of doing ... this. Again," I added in a watery voice.

"I don't know how to do this either, Julia. There's no rule book, no precedent for us to follow." All the while, his hand smoothed up and down, up and down. My shirt covered my skin, but the heat of his hand seared through it like it was nonexistent.

"Don't you feel it hanging over us? These awful words and unresolved feelings. It's like I can't breathe while it's still between us."

His hand tightened when it came up and over my shoulder, and I got the sense that he wanted to cup the back of my neck like he used to, let his fingers tangle in my hair. Only he didn't. He watched my face, so patient and so calm, only the slightest hint of manic, bald emotion in his eyes while I spoke.

Words spilled out of me, with no filter or no second guessing as to how he might take it, how it might sound. "And it's so *big*. Everything that happened is so much bigger than us, and I can't even imagine how we sit down and start that conversation. Is it as simple as I'm sorry? To admit where we went wrong and just move past it? Cole, I don't know how we're supposed to *do* this." My breath came faster, my pitch rising, the tears drying up in favor of a panic gripping my throat. "And I don't even know if it matters, because once Brooke has a house ... once we find the house, why would we have a reason to see each other? And I don't even know if we *should* or if you want to..."

"Julia," he interrupted, voice firm and touch steadying on my arm. "Take a deep breath." Okay. Right. Breathing was good. I did as he asked, watched him nod approvingly when I repeated it. "Good. That's better."

That's what I missed about Cole. That right there. The intent behind every single thing he did. The way he spoke and how he moved, the words he spoke were all so full of intention. He was one of the least flippant people I'd ever met. And he watched me with so much intent that my heart sped up inexplicably. The string tugged, knotted tight around my spine and I followed, just enough that I reached a hand up and gripped the lapel of his suit.

His eyes shut briefly, and when they opened, I had to suck in a breath because there was so *much* in them. "You're right. We don't have to see each other after this if we don't want to."

Disappointment was a sharp slice against my heart, and my mind raced to figure out if it was real, or if I was just caught up in this overloaded moment. And then guilt, because I didn't have the right to feel disappointed. I'd left him. So I nodded slowly, stared at the knot of his bright blue tie. "Right."

His hand slid from my shoulder up to my face, and gently, so very gently, he swept his thumb over my cheekbone. My heart rioted, my stomach pitched and all the skin on my body sprang with goosebumps. The desire was swift and unexpected and I worked to breathe through it.

"Julia," he said quietly, a command to quit avoiding his eyes. It took another beat, but I looked up. "I know that I want to see you again. Okay? It can be as simple as coffee. Just coffee and conversation. I think we can manage that, don't you?"

"I don't know," I answered honestly. "Can we?"

Cole considered his words before he spoke, watched his hand on my face before he opened his mouth. "I think we owe it to ourselves to try. Sit down and talk, figure out what normal might look like for us now, with the people that we've become."

When I could finally swallow past the lump in my throat, his thumb moved again and my eyelids fluttered shut. "Do you think we're so different?"

He didn't answer right away, so I looked up at him. Then he nodded. "I do. It's inevitable."

"I hope that's not the case," I whispered, hardly able to believe that I was having this conversation with him. Because I wanted to, because I dared to, I lifted my other hand and touched the knot of his tie, coming so close to the warm skin of his neck that I could feel the heat of it on my fingertips.

"Why not?" he said roughly, stepping closer to me. Closer, and closer again. A breath between us, and it felt like too much. I didn't answer, so he said it again. "Julia, why not?"

I swallowed audibly, tightened my fingers where they still gripped his suit. "Because there's so much about you I would never want to change, and if I think too hard about the fact that my thoughtless actions, my selfish decisions might have pulled those things out of you, it makes me hate myself more than I already do for leaving you."

"Julia," he said on a loaded exhale and leaned his head down. His lips were so close to my forehead that I felt every puff of air, each one seeping through my skin, into my veins, gathering strength to my heart. Enough strength that I pushed away all the reasons why we shouldn't, why I was afraid to, and lifted my chin so that his lips found purchase.

He pressed a kiss to my forehead, wrapped his arm tightly around my waist to gather me to him. My hand smoothed up and over his chest, only stopping when I cupped his hard jaw. Cole kissed along my temple and across my cheek, the throbbing of his heart audible underneath my other hand. He whispered into my skin, and I couldn't understand what he said above the roaring of my blood. My hand moved from his jaw to the back of his head where I sifted my fingers through his silky hair.

"Please," I begged him quietly. Before my heart could beat a single time, our mouths met in an achingly slow kiss. He groaned, a tortured sound that came from so deep in his chest that I couldn't help but match it with a relieved sob of my own, just from the touch of our lips.

His taste was so familiar, his lips so firm and sure, that my eyes burned with new tears. Home. It felt like home. Our lips moved against each other in an unhurried push and pull, slow sips that spoke of familiarity and a banked passion. I wound myself around him, both arms around his neck and reveled in the way he deepened the kiss, the way he slid his hands up my back and gripped my hair the way he loved to, the way I loved, too.

I went up on the balls of my feet, needing to get closer, unable to fight the tidal wave of overwhelming feeling of being wrapped in his arms again. After so long, an impossible distance, I was exactly where I wanted to be. My hands tightened, so did his. Just as I started to tilt my head, to chase his tongue with my own, he pulled back.

Not too far, just enough to brush his nose against the length of my own. His eyes were still closed, but I couldn't do the same. Wasting a moment, forgetting a second of this would only be something to add to my list of things I'd done wrong. So I savored it. Breathed him in, enjoyed the feel of his hair in between my fingers, the iron band of muscles in his arms where they encircled me, clutched me to him.

Unable to stop, I pressed another soft kiss against his mouth and smiled when he sighed audibly against my lips. His hands moved so he cupped both sides of my face and he finally opened his eyes.

"Hi," I whispered, loathing the thought of moving away from him.

He let out a low laugh and tilted his forehead against mine. "Hi."

Instead of kissing him again, I wrapped my arms around his waist and settled against him. Cole stroked a hand down the length of my ponytail and took a deep inhale against the top of my head before he took a step back. Instantly I felt cold, but the look on his face told me that he hated it as much as I did.

"That was probably stupid, huh?" I asked, giving him a sheepish smile.

"Not stupid. Just, I don't know," he searched for the right word, as he held my eyes. "If this is on the table, all of it, then we talk first. Coffee first. Somewhere incredibly public." His thumb traced the bottom edge of my lip and I shivered. "Some people could jump in without looking first, but we are doing this the right way."

Cole was so sure. I could see it in his face. So sure that no matter what had happened between us so long ago, it was something that we were capable of overcoming. I hadn't trusted him before, not enough. Not like I should have. I should have trusted my husband enough to tell him how I was feeling without using my emotions as a weapon, as a shield against him because I hated his different opinion, felt insecure about the fact that he knew exactly what he wanted to do and why and I wasn't able to do the same.

"The right way," I repeated with a tiny smile. "Brooke told me that I needed to just talk to you. I hate it when she's right."

He smiled so brilliantly that I laughed, my head spinning and my heart clenching in my chest. We walked out of the kitchen with our shoulders brushing. "This isn't her house, is it?"

I loved that he knew. I shook my head. "Nope."

"The one from yesterday?"

"Yup."

Cole locked up behind us and opened my car door for me. After I was buckled in and rolled down the window, he closed the door and braced his hands on the car so he could lean his head down. "I'm going to call Brooke, maybe set up a time to come to her place so I can see her face to face when we talk about putting in an offer. Will you be there?"

The smile threatened at how silly this felt. Like a date, but so much weirder, because divorced couple right here. Thankfully, I kept my cool and nodded. "I'll be there."

Cole stepped back so I could pull out, but I pointed a finger at him through my open window. "Don't think I don't know what you were doing with your tie choices."

"I expected you to know." He rapped his knuckles on the top of the car and winked at me. "I'll see you soon, Julia."

It was a miracle that I didn't puke, that I was capable of calmly driving away. My fingers fumbled with my phone when I hit a red light, and I pulled up Rory's contact info, in desperate, holy-shit-what-is-happening need of another female opinion that was not Brooke. Rory was unbiased. Brooke would shove me to our coffee date faster than I could say "meddlesome".

Thank the Lord, sweet baby in a manger, Rory picked up on the first ring.

"This is Aurora," she said politely.

"How serious was your offer of friendship? Because I'm about to go park myself at a bar to stem the oncoming freak-out that I have brewing in my head."

After a beat, she laughed. "Well, hi Julia. Good day?"

I whimpered in answer.

"Of course my offer was serious. I can safely escape the office in," she hummed, "about an hour, give or take. Does that work?"

"Yes," I said on a rush. "Thank you."

"Text me where to meet you. Try not to drink too much before I get there."

"No promises," I mumbled, my belly swarming with butterflies. Lots and lots of butterflies.

Fifty-eight minutes later, Rory edged around a high-top table at the country bar I'd chosen. I laughed at how out of place she looked. Both of us, I guess. But her especially, in a tailored black dress, wide cheetah print belt and ice pick-heeled black patent shoes.

"Nice choice," she said dryly when she sat opposite of me.

I shrugged, not even feeling self-conscious about it. "Can't get good country bars in Connecticut. It was also the first one I saw, so there you go."

She assessed me carefully, obviously noting the *I've been recently crying* treatment to my eye makeup. Her eyes only widened slightly at the two drinks in front of me.

"I couldn't decide," I said, only the slightest defensive edge in my voice.

"One of those days, huh?"

I blew out a long breath. "Abridged version?"

"If that's what you prefer."

"My sister tricked me and Cole into house-hunting for her together, we did a pretty spectacular job of avoiding anything of substance until today, when we kissed in the kitchen of someone else's house and I think possibly agreed to start dating. But I don't really know for sure."

Rory choked on the sip of water in her mouth. When she'd succeeded in swallowing it without spewing all over me, she leaned in. "Umm, what?"

"I'm still not sure how it happened," I cried. A guy at the table next to us turned to glance at me and Rory nailed him with a glare so effective that even I shrank in my seat. "And I can't talk to my sister about it because she's so Team Cole that it won't even be something she thinks I need to think over. But it's ridiculous, isn't it? We're divorced, for crying out loud. We haven't had a single discussion about what happened between us, and we kissed. Like, tongue kissed." Then I pouted. "Well, almost."

I knew it was bad when, in the process of my little outburst, Rory's mouth slowly fell open and she grabbed the fuller of my two drinks. "Mind if I have a sip?"

"Help yourself," I said miserably.

She took a long drink and winced. "That's terrible."

"It is."

Rory sank back in her seat and stared at me. "I must admit I'm at a bit of a loss here. One, I've never been divorced. Two, I don't know either you or Cole all that well. And three, I sure as hell didn't expect you to say what you just said."

She chuckled when I dropped my head into my hands. "I'm glad you find this funny."

"I find your theatrics funny," she clarified.

In my head, I glared at her, but I didn't have the strength to lift my head. "I think the situation warrants some theatrics."

"Can't argue with that. But they won't help."

That helped me lift my head. "No, I suppose they won't."

"Do you *want* to date your ex-husband?" she asked matter-of-factly.

"Is it really that simple?"

"Yes."

"Who? Who would this be simple for?" I shrugged. "I'm still sifting through how I feel about all of this, and that feels like a really loaded question that I am not at all equipped to answer."

Rory regarded me for a few seconds. "I don't know you that well, of course, but if you kissed him, then you want him. Right? You're attracted to him?"

Now that wasn't hard to answer. "Yes." I said it so miserably that she grinned. I chucked a napkin at her. "But that's a separate issue."

"Is it?" It was Rory's turn to shrug. "Seems like a pretty good starting point to me. You date someone that you know you have things in common with, that you're attracted to. If that's the lens that both of you are willing to view this through, it seems like you might be complicating this."

"Maybe," I hedged.

"So," she said, "let's try this again. Do you want to date Cole?"

His kiss. The way he winked at me before I drove off. The way he wanted to do this the right way. It wasn't hard for me to answer. "Yes, I do."

Rory smiled. "That wasn't so hard."

"Oh, sure. Are you going to be my fill-in for the big convo that we're destined to have?"

"Ha. You couldn't pay me enough." She flagged down a waitress and ordered a chardonnay. "Who says it has to be hard?"

I held my hand out to her, which she regarded warily. "I'm not sure we've been properly introduced. My name is Julia and I left my husband in a spectacularly callous fashion, and we still have yet to discuss why. Also, I don't deal well with emotions that scare me."

Rory let out an indelicate sound that might have been a snort on a less-polished woman. "Tell me who *does* deal with scary emotions well?"

Fair point. Ugh. I hated logic in moments such as these. She laughed at the expression on my face.

"I'm a wreck."

"No, you're not," she countered instantly. "There's not exactly a road map for this, but the bottom line, the only one that matters is if you want to do the work. If you don't, there's nothing wrong with that. If you don't want to revisit everything that happened, don't want to wade through the sludge even though Cole is on the other side of it, then don't."

The way my heart squeezed painfully at her easy out gave me my answer. Of course, I didn't want to wade through the sludge. Didn't want to rehash what I considered the greatest shame of my entire life.

"If Cole is on the other side," I said carefully, "then yes, but…"

"But nothing. I'm serious. That man loves you. What could be so hard about one conversation?"

"It's more than that." I held up my hands when she gave me a doubtful look. "It is."

"How so?"

I swallowed heavily, because it took a lot for me to put a voice to my fears. "Even if we have that conversation, how do we ever really get past it? Where I won't constantly feel like I need to make up this giant awful thing to him?"

"The balance of power."

I nodded. "Yeah. It seems like I'll always feel that Cole has the upper hand in our relationship, that black mark that he can throw back in my face, because I took away our marriage. I took away *time*. How does someone ever forgive that?"

"Or forgive themselves for that," she said quietly.

I stared down at the table, unable to admit the truth in her words. "He may not forgive me when he realizes the extent of how cowardly I was," I admitted quietly, hoping she couldn't hear me.

"You think he doesn't already know?"

My head whipped up. Okaaay, I guess she heard me. There was blatant challenge in her eyes, but her smile was sympathetic.

"I'm sorry if that sounds harsh," she said. "But think about it. If he's the one you left without a single word, don't you think he already knows the worst side of you?"

I pulled in a shaky breath. "I suppose. I've never thought of it that way."

"Nobody likes to think about it that way. But there's a reason that we place our trust in a select few people in this world, why we let them truly love us. It's because they see us at our lowest and still find us worthy. The dark, the yuck, the awful, it doesn't scare them away. That's a hard pill to swallow sometimes, because we don't *feel* like we're worthy. And I know Cole still loves you, even though you left him. Real love forgives the unforgiveable."

I actively willed away the tears that really wanted to escape at her gently spoken words, harsh though they were. They also happened to be true. "Why are you so smart?"

She smiled. "Annoying, right? Garrett thinks so too sometimes."

"I'd like to meet him someday."

"You will," she said, and I could tell she believed it. "You'll meet all the guys. They're great."

"I'm glad Cole has had that in his life. He probably needed it. Needed them."

Rory's wine arrived at the table, and she gave the waitress a polite smile. "You need it too, Julia. And I'm glad you called. I'm not a hugger, otherwise I'd be giving you one right now."

I laughed. "Fair enough. I am a hugger, so I might force you when we're done here."

Her nose wrinkled. "Lovely."

"Thank you though," I told her sincerely.

She waved off my thanks, but I can tell she was pleased. "While you're feeling generous toward me, I've been wondering something."

"What's that?"

"Why didn't you ever change your last name?"

I laughed under my breath before taking another drink. "Couldn't bring myself to do it. Always had an excuse why I couldn't go through the process." Briefly, I lifted my eyebrows. "I hated the idea of letting go of that part of me. Letting go of Cole, I guess. I know it sounds insane, but that felt like something even more permanent than divorcing him."

"Exactly how much denial have you been living in these past years?" she asked dryly.

I chucked a balled-up napkin at her, and we laughed.

Rory gently set the napkin onto the table. "Now that the hard part is over, tell me exactly why your sister is an amazing, evil genius."

I told her, and we laughed, but the whole time we sat there, I kept replaying the kiss, replaying his words and Rory's words. Maybe I was complicating things. It certainly wouldn't be the first time in my life that I'd done so. But this was Cole. The only man I'd ever loved. And breaking his heart once was bad enough, I'd never forgive myself if I did it again.

But if he was willing to take a chance on me, then I could pull my big girl pants up and do the same. He said he'd see me soon, and suddenly, it felt like it couldn't be soon enough.

CHAPTER FOURTEEN

JULIA

"I think I'm going to puke."

"Not in the muffins, please," Brooke called from the couch. "Aren't I supposed to be the one with that particular issue?"

I blew out a hard breath so that the chunk of hair that had fallen in my eyes moved out of the way while I scooped muffin batter into the tin. "You're not exactly in the same position that I am right now."

"Ahh yes. The position where your charming and handsome ex-husband is about to knock on the door to this apartment in about five minutes?"

Yup. That was the one. And maybe there was the teensy little addition of the kiss, the one that I had yet to tell Brooke about because I didn't want her to go into early labor when she found out. "Yeah, maybe."

"It'll be fine. Cole will be so excited to see me that he won't even notice that you've baked five dozen muffins and can't stop fluttering around the room." She smiled at me when I glanced at her over my shoulder from the shoebox-sized kitchen.

"Thanks."

Brooke stretched and pushed a fist into her back. "You're welcome. Lord, I swear there won't be room in here for much longer."

Instead of responding, I stared at the clock while it ticked past another minute. Cole would be here any second. My stomach rioted with nerves, so buoyant that I thought it might float right up my throat. Rory's advice the night before never stopped chipping away at my brain, so I only managed a few fitful hours of sleep. Besides the unintended glimpse in the grocery store, this was the worst I'd looked since Cole first saw me again. That was okay though, because he'd already seen me at my lowest. Rory was right about that.

We were past the point of needing to impress each other. What we needed to do—decide if we *could* do—was see whether we had enough of a foundation to rebuild. Whether the attraction we felt wasn't a symptom of missing each other, missing the intimacy we had, or if it was real.

It sure as hell felt real to me, that gnawing pain inside of me when I thought of him now. Cole had well and truly been released from the prison I'd kept him in for so many years. Now he was everywhere, coursing through my veins, my heart, my mind.

"I kissed him," I said quietly, hoping that maybe Brooke wouldn't hear me.

"What?" she screeched.

With a wince, I turned to face her. "Yesterday. At the house."

Her jaw fell so far open that I could have punched her in tonsils if I wanted to. "You dirty, lying little slut. How could you not tell me?"

Nothing like a loaded question to answer two minutes before Cole walked in the door. I washed my hands and took my time drying them on the towel she kept hanging on the handle of the stove before going and sitting next to her on the couch. "Because I knew once I did, he and I would be a sure thing in your mind."

"Sweet cheeks," she said condescendingly, "you've been a sure thing in my mind since the day you saw him at King Soopers."

"You know, I get the distinct impression that if you could reach that far, you would've patted my head when you said that."

Brooke eyed the distance between us on the couch. "Possibly." Then she grinned. "Was it good?"

I couldn't stop the smile. Didn't want to. "Yeah. It was."

Her head dropped back on the couch and she sighed. "I know I'm supposed to be a man-hater right now because of Kevin, but man, that right there restores my hope in humanity a little bit."

"How so?"

"The smile on your face is something that I have not seen in years." As I opened my mouth to answer, there was a sharp knock on the door. Brooke winked at me. "Go get him, tiger. Just please don't mate in the doorway while I'm stuck here on the couch."

Behind my back, I held up my middle finger, which made her laugh. Smoothing my messy hair or fidgeting with my hooded sweatshirt felt ridiculous, so I just opened the damn door, finding him smiling widely on the other side.

"Come on in," I told him with a shy smile. His eyes were so warm, so *happy*, that all my nerves evaporated in an instant. How he could be so happy to see me, looking exhausted and terrible, was so far beyond my powers of comprehension that I decided it simply didn't matter.

There was no mating in the doorway, not even a hug in greeting. But it was okay, because the way he held my eyes before walking in was enough to reduce my knees to a pitiful pile of gelatin, barely enough to hold me up. Then he smiled over my shoulder.

"If it isn't the master plotter herself," Cole said to Brooke. She laughed and held her hands out so he could help her up. He took them, but looked over at me. "This okay, or should I ignore the nice, pregnant woman's request to stand?"

"The nice pregnant lady can talk, thank you very much," Brooke said with absolutely no heat. Cole let go of one hand to grip her elbow and help steady her. My sister cupped the side of Cole's face and I blinked away tears. "Hey, bro."

He leaned in for a hug, wrapping her up so completely that I almost felt like I was intruding. "Thank you," he whispered, but I heard him. Then he pulled back and looked at her basketball-size belly. "May I?"

Brooke nodded, still smiling at him. Cole's large hand spread over her stomach, and my heart tingled, sadness and pride warring frantically. Pride in him, that he was such a good man after everything. Sadness because I'd never felt that from him. Thankfully Cole didn't turn to look at me, he wouldn't need to, he knew me well enough to know what I'd be thinking. He simply shook his head and made an awe-filled sound. "Two in there, huh? You always were an over-achieving little shit."

She laughed. "Good to see you, too. And yes, two. Hence the reason I'm stuck inside this apartment. If you want me to knit you a scarf or something, I'm about to take up a new hobby before I lose my mind."

Cole helped her sit back down and shrugged off his jacket before laying it over the back of a chair by the small kitchen table. "You won't need a new hobby."

I busied myself in the kitchen, pouring water for Cole and refilling Brooke's jug. "Why not?"

He looked at me, looked down the length of my body, and smiled. I was still wearing my fuzzy black slippers on my feet, and my leggings had ducks on them, a far cry from how I'd looked the last time I saw him. "She's about to buy a house and move. That should keep her busy for a bit."

"Is it insane that I'm about to put in an offer on a house that I've never seen?" Brooke asked.

Cole shook his head. "I don't think so. You're certainly not the first client of mine that's done it. And you're right to trust Julia, it's a great property. You'll be able to grow into it, give your kids a nice place to grow up."

I gave him his water and took a seat by Brooke. "How much do you think she should offer?"

Cole pulled out his laptop while we discussed that, the comps in the neighborhood and how long it had been on the market. Brooke asked to see some of the pictures he'd taken after I left and he flipped through them, pointing out things that might get brought up in the inspection. In the end, Brooke decided to offer the asking price since it was within her budget and she didn't want to lose the house.

"I think that's smart," he told her with a smile. "The listing agent said she's shown it quite a few times since they lowered the price a couple weeks ago."

"If they accept the offer, when would she be able to move in?"

He turned to me, the warmth in his eyes the only difference in how he looked at Brooke. "We can negotiate that in the offer. But I don't see why it couldn't be soon. The owners are already out. As long as there's nothing major that comes up in the inspection that we need them to fix, and we can schedule the closing date ASAP, you might as well start packing."

I looked around the tiny room. "Okay, that'll take us about an hour."

Brooke laughed. "Don't be such a snob. It's not that bad."

"Is all of this furniture coming with you?" Cole asked, eyeing the sectional couch we were sitting on.

"Yeah, plus some of Julia's stuff that's in storage," she said. "I guess we'll have to hire a moving company."

"No need," Cole said quickly. "I've got a handful of friends and two trucks we can use, if you're okay with that."

"Oh, we couldn't impose on them," I said immediately, then swallowed, hoping it didn't sound rude to so easily dismiss his offer. I held my breath and held his eyes before looking over at Brooke. She had her eyebrows raised, clearly not expecting the offer either. I'd just mentioned to Rory how much I wanted to meet his friends, but I certainly hadn't expected them to help move my sister across town when they'd never met either of us.

But he only smiled. "It's not an imposition."

"Yeah," Brooke said. "Especially if they're hot. Are they hot?"

"Brooke," I admonished under my breath.

Cole rubbed his jaw. "I refuse to answer that question." We laughed, and then he pinched his eyes shut. "But objectively, I'm sure that you would find at least one of them attractive, yes."

Brooke hummed. "How many of these objectively handsome friends do you have to perform manual labor for me while I sit on my chair and dictate like a queen?"

He gave her an amused grin. "Depending on what day we do this, there are four, five including me. But only Michael and Tristan are single, so you'll have to rein yourself in with the others."

My stomach swooped. Brooke flicked her eyes over at me and widened them dramatically. Cole clearly hadn't caught the implication of what he'd said. He was so in, all in, and it boggled my mind. Every day, I mentally struggled with hurdling those obstacles ahead of us, but it didn't seem like he doubted us in the slightest.

How. The. *Eff* was it possible? It lit the smallest fire of panic in my belly.

"Oh, I only want to look," she said breezily. Then she waved at her stomach. "Plus, it's not like I'm going to sweep anyone off their feet like this. I've got the world's two best mood killers in there."

"Regardless, you look amazing, Brooke," he said sincerely. "I'm happy for you."

My heart. No matter what was in my belly, my heart didn't stand a chance with this man. I don't think Brooke did either, because she sniffed and looked down at his laptop again, probably hoping he didn't notice. My sister was not a crier. Quite unlike me, obviously.

While we sat there, Cole emailed the listing agent with Brooke's offer, her desire to close and move in quickly. When Brooke started knitting her fingers together, I reached out to steady her.

"You'll get it. That house was meant for you."

She smiled. "I guess this is one time I can be happy that Mom and

Dad are loaded, huh? Didn't think I'd touch that trust fund for a long time."

Both Brooke and I received trust funds when we turned twenty, with stipulations of how we could use it before we turned thirty. Education and real estate were about the only reasons we could draw from it in those first ten years. I'd purchased my small bungalow in Connecticut with it, and got my Master's in communication, without the slightest compunction about paying those debts with money that came from our family. The way I looked at it was they damn well owed us something good, something of worth, because as parents, they kinda sucked.

No matter what Brooke or I did, it wasn't good enough. For me, divorcing Cole without a backward glance was my saving grace. Brooke's was contributing to the family line. They were a dichotomy, my parents. They had old-school values, a thick guilt vein born from the Catholic upbringing they'd both had, that they gave us in only the slightest, watered-down version of the faith.

My divorce from Cole was one of the strangest things they could have supported, but they did. Support being the leanest word I could think of. In reality, they bludgeoned me over the head with the reasons why I should do it. He had no family, he was no one, he couldn't give me a child, didn't support me in wanting to do it the 'right way' (according to them), and he didn't respect our family. That was the biggest sin of them all.

Their perception of his 'disrespect' was too much to overcome in their eyes. Even though I'd long ago given up trying to understand them, they'd attempted to lay out all their reasons.

So sitting there, watching him with Brooke, was almost more than I could handle. Cole never judged the trust fund we'd received, but he wasn't in a rush to touch it either, when we'd been married. Buying a house had been our only goal with it, and after the lack of support from my parents', he said he'd never taint an adoption with money from them.

Harsh words at the time, but I couldn't argue the truth of them now. The shame returned, slow and cold through my veins. I couldn't blame my age on how much I listened to my parents. I was old enough to make my own choices, but the sheer exhaustion of what Cole and I had gone through weighed on me so heavily that I didn't have it in me to fight him anymore.

When your mother and father, who never truly supported you in any of the ways that mattered, start rubbing your back and wiping your tears, telling you that you're doing the right thing, it's heady. So I'd rested in that, instead of walking back through the door to Cole.

"Julia?" Brooke asked.

I blinked, giving her a smile. "Sorry. Blanked out for a minute."

Cole was watching me carefully, the warmth in his eyes cooled by a wary expression that I recognized from the first house we wandered. Unsure of what I was thinking, what I was feeling. He must have read the expression on my face, one that I'd unconsciously formed. Sure enough, I rubbed at my forehead and felt the tightness there from the way my brows furrowed.

"I just said that we were done here," Brooke said. "And I asked if you wanted to walk Cole out." She gave me a meaningful look. A *don't you freaking dare not take this opportunity* kind of look that only a sister can deliver with the correct amount of murderous intent without looking psychotic.

"Sure. I'd be happy to."

Cole stood and placed a quick kiss on the top of Brooke's head. "Good to see you, kid."

She beamed up at him and I couldn't help but roll my eyes. Lately, the only thing that made her this level of happy was a new carton of Ben and Jerry's hand-delivered to her bed. "You too. Let me know as soon as you hear, either way."

"I will," he promised and slung his laptop bag over his shoulder. This time, I did smooth out my sweatshirt while I walked to the door, then I looked down at my slippers, wondering if I should switch to shoes. Cole spoke over my shoulder, a low rumbling voice that did interesting things to parts of my body that were definitely not my stomach. Little bit lower. Little bit higher. "Keep 'em on. I think they're sexy."

I was about to smile over my shoulder when Brooke groaned. "Oh em gee, I told you no mating in the doorway."

Cole choked on a laugh and I opened the door before turning and pinning her with a glare. "I'll be right back."

"Don't hurry on my account."

"The muffins will burn if I don't come back in."

She lifted her eyebrows at me. "I think your muffin could do with a little bit of that."

Lord save me from little sisters. I couldn't meet Cole's eyes while I shut the door behind me and we walked down the stairs to the half-empty parking lot. His shoulder brushed against mine and all around me was his scent, despite the fact that we were outside. Maybe no one else would have noticed it so strongly, but I knew I was attuned to it in a different way than anyone else might have been.

We reached his car without a word spoken between us, a vibrating tension strung tight between our bodies.

"Remember that coffee we talked about?" he asked me, dipping his chin a little so that I had no choice but to meet his eyes.

"Yeah," I managed, voice catching only the slightest bit.

"How about now?"

My head snapped up. "Now?"

His smile was slow, amused, and took its sweet time stretching across his face. For the first time, I noticed that he had the faintest of laugh lines around his eyes when he smiled, a small stamp of age that he didn't have before. Yeah, they worked for him. Ass.

"Too soon?"

"Yeah," I said, then shook my head. "No, I mean, I think I'd like to look a little more ... presentable."

He studied my face in a deliberate way, taking his time on every separate piece, settling on my mouth the longest. The dark brown of his eyes heated, making my blood boil into something unrecognizable. "You're beautiful."

I blushed. I couldn't help it. "Can I meet you somewhere in an hour?"

Cole nodded. "That's fine. Somewhere busy or quiet?"

My breath stretched between us, and I saw him inhale it, as if it were a tangible piece of me that he could slip under his skin. A tiny part of me that was just for him.

"I think ... I think we should go somewhere busy."

He let out a low laugh and then hissed in a breath, dropping a quick, impossibly innocent kiss on my forehead. His lips were dry, warm, and they didn't linger like I expected them to. "You're probably right. I'll text you an address."

I turned and walked back up the steps, his eyes on me the entire way, and it wasn't until I shut myself back in the apartment to the unrestrained laughter of my sister, that I could breathe fully again.

"Shut up," I said to Brooke. "We're just going to talk."

"Okay," she replied, then broke out in peals of laughter again. I pinched my eyes shut and thunked the back of my head against the door.

An hour.

I could do this.

For once, I had to try to earn the blind faith that he'd seemingly never lost in me. For *him*, I could do this.

CHAPTER FIFTEEN

COLE

Table or massive leather chairs? The choice of seating had never, ever felt so vital to me as it did while I waited for Julia to show up at the coffee shop I'd randomly picked because it was only about ten minutes from Brooke's place and close enough to the office that I was still able to get there and get a little work done before we were supposed to meet.

If we sat at a table, there would be a stretch of lacquered wood separating us and hard, uncomfortable chairs to hold us up. But those chairs were move-able. There was the possibility for slyly moving my chair closer to hers, to be next to her at the table instead of across. And I could stare straight at her, face her head-on and have the ability to stare, unabashedly, to my heart's content.

Speaking of my heart, I rubbed at my shirt, making a mental checklist of whether I was having heart attack symptoms when I realized the appointed hour was up, that she'd be walking through the door any minute. It felt like a first date, but about a thousand times more stressful.

I turned to the brown leather chairs, at their stationary positions, at the way they didn't face each other, and made a sharp pivot to the table next to me. My hands smoothed out on the surface while I sat, my fingers tapping a frantic rhythm while I waited. Since I was waiting to order until she got there, there was very little to do except stare at my phone, but that made me feel like an idiot who wasn't capable of leaving it untouched for more than a few minutes.

Bright sunlight streamed in through the massive wall of windows that faced toward the west. People spoke in a low, pleasant hum from the groups of seating around the coffee shop, one of the more generic ones sprinkled around Denver. I could have picked something newer, something with fancy brews and sleek minimalist design, but that didn't feel right. Not for this.

What was this? I wasn't even sure I knew. Brooke had told her to talk to me, and given that we were in public, my guess is that we could start with the basics. So far we'd managed to ignore the reality of what faced us, or try to kiss it away, which was not a bad plan, but also not the healthiest.

I smoothed a hand down my face when I glanced at the door again. I could survive on that one kiss for another few years if I needed to. The way she felt in my arms, pressed up against me, was the kind of soul-calming happiness that I never thought I'd experience again. The singular taste of her, something I'd never forgotten, was now so fresh in my mind that I was equally relieved and pissed off that we were somewhere public. If we were anywhere else, without strangers' eyes on us, I wouldn't be able to hold back.

The bell over the door chimed causing me to look up. Julia was standing there, staring at me with a tiny smile on her face. She'd changed into jeans and a fitted shirt, her hair damp and braided over her shoulder in a thick rope. On her face was little to no makeup, which made my heart swell, because she looked even more beautiful to me that way. Her smile grew, and the dimple on her left cheek popped.

I stood from my chair and closed the distance between us. Was I supposed to hug her? Kiss her cheek? Grab her ass and feel her tongue against mine? Honestly, they all felt like pretty damn good options. Julia answered the question for me and leaned in to give me a quick hug. Too quick. But her arm snuck around my waist and I was able to press a kiss to the top of her head since she was wearing flats, so it still felt like an embarrassment of riches to me.

"You didn't order yet?" she asked.

"I was waiting for you."

Julia blushed and I laughed a little at the unintentional meaning to my words. She gave me a quick look under her lashes and headed toward the counter. "Then I'm sorry I took so long."

Okay. Massive subtext and double-meanings was going to be the name of the game today. We both ordered from the chatty barista behind the counter, and didn't say anything while we waited for our drinks. I picked up her chai tea latte and my Americano, nodding to the table where I'd been sitting when she arrived. While we sat and took the first tentative sips from our respective drinks, it felt like we were studying each other in a weighted, significant way that we hadn't done yet.

No unexpected kisses here, no sister with prying eyes, no surprise sightings. Conscious, intentional conversation. Something premeditated and thoughtful. We probably hadn't had that for the entire last year of our marriage, if I was honest.

"So," I started, feeling the weight of the moment like a car had parked itself on my chest. Not in a bad way, but heavy all the same. "Tell me what I've missed."

Her eyes were kind of sad, but she still smiled at me. "Nothing like jumping right in."

"I guess that was kind of broad." I took another sip of coffee, barely tasted it when I swallowed. All of my senses were on her. Everything I smelled was her, even through the thick aroma of coffee. Nothing had ever affected me the way she did, so the fact that I was so tuned into her, the way that everything blurred around me when she was sitting in front of me, was welcome in its familiarity. "We're just going to take this one thing at a time. Okay?"

"One thing at a time," she repeated, holding my eyes. I nodded and gave her a quick, comforting smile, which she returned. "I got my Master's from UConn."

"Good for you. I know that was important to you." Pride in her accomplishments was easy, something I was also familiar with. But I couldn't stop the dull, throbbing ache of what we'd missed in each other's lives.

"It was. Helped me get the kind of job I really wanted. I was the director of marketing for a small non-profit that focused on children's health and literacy in under-served populations. I loved it," she paused and took a deep breath. "They lost the grant they relied on, so I was kind of in limbo when Brooke called me. It felt like an easy decision to come out here and help her."

"How long did you work there?"

She lifted her eyebrows briefly while she thought. "Hmm, I think I was just shy of four years when we got the call. It was tough to see it close, but I guess the timing worked out."

"I'll say," I mumbled, but caught her quick grin in response.

"What about you?"

"You already know what I've been doing."

"So nothing has changed. You've done *nothing* new?"

"I moved," I told her. "Bought a house. Worked a lot. Probably more than I should have," I admitted. "Made some friends, some really good friends, and kept waking up every day. That's about it."

Her eyes were focused down at her drink while she took a few deep breaths. The way I said it couldn't have sounded more monotonous, which wasn't how I meant it. But I guess my life did hold a sameness to it, something that was comforting in her absence.

"No girlfriends?" she asked lightly.

"We really want to go down this road?" I said back, just as lightly, just as conscious of all the people around us as she probably was. "Here?"

"You're saying you're not curious at all?"

I regarded her steadily, something tight and sharp balled up in my chest when I thought of her with a hypothetical boyfriend. Of course I was curious. "No girlfriends."

"Dates then," she countered.

My Julia was nothing if not stubborn. And she'd hold onto this bone until her jaws cracked in half if we didn't just hash it out. So even if she thought I was pathetic, I held her eyes and answered. "No dates. No girlfriends. No nothing."

Her face lost a little bit of color, but she didn't so much as blink. "Nothing," she repeated, a tinge of disbelief in her voice. One of her hands dropped from where it was curled around her cup, and I stared at the pale pink rounded edges of her fingernails before slowly reaching across the table sliding my pointer finger underneath hers.

Neither of us said anything when I curled my finger around hers and used it to pull her hand closer to mine. With my other hand, palm facing up, I slid it completely under hers, so that her fingers rested on my wrist, and mine on hers.

Julia curved her fingers in, just a touch, and the tips of her fingernails scratched the thrumming of my pulse under my skin. I had to close my eyes, pull at every molecule of self-control. She used to do that, use just the edges of her nails and drag them down my stomach, over every edge of my muscles, tracing them until I'd crack.

"Nothing," I said in a rough voice. I opened my eyes, saw her pupils dilate. "No one."

"Oh, Cole," she breathed, let her fingers trace the veins in my wrist for a moment before pulling away. "I dated someone. For about nine months."

Any stirrings of desire, of the need to sling her over my shoulder and find a quiet, private spot were doused instantly, the hypothetical relationship acting like a bucket of ice cold water over my head. It wasn't that I was surprised. Not exactly. Definitely not *happy* to hear it, judging by the complete shutdown of my brain, but I wasn't surprised. Julia was smart and beautiful, kind and witty. Men gravitated to women like her with ease.

But she had always felt like mine, too. Even when I didn't see her, when I didn't know where she was, she was mine. And I was hers. The thought of someone else looking at her in the same way—even for a brief amount of time—had my stomach curdling, my blood slowing through my veins.

"What happened?" Wow, I managed to say that and not sound like a psycho. Good job, me.

"Just … ended. He wanted something more serious than I did. And the other dates I went on weren't, I don't know, they didn't feel right."

"Because…" I prompted, actively banishing the thoughts of her in bed with another man. For my sanity, and for the sake of the table between us, because I'd probably break that if I thought about it for too long.

"Brooke said I was too picky," she said, watching me carefully, with a massive amount of guilt in her eyes, and a little wariness too. Couldn't blame her. I was feeling just a bit touchy with the current subject. Not because I'd ever, ever expected her to not move on, not find someone else. I knew the way I lived my life while she was gone was borderline insane. To wait for someone for seven years probably put me in the *Guinness Book of World Records* for Man Who Pined the Longest. Poor sucker, someone would think, when they saw my picture.

Truthfully, I didn't even feel the need to tell her that her pickiness was because those guys weren't right for her. And they weren't right for her because they weren't me. Just like no woman ever caused the slightest bit of interest for me because they weren't her. But Julia didn't need me to tell her that. Whether she'd admit it yet or not, she knew. I could see it in her eyes, in the way she watched me earlier at Brooke's, like she wanted to devour me. With her messy hair and ridiculous leggings, massive sweatshirt that covered the body I loved so much, I would have let her.

But this was good. It was necessary. It also felt like we were treading dangerous ground, our thoughts both skirting the edge of what we were capable of withstanding. And there was one surefire topic that I knew would douse those thoughts in ice about as well as Julia dating another man.

"How are your parents?" The question almost lodged in my throat, because the truth was that I didn't give a shit about them. Her parents felt the same way about me as I did about them. It was quite possible that Julia didn't realize the extent of my bitterness toward them, and I still could feel it like a coil of iron around my spine.

Her cup froze in the air in front of her mouth, her eyes lasered onto me. The cup went back down to the table without her taking a drink. "Do you really want to know?"

Okay, maybe she did know. I breathed out a laugh. "Sure, why not."

Julia's brows bent in a V over her eyes, but she answered. "Currently in Italy for a few months, which is why I'm here to help Brooke. It wasn't ... convenient for them to cut their trip short."

The coil of iron, reserved only for them, took on a cold temperature. It didn't even surprise me, but it still pissed me off. "I'm glad you can be there for her, then."

"They're assholes," she said. "You can say it."

I laughed. "I've certainly thought it over the years, I never realized you agreed."

She swallowed then, and her eyes darted away to the table next to us, where a young couple sat down and started unloading shopping bags onto the floor around their seats, chatting loudly about traffic and urban sprawl and something else that sounded ridiculous and pompous. Julia leaned forward and knit her fingers together on the table before speaking. "I do agree now. Cole, it's hard to label your parents as self-absorbed, impossible to please. And those are kind ways to put it. Manipulative and selfish are even harder things to lay at their feet."

I took a moment to digest that, because she was right. My parents had been simple people. Hard-working and kind, not the parents to coddle me or spoil me, but always supportive. They were all I knew, until I married Julia and saw what she'd been raised with. And that was all *she* knew.

"But," she continued, "I can't blame my parents for what happened. They influenced me, how I acted, and I won't deny that. But I can't shift ownership of my decisions to them." She held my eyes and I had to clench my jaw from the pain I saw inside of her. "It would be too easy."

"Our decisions," I told her. "You and I both have to take ownership."

I expected her to smile, or look relieved, but she didn't. She shook her head firmly. "No, I mean at the end, that was on me." When I started to protest again, because I could have fought harder for her, not let her ignore me, she held up a hand to stop me. "No, Cole. It was me. At the end of the day, *I* am the one who needs to make reparations, make apologies, beg forgiveness."

Her voice wavered, and I reached out to take her hand again, needing the feel of her skin against mine. "That's not tr-" A raucous burst of laughter came from behind us, and Julia practically flinched. "I wish we didn't have a table in between us right now," I said quietly, watching her fingers while I wrapped them in between mine.

"Earlier, you gave me the option of busy or quiet."

I nodded, tearing my gaze from our hands up to her face again. "I did."

"What was the quiet option?"

Tension bloomed, in my gut, in my heart, all over my skin, the kind of tension that I hadn't felt in a pathetically long time. Not since Julia. "My house," I managed to get out. "The quiet option was my house."

That hung between us, I watched her process it for a few seconds before she nodded slowly. "I'd like to change my answer. I can't have this conversation here."

Indecision warred inside of me. She was right, it was difficult, almost impossible to imagine finishing out the conversation we were having with everything that was going on around us. But the flip side was whether it was prudent, whether it was smart to trust us there.

But in the end, I knew what my decision would be, because I knew that if she could withstand this heady tension, then I could too.

"Okay. I can text you the address just in case we are separated by a light or something." I swallowed. "Or you could come in my car, and I'll bring you back later."

Only the slightest sliver of me felt desperate for her to choose the latter, because if she drove herself, I couldn't guarantee that she wouldn't change her mind on the drive over. Stop her car and realize that we were insane for tempting ourselves this way, for thinking that an empty house, my empty house, was the best choice for serious conversation.

"I think I should drive myself," she said after a minute. I nodded, trying to push the thick beat of disappointment from my stomach. We stood and discarded our half-full cups, I reached around her to open the door and hold it for her. Julia smiled over her shoulder, and the disappointment fled.

"Okay. I'll send you the address."

She nodded and walked to her car. I got to mine and took a second after sitting in the seat to gather myself, then I sent the address to the number she'd given me.

Julia: I'll see you there. Try not to drive too fast.

When I pulled away from the curb, I was grinning.

CHAPTER SIXTEEN

JULIA

The neighborhood that Cole lived in wasn't what I expected. The landscaping was mature enough that I knew the homes weren't brand new, but they certainly looked it. There was a mix of families with kids, older couples that I could see as I wound down the curving street behind his car. When he pulled into a driveway, I took a deep breath and let it out slowly.

Must. Not. Pass. Out.

His home was beautiful, dark gray siding and crisp white trim. A black, glossy door with windows flanking either side, and an aspen tree planted off to the left of the house, decked with the bright yellow leaves of autumn in Colorado. What it didn't look like was a place that a bachelor would live, but then again, Cole didn't fall into the cliché category. His career was established, and more than anything, he'd wanted a home that was *his*.

While I parked my car, I stared at the peaked roof over the two-stall garage, the welcome mat in the front of the door on the small porch. There were no flowers planted along the front walk or in planters by the door, but there was space for them. In fact, I couldn't deny that this was precisely the kind of place that would have appealed to us when we were looking so many years ago.

That didn't help my active avoidance of unconsciousness, because holy shit. I was about to walk into Cole's home. With no one to buffer us. No reason that we were together in that place other than the desire to spend time together.

I laughed. I couldn't help it. I laughed hard and long, not even caring that he could see me from where he waited, leaning up against his car like he was a freaking model or something. Lord, I'd buy whatever he was selling, if that was the case. The white oxford that he wore stretched across his broad chest when he inhaled, and the bands of muscle wrapped around his biceps flexed under the fabric while he crossed his arms. His face held a trace of amusement, but a lot of nerves too. It was obvious in the tightness of his sharply angled jaw, the slight narrowing of his dark eyes.

When I was reasonably sure that I could contain myself, I got out of my car and tucked my keys into my purse. He pushed off of his car and walked over to me.

"Ready?"

"To go inside?"

He smiled. "That was my plan, yes." I swallowed and blinked up at the house, then back at him. His face sobered. "We don't have to, Julia. Not if you're uncomfortable."

"No," I said quickly. "It's just ... it's very *real*. Being here. Does that make sense?"

"Yeah. But we can still sit outside, or go find another coffee shop or something if you'd rather do that."

There was no empty offer buried in his words. I knew he meant it. So I held out my hand, waited for him to wind his fingers in between mine. "Show me where you live," I told him.

And he did.

We cleared the doorway, and the large open room was warm and perfectly—I mean *perfectly*—decorated. I actually side-eyed him for a second when I saw some of the accent chairs, which I would have killed for about ten years ago. Glossy hardwood floors stretched from wall to wall, broken up by area rugs to delineate the separate areas. My fingers trailed along the granite on the large kitchen island, and I shook my head at how little he probably used all this amazing counter space. Unless he had figured out how to boil water in my absence, not much cooking happened in this kitchen.

"It's beautiful." I smiled at him. Unable to not look, I opened one of the cherry cabinets and laughed a little that it was completely empty. "Still not much of a cook, I see."

"Hey," he said, "I'm exceptionally talented at opening takeout containers."

I shook my head again. In the middle of the large square dining table, there was a beautiful vase, but nothing that I saw screamed Cole to me. "It looks like a model home." When he didn't answer, I glanced back at him to see that he was rubbing the back of his neck. Pink tinged his cheeks and I turned to face him fully. I narrowed my eyes. "What's that look?"

"I uhh, I hired the same interior designer that did the model home in this neighborhood." Then he shrugged. "Never saw much reason to change it."

Embarrassed Cole was too much for my heart, so I smothered my smile. "Can't blame you. She did a good job. How long have you lived here?"

He cleared his throat and pointed to the stainless steel fridge. "Water? Wine? I've got some beer, too."

"Oh, um, water is great, thanks." For a moment, I wanted to change to wine, to settle my racing nerves, but Cole handed me a bottle and tapped his fingers on the counter while I took a drink. "Six years."

"What?"

"That's how long I've lived here. Six years."

The pleasant lightness of our interaction tempered a bit with that.

So shortly before I had him served with divorce papers. The financial transaction wouldn't have registered to me. Much to my lawyer's chagrin, I'd wanted nothing from Cole. Just wanted it to be done as cleanly and as quickly as possible. If he'd dropped the coin on a place like this six months before the papers were filed, I hadn't really cared enough to notice.

"Oh." Lame. So lame. It stopped me short though, just a bit. Had he expected me not to come back and wanted to start fresh? That didn't really make sense. But for him to do this before we got divorced threw me a little.

And Cole being Cole, he watched all of that play across my face. "I bought it for us. I saw it when I was showing another client something in this neighborhood, and it had everything we wanted. Exactly what we couldn't find for all those months." He rubbed his jaw and sighed. "I know that sounds crazy, but I thought you might come back to me, and I wanted us to have a place that we could call our own."

I looked around again, seeing things through Cole's eyes, how he waited for me, thinking that I might walk back through the door of his life at any time. I covered my mouth with a shaking hand when I realized the walls were all painted the color that we had in our apartment, the one that I had told him was the perfect neutral, that I'd told him I'd be using in our house whenever we found one.

"Cole," I whispered, running my hands along the back of the stools that were pushed up against the island, the exact same style of stools that I'd showed him online once.

Once.

"This feels so much more pathetic now that you're here," he admitted quietly. He didn't move toward me, just let me look my fill. I turned the corner past the kitchen and swallowed when I saw the guest bathroom. Or, I assumed it was, by how little use it showed. The gray counter tops, the mirror framed with a thick, heavy frame. The light fixture that I'd picked out at Home Depot.

He wasn't pathetic, I thought with a fierce, protective beat of my heart. He was *mine*. And all these days, months, years, he'd waited for me. All I'd managed to get out in the coffee shop was that I was the one who needed to make amends, because it's truly how I felt. Cole contributed to our issues, of course, but at the end of the day, it was my fault that our marriage ended.

Suddenly, I needed to see every room. Needed to see the home that he made for us, when I never gave him a single speck of hope that we might use it together. The guest bedroom had the small writing desk tucked into the corner, just like I'd wanted, and a queen bed up against an upholstered headboard, just like I'd wanted. The stamp of the designer was clear, but underneath those small touches was the foundation that Cole and I had dreamed of for years.

Before Pinterest boards were a thing, he and I had pored over magazines, surfed through websites and bookmarked the things we loved. Some that we agreed on, others that we didn't. And when I turned the corner to the master bedroom, I almost lost my breath. There, dominating the space in the middle of the large bedroom, was the thing I'd wanted, the thing he hadn't. The four poster king-sized bed, solid mahogany, from the looks of it. Each poster stretched up at least six feet, the white duvet of the bed stark and bright against the wood.

Every night, he slept there. I breathed deeply, tried to calm my emotions, but it was impossible.

"Holy shit," I said under my breath, and the tears were thick in my voice. The dark gray of the walls, the bright white of the trim, the warm wood of the floor, it was all perfect. Under the large windows facing east were two deep chairs, gray and soft-looking, with a small mahogany table in between them. A tear hit my cheek and I swiped it away. I didn't want to cry today, and that one would be the only that I allowed myself.

"Chairs in the master bedroom?" he'd asked one afternoon that I was looking at home decor magazines.

"So we can have our coffee together in the morning," I'd told him, rolling my eyes like it was obvious. "Won't that be romantic?"

"Terribly," he had mumbled and gone back to looking at the paper. But he had smiled, and I knew we'd have chairs in our bedroom.

The master bathroom was around the corner, and the walk-in closet was to the side. But I was still frozen in the doorway of the bedroom that I'd dreamed about for five years. Longer, if I counted my days house-hunting in Connecticut.

"You really never gave up on me," I said, very much in a daze.

"Of course not," Cole answered from behind me. "How could I?"

Being in his house, in the house that he bought in order for us to have a home, loosened my tongue and girded my heart for however he might react.

"I'm so sorry, Cole," I whispered.

"Oh, Julia." His hands cupped my shoulders, and my hair ruffled when he exhaled into the crown of my head. "Look at me."

Slowly, I turned, and he slid his hands down my back while I stared up at him. "I'm *sorry*. For everything."

"I know you are."

"No," I said firmly as he cupped the sides of my face with his warm, big hands. "Don't let me off easily." My hands moved until they were laying on his chest. "I *owe* you these words, Cole. I owe them to you a thousand times."

"There's no debt between us." His thumb brushed under my lip and I kissed the pad of it.

"I'm sorry," I said again, resting my head against his chest and gripping his shirt in my hands. "I'm sorry. I'm sorry, I am so, so sorry."

"Shh, it's okay." He wrapped his arms around me and I swallowed back tears. This time, this time, I could hug him back while he comforted me. And I did as tightly as I'd wanted to the first day I cried to him. "I'm here. It's okay."

We stood there, doing nothing but breathing each other in, my apologies still coating the air between us. I didn't know if it was enough right now, but it was something. I tightened my arms, felt every shifting muscle in his back by spreading my fingers and moving my hands in slow circles. Cole buried his nose in my hair, and all the unsettled parts of me smoothed back into place, every raw edge soothed by his mere presence. It wasn't until that moment that I realized how much of me had been hibernating, buried somewhere deep and dark where I couldn't be bothered by the outside world. That cocoon burst open, and everything slid back into its rightful place.

It felt too good to be true, too perfect in a way that I never could have anticipated.

"You really never moved on," I said into his chest, unwilling to pull away from him. "Not even a little."

"Have I scared you off?"

I laughed and nuzzled against the solid heat of him, the scent of his skin so potent that I could smell it through his shirt. "Clearly."

Cole was the one who pulled back and I tried not to pout. His eyes searched my face. "There was no option for me to move on from you. From the day I met you, you were it for me." He traced the tip of one finger down the bridge of my nose, followed the line of my lips when they opened on a soft gasp, felt along the curve my jaw until he could follow the edge of my ear. "Even if lived out the rest of my days on this earth without ever seeing your face again, you are *it* for me, Julia."

Speech wasn't an option with all the massive, swamping emotions clogging my throat. I cupped his face, drew my fingers along the dark hair sprouting up on his jaw. So precious to me, every part of him. "I don't know how you can forgive me," I admitted, unable to move this even a millimeter further until I forced myself to say it out loud.

He didn't say anything right away, didn't even blink while our eyes held. Then he took in a deep breath, and my breasts brushed against the front of his shirt. "I can forgive you because I love you. It wasn't conditional when I promised that to you. It's unyielding, inflexible, unstoppable."

My eyes fell shut, another tear snaked down my face, but Cole caught it with his fingers and brushed it away so gently, so tenderly that my heart squeezed in my chest. "I don't deserve you."

"Julia," he said. "Look at me." I did, and he smiled. "I know that we could stand here and rehash all the awful things that we *both* did, that we *both* said."

"Do we have to?" I asked glumly, hooking one side of my lips up in a smile.

"No, we don't have to. I meant it when I forgave you, and I did that long before you ever asked it of me."

I sighed, hugged him to me again. "Thank you."

"Do you forgive me for the things I said and the things I did?"

My answer was so easy, that it came out on a rushed, relieved breath. "Yes, I do."

"Then that's all I need."

His finger found the edge of my chin and tilted up gently, until I was looking up into his wonderful, handsome face. Cole's eyes locked in on my lips, and suddenly, we were too far away, so far that I didn't think I could survive it anymore.

I lifted up just as he swooped down and our lips crashed together.

CHAPTER SEVENTEEN

COLE

Her tongue against mine, slick and wet, almost brought me to my knees. My heart thundered in my chest, my brain chanted her name over and over in the same frantic, furious rhythm. Julia was up on her tiptoes, wrapped around me so tightly that there was no space between us, not for the entire length of her long, lean body.

Her breasts pressed against my chest made me feel eleven feet tall, like I could conquer the world. My hands gripped her bottom while I pressed her back up against the door frame leading into my bedroom. The ridiculous shrine that I'd created to the home we dreamed of hadn't scared her off, hadn't even made her blink. Because it wasn't ridiculous to her.

To anyone else it might have been. Sad, pathetic, pitiful. Those were adjectives that I pondered on a regular basis, but despite that, despite everything that went wrong and the years apart, she was here. In my arms. That alone should have forced me to slow my tempo, not grab her so roughly, moan into her mouth like I was dying.

But I *was* dying. Dying from everything she made me feel. I'd lay myself on that altar every single day, given the choice of how I had been living before. The emptiness without her was swept away with every touch of her soft lips against mine, with every sigh and whimper that slipped from her mouth into mine. When I nuzzled her head to the side to expose the arch of her throat, sucked on the sensitive spot over her pulse, she slumped against the door. I smiled into her skin, gave her another deep, searching kiss when she wrapped her fingers into my hair and yanked my head up.

"Oh," she sighed when I cupped her breast with one hand. "What are we *doing*?"

I froze. "Do you want to stop?"

Julia laughed and ran her thumb over my lips. "No, I don't. It was one of those inconveniently timed hypothetical questions that I didn't really expect you to answer."

Then she arched her back and I unfroze. Pretty easily, actually. "Good. Because my brain isn't working all that well right now."

She kissed me, soft and quick, then met my eyes. "Take me to bed, Cole."

"Are you *sure*?" My heart was *pounding*, my skin vibrating.

With steady hands, she began unbuttoning my shirt and not once did she waver, did she hesitate. Not while she pushed my shirt over my shoulders and ran her hands lightly over the skin and muscle that she uncovered, or when she trailed a finger down the line of dark hair underneath my belly button. Not when my hands shook pulling the shirt over her head and raised arms. Not when she unhooked my belt, let it fall to the floor with a loud, awkward clang in the quiet room and my breath heaved between us.

Julia laid her hand over my heart, and my head bowed so I would be able to look at it. The pale slimness of her fingers against my darker skin made me close my eyes for a few seconds, thinking of how empty that space had felt in her absence, like my dream had somehow been realized. Not anymore. I covered her hand with my own, then lifted them both so I could kiss the tips of her fingers.

With a smile on her face, she gently nudged me toward the bed, and turned to unhook her pale pink bra. While her back was still turned, I dragged my finger down her spine, feeling each bump underneath her soft skin, leaning over to kiss the small freckles on the slope of her shoulder. Julia leaned her head back on my chest and shivered, so I wrapped my arms around her and held to her to me. She gripped my forearms with her hands and sighed.

"Is this real?" I couldn't help but whisper. "You feel real. The way your heart is pounding under my arms feels real, but I can't get over the fact that I might be dreaming this up."

She tilted her chin so she could look at me, and I dropped a kiss on her upturned mouth. Her smile was soft and understanding. "I'm right here," she whispered against my mouth. Then she turned and hooked a finger into my empty belt loop, walking us backward to the bed. When her knees hit, she crawled up the bed, and I followed, unable to be too far away from her.

Now the tempo had slowed, and we pulled off the remainder of our clothes, her hands on mine and mine on hers, like we were unwrapping a present. Stretching out the moments with a patience I didn't believe I was capable of, especially when we were fully pressed against each other without a single barrier. My hands shook again, the tremor something I couldn't even bring myself to be embarrassed about. Because it was her, and it had been so long since I'd touched the naked skin of her back, her breasts, the softness of her stomach and the firm, toned length of her legs.

We kissed and kissed and kissed. Soft kisses, sucking, biting kisses and kisses so deep that she had to break away simply to breathe. My skin was on fire when she begged me, and like it was with anything else, I could never have denied her. I pressed her leg up against my chest, bent at the knee, and still our mouths didn't part.

Julia sobbed out a breath when I pushed inside her, and I dropped my face into the curve of her neck while I held there. Perfection, relief, blinding desire, and love. The feeling of it was so deep that I felt it stir in the marrow of my bones.

"Please," she said into my sweat-slicked temple.

I kissed up her neck, stopped to nibble at the corner of her jaw. "Please, what?"

She laughed, squirmed under me when I still didn't move. "Cole," she whined and bit at my lower lip.

That sharp tug of her teeth pulled goosebumps along my arms. But it wasn't until she scratched her fingernails down my back that I finally moved. We moved together, breathed together, so slowly and so achingly tender, like neither one of us wanted it to end.

I bit into the tendon on her neck when she fell apart around me on a soft cry, and she cradled the back of my head while I did the same. The way I slumped on top of her made our sweat-slicked skin stick together, but neither one of us pulled away. Her legs wrapped around my hips and I buried my face into her hair, where it was only half held into the braid from earlier.

Finally, I rolled to my back and let out the kind of deep breath that felt like it came from my soul. Any adult male who'd broken the sex-free streak that I'd just endured would have done the exact same thing. It was so deep and so loud that Julia looked at me and started laughing, she pressed her forehead against my shoulder and reached for one of my hands. She rolled to face me, our hands still woven together when she pressed them against her chest.

"Feel better?" she asked with a smile.

I could barely open my damn eyes. But I refused to miss a second of her like this. She might leave, go back to Brooke's, she might freak out because we ended up in bed after the first legitimate conversation we'd had since seeing each other again. Instead, she pleasantly surprised me by unwinding our hands so that she could loop my arm around her shoulders and press herself up against my side, just like she used to. Her arm snaked around my waist and she draped her leg over one of mine so we were well and truly entangled.

Once she was settled, I kissed her forehead. "Yeah. I feel better."

I could feel her smile against my skin in the lift of her cheeks, but she didn't say anything. There were no sounds around us except the ticking of the clock on the wall and the low hum of the furnace kicking on.

Julia propped her chin on my chest and watched me. Her hair was a disaster and her lips were red and swollen. She was perfect. "I bet you'll feel even better in about ten minutes."

One of my eyebrows lifted. "You give me much credit, woman."

She laughed and pinched my side. "I just heard your stomach growl, perv. I meant that I was going to go make you some food."

"That so?" I murmured, imprinting the moment in my head, sliding memories around so that it could fit into the top tier, the one reserved for the short snippets of time that were the very best, the happiest, the kind that made you feel like every bad moment in your life was worth living, just so that you could be in that place.

"Yeah." She smiled one of those no-teeth smiles that crinkled the skin next to her eyes. "Is there any food in the fridge that I can work with?"

I closed my eyes and smoothed my hand along the curve of her waist. "Sorry, you've zapped my brain of any possible functionality. I can't be expected to know anything beyond my name right now. I'm not even sure of that."

She laughed when she leaned up on an elbow. "Cole," she kissed the tip of my nose. "Andrew." Kiss on my chin. "Mallinson." Against my mouth again, lingering long enough that I wrapped my arms around her.

I'd wondered, of course, about the fact that Julia never changed her last name. When Rory said it, that she had a potential candidate by the name of Julia Mallinson, I hadn't thought through the implications of the fact that she'd kept my last name. The question fairly itched its way off the tip of my tongue, but I swallowed it down, not wanting to break the moment.

Call me a coward. Maybe that's what I was. Or selfish. That was even more appropriate. My hands were on her naked skin, it was a simple trek up her waist and I could feel the weight of her breast under my fingers. Did I want to keep it there?

Damn straight. So I kissed her, laid back and watched her roll off the bed in search of clothes so she could go make some food. Leisurely, she pulled on her underwear and held my eyes, unashamed in her nudity. But she'd always been comfortable in her skin, something that blew me away when we were younger because I'd felt a certain awkwardness in my gangly height as a teen and even as a young man.

There was a confidence in Julia, even back then, that somehow seeped its way into my own skin. The way she loved me, the way she felt the exact same thing that I had felt at the time, gave me a confidence I hadn't expected. I wasn't an insecure person, but sometimes I felt more like the loss of my mother made it so that I missed out on something valuable. She and I only had a handful of conversations about women, the one about the woman I'd marry was really the only one that still stood out in my memory. My dad was a quiet man, simple in his tastes and how he lived his life.

Telling me how to woo a woman, how to project myself with confidence, wasn't something he felt the need to teach me. That's why Julia was such a revelation for me. I didn't need to be anything other than myself with her. Didn't need smooth lines, or clever ways to get her to go out with me, she just looked at me and saw *me*.

Julia slipped her bra up and reached behind her to hook the clasp, shaking her head when I narrowed my eyes. When she passed the bed on the way to the bathroom, she leaned over and kissed the top of my head. I rolled onto my side and propped my head in my hand so I could watch her pull one of my t-shirts over her head and then fix her braid in the master bathroom mirror. She finished and looked around the gray-tiled room, lingering on the sunken tub that I'd used approximately zero times since I'd lived there.

"That tub could fit four people in it," she said.

"Two, for sure."

Julia glanced over her shoulder at me, eyebrow raised. "Is that an invitation?"

"Always," I told her honestly. Given how I felt, loose-limbed and relaxed, a bone-deep sense of satisfaction that couldn't be manufactured by anything other than her, I would've given her anything.

"Maybe after we eat." She flicked off the bathroom light and skirted past the bed, laughing when I reached out and tried to grab the hem of my shirt where it fell to her thighs. To the sounds of her rifling through my kitchen, I flopped back on the bed and laid my hands on my stomach.

The smallest of doubts niggled at the back of my brain. The first day we saw each other, I told her I still loved her, and even now, I didn't really know how Julia felt about me. Wanting me was one thing. Feeling guilty about how things played out between us was another thing entirely. Granted, I did still know Julia enough to understand that falling into bed with me would never be flippant or impulsive. But that was still light years away from love. From committing to a future, committing to a second chance.

"Your pantry looks exactly like it did in college, Cole. This is pathetic."

I laughed and rolled out of bed, yanking my cotton sleep pants out of my dresser and pulling them on without bothering with a shirt or boxer briefs. When I got into the kitchen, I was scratching my chest and froze at the sight of her on tip toes, shirt rising up the length of her toned legs.

Since she was rifling through a cupboard, she didn't hear me come in the room, so I snuck up behind her and slipped my hands underneath the shirt. She shrieked and turned around when I caged her in against the counter. I pressed my mouth against her neck and Julia sighed, melting into me. Her hands slid up my stomach and rested on my chest.

I shivered. "Your fingers are freezing, woman."

"Oh, so I shouldn't do this?" And she shoved them down into my pants. I dug my hands into her side where I knew she was ticklish, and she started laughing. "Stop! Fine, okay, I give."

The front door of my house slammed shut and we both froze. "Well, well, well," Michael's voice said from behind me, sounding entirely pleased and completely annoying. "What do we have here?"

I gave Julia an apologetic look and turned around so that she was behind me and hopefully blocked from sight. "Breaking and entering, from the looks of it."

"Ouch," he said, not concerned in the slightest. Asshole smiled. Widely. "Aren't you going to introduce me?"

"Should I go grab some pants?" Julia whispered against my shoulder.

"Not on my account," Michael mumbled as he sat on one of the stools by the kitchen island. I gave him a dry look, which he ignored. "I'm Michael Whitfield, oh mysterious one. I'm assuming you're Julia."

I sighed. Julia laughed.

"How did you get in here?" I asked him.

He held up a keychain that I recognized from a spare I'd given Garrett. "You weren't answering your phone and I needed to borrow your chainsaw. Figured you weren't home." He smiled again. "Guess I was wrong."

"And the cars in the driveway didn't make you pause in the slightest?"

"Dude, you practically regenerated your virginity since I've known you. You getting laid was *literally* the last thing that entered my mind."

Julia must have decided that he was harmless, which was entirely debatable, so she laid her hand on my back before sliding out from behind me. Michael's eyebrows rose on his forehead at her wearing my shirt and I debated only mildly painless ways that I could kill him.

"I'm Julia." She held out her hand to him, which he took and brought to his mouth for a kiss, which drew a surprised laugh from her. Raise mildly painless to disembowelment.

"I cannot even begin to tell you what a pleasure it is to meet you," Michael said after I'd glared long enough that he dropped her hand. "We were beginning to think you didn't actually exist. That you were a figment of Cole's imagination."

"The chainsaw is in the garage," I said when Julia laughed again. "Help yourself."

"I'll get it later. What are we about to eat here? I'm starving and suddenly find myself in need of entertainment."

Julia looked at me with a question in her eyes.

"No," I told Michael. "Get the saw and go."

"Figured he would've been a lot happier post-coitus," Michael said to Julia.

She smiled at him sweetly. "He was plenty happy before you walked in."

"Touché, lovely lady. Touché."

"So is he one of the friends you mentioned that could maybe help Brooke?" she asked me.

I nodded. "Yeah. If he lives that long, I'm pretty sure he'll owe me."

"Is 'he' me? And can we stop referring to me in the third person while I'm still sitting here?" Michael asked.

"Julia's sister will need help moving in a couple weeks, if her offer gets accepted, which I think it will. Trying to keep her moving costs down. I said maybe you and the guys could help out if you're free."

He pursed his lips. "This sister ... is she as beautiful as you, Julia?"

Julia smiled at him. "Brooke is a very beautiful woman. Long dark hair. Big brown eyes. Funny, too."

"Single?"

"She is."

Michael rubbed his hands together. "Then I'm one thousand percent free. You name the date."

Julia walked around the island and slung her arm over Michael's shoulder while I watched, completely amused. "She's also seven months pregnant with twins."

Michael held his hands up. "And just like that, you've got yourself a completely innocent and friendly mover. Well played, sis."

She smacked the side of his face just hard enough that he winced. "I like you, Michael. I'd hate to have to castrate you if you hit on her."

He rubbed his face while she walked back over to me. "I'm impressed. Not everyone can be intimidating when they're not wearing pants."

Julia slid her arm around my waist and smiled up at me. "Just one of my hidden talents."

I leaned down to place a lingering kiss on her upturned mouth. "And you have a lot, believe me."

Michael smacked the counter before he got off his stool. "I'm out. I'll come back to get the chainsaw when you're not attached to her lips."

He slammed the door again on the way out and we both started laughing.

"He's somethin'," Julia said.

"He's a good guy, just slightly allergic to commitment."

My phone buzzed on the counter and I picked it up when I saw it was the listing agent for Brooke's house. While she talked, I smiled and gave Julia a thumbs up. She sighed in relief and sat in the stool Michael had just vacated.

"Thanks, Amy, I appreciate you getting back to me so quickly. My client will be thrilled. I'll call you when we've got the inspection ordered."

"Thank goodness," Julia said when I hung up. "They didn't counter?"

"Nope. Should be a pretty easy process from here. Do you want to call her or shall I?"

Julia hesitated and gave me a wide-eyed look. Before she even opened her mouth, I had a feeling I wasn't going to like what she was about to say. "You can call her. But ... are you okay if I don't tell her just yet about this? About us?"

I let out a heavy breath and sat on the stool next to her, irritation tightening the space over my heart.

"Julia…" I said slowly, unable to meet her eyes for fear of what she might see there.

"I'm awful, aren't I?"

I was going for sainthood at this rate, but I swallowed back my immediate refusal, which was a huge deal for me. "I get that you're scared, I do. And I don't think you're awful, but it's frustrating."

"Cole," she said feelingly, and she turned to face me, laid her hands on my face so I had no choice but to look at her. "It's not a reflection about you and me, it's not."

"Isn't it?" I was feeling petulant, sounding petulant, but all I wanted to do was shout from the roof that we were getting this second chance, and she was asking for me to keep it quiet.

Julia leaned forward and gave me a soft kiss, flicking her tongue against the bottom edge of my lip when I didn't deepen it. Her eyes were huge and pleading when she pulled back. "No, it's *not*. It's about my crazy sister."

"You say that like I don't know her." I lifted my eyebrows when she opened her mouth to say something. "Why is it so important to you that she doesn't know?"

"You do know Brooke, I'd never disagree with that. If I tell her what happened, she'll have me marching back up the aisle tomorrow, and I'm not sure I'm ready to bear the weight of her expectations. Not that I don't have any for us, or that you don't. But I can handle yours and mine. Anybody else's seems like too much. Does that make sense?"

It did. And it didn't. It made me feel like I was walking a fishing line for tight rope. "As long as I know that you're not keeping it from her because you're ashamed, or you regret what happened." I held her eyes. "That I couldn't handle."

"No," she said quickly and cupped the side of my face again. "I'm

KARLA SORENSEN

not ashamed, and I don't regret it. Not a second of it." Julia searched
for what to say next, I could see it in her eyes. "This is a big deal, what
we're doing. We both feel it. But we still need to take one thing at a
time. Brooke is a couple things away, at least to me."

"One thing at a time," I repeated quietly. I couldn't deny that there
was a throb of disappointment deep in my gut that I couldn't quite
extinguish, but I'd been mentally prepared for what I felt if Julia ever
came back into my life. I'd sorted through the tangled knot of emotions
that she'd left in my chest. Julia probably hadn't done that, because I
knew enough that she put off processing those sorts of things unless it
was entirely necessary. If I could help her, then I would. "One thing at
a time," I said more firmly, only when I knew that I meant it.

Julia stood off her stool to stand in between my knees and wrapped
her arms around my neck. I gripped her around the waist and buried
my nose in her hair. "Thank you," she whispered into my ear. "I know
this is hard."

"It's not harder than living without you." I kissed her shoulder
and pulled back. Her eyes were clear, not clouded with hesitation or
uncertainty. We could do this. "I'm going to switch the lineup, if you're
okay with that."

"Oh yeah?"

"Bathtub, and *then* food."

She smiled and kissed me. "I can get behind that."

CHAPTER EIGHTEEN

JULIA

"I'm dying," Brooke moaned, turning her face into her sweat-soaked pillow. I flipped the damp washcloth over on her forehead and smoothed it down her neck.

"You're not dying. It's just the flu. Your doctor said as long as we can keep the fever going down with Tylenol, if those babies keep moving around and you're not puking constantly, there's no reason to come in."

She glared at me, effectively too, which was surprising considering how hazy her eyes were from lack of sleep and the fever that had ebbed and flowed over the last two days. "Easy for him to say. Asshole. It's his fault anyway. If he didn't make me come in for a checkup, I wouldn't have been in his germ-infested waiting room." She moaned again. "Why do I have such an asshole doctor? He's hoarding drugs that will help me, I know it."

"Can you sit up and try and drink some more 7-Up?"

"No."

I swallowed my smile at her surly tone, and my fingers stroked down her tangled hair before I stood. "Okay. You can have more medicine in an hour. Try to rest."

"I've been resting for six weeks. This is bullshit."

"Good to know you've maintained your positive attitude."

She flipped me off right before I shut the door to her bedroom. The couch/my bed was a welcome sight after tending to Julia around the clock since she'd sprung a fever and horrible body aches. We'd both gotten the flu shot, but so far, I was the only one who'd avoided getting sick. Yes, she was dramatic when she didn't feel good, but it was hard for me to argue with someone who'd been stuck in bed for weeks and now had a hundred and one fever while also worrying about the health of her babies.

This bout of sickness was inconvenient for her, of course, but I couldn't deny that it was for me as well. She got sick the day after I left Cole's house (her fever probably the only reason she hadn't truly pestered me about how long I was gone 'talking' to him) and I hadn't seen him since. I pressed my face into my pillow on the couch and smiled. My heart kicked every time I thought about the few hours we'd spent there. We took a bath together and I drove him nearly out of his mind from the opposite side of the bubble-filled tub before I put us both out of our misery and straddled his lap while the water cooled. After that, we ate omelets in bed.

Even though we'd texted every day since then, I couldn't leave Brooke. Until her fever broke, which could be up to week, according to her doctor, I was on nurse duty. Taking her temperature every four hours, around the clock. Forcing her to drink clear liquids, keeping her as comfortable as possible, making sure the babies were moving normally.

Suffice it to say, I was so effing tired. But still I smiled. The smile stayed on my face while I started drifting off to sleep, a welcome break from the last few days.

Until someone knocked on the door. I whimpered into my pillow and rolled off the couch. But when I looked through the peephole and saw Cole holding a bag of groceries, I flung the door open.

"What are you doing here?" I said, happiness lighting me up like tiny little fire crackers were strung through my veins.

He dropped a kiss on my forehead before he walked in. "Thought you might need some supplies." Cole set the brown paper bag on the small table and pulled out Gatorade, saltines, chicken noodle soup, cough drops, Tylenol, hot water bottle, and some magazines. Then he glanced up at me and pulled out two bottles of my favorite wine, laughing at my stunned expression. "And I might have missed you a little bit."

Tiny. Little. Firecrackers. They went off one by one, microscopic explosions that rocked me to my core. How was it possible that I ever thought myself not in love with him? I'd tricked myself over the years, when I actively ignored the thought of him, but I'd never really stopped, had I?

I opened my mouth to say it, but closed it again when he looked away.

"How's she doing?"

Brooke calling me a chicken shit rang through my head, but I willed it away. One thing at a time. Plus, it wasn't exactly the most romantic time to tell him that I did actually still love him. When I was un-showered for the, ohh, third day in a row, and wearing a t-shirt with chicken soup stains on it. "Same. I still need to keep a close eye on her temperature. If it goes above one-oh-one point five, her doctor said to take her into the hospital, and I know she'd like to avoid that." I lifted my eyebrows. "So would I, I guess. At least here, I get to sleep in my own bed."

He snorted. "That couch is not a bed." Cole stepped into me and slid his hands around my waist until they settled on the curve of my butt. "I bet you liked mine better."

"You're so cocky now that you've gotten laid," I said, right before he brushed a kiss across my mouth. Neither one of us deepened it, content to simply feel each other in such an innocent way.

"That going to happen again?" he asked against my mouth.

"Not here." I didn't actually think he'd want to screw me on Brooke's couch, but I figured it was worth saying anyway. I kissed him again, just to soften it a bit, make sure he knew I wasn't upset.

Cole sighed and pulled back. "I know." Then he lifted an eyebrow and gripped my ass a little tighter. "That would certainly be one way to let Brooke know about us, huh?"

"Ha, ha. Not happening." I shook my head when I looked over the groceries he brought again. "This is amazing, thank you."

"You sounded pretty beat in your last text." His eyes searched my face, lingering on the dark circles that I knew were increasing exponentially with every night of lost sleep. If Brooke didn't improve quickly, I swear they'd cover half my face in another couple days. "And I got Brooke's closing scheduled for next week Friday, figured I could kill two birds with one stone."

"Inspection went well?"

He nodded and pushed me to sit in one of the chairs. "Yeah. She could probably push for a couple things to be fixed if she wanted, or have them chip in for some of her closing costs if they don't want to mess with it."

"Nothing major though? I know she was worried about the roof."

"Nope. It looks good. When they replaced it last, it was done well. She'll get a lot of years out of it yet."

I sighed and rested my head in my hand, tilting my chin up so I could still look at him. "That's good."

Cole felt my forehead with the back of his hand. "You're not getting sick, are you?"

"Just tired. I'm not sure which sounds better, getting out of the house for a few hours or sleeping. Rory sent me a text about grabbing a drink, and I swear I almost wept at the thought of a martini."

He laughed and took the seat across from me. "I can stay with her if you want to go. Just tell me what I need to do."

I sat back. "No way, I'm not going to make you do that. Besides, if I was in possession of a get out of jail free card, wouldn't you want me to use it with you?"

Cole braced his elbows on the table and I eyed his shoulders when the fabric of his shirt stretched across them. He was so much bigger than when we first got married. Just a boy then, really. This ... this was a man.

"I'm not worried about us finding time." He smiled. "I'm good at being patient. Besides, I know you don't really have any help here."

My parents. Ugh. I'd muted their asses on my cell phone when my dad started texting me links of articles about how flu in pregnant women could cause birth defects. Cole's statement didn't have much of a veil over it. We both knew he thought that my parents were self-centered assholes. Not far off the mark, of course, but it was still a burr in the saddle of our relationship.

And yes, Cole was good at waiting, something that never stopped stealing my breath if I thought about it too long. While I was still sifting and searching through my vast emotional repertoire when it came to him, he was as clear as could be. No muddled emotions or mislabeled feelings. Cole loved me. He'd be patient with me. He'd wait for me to be ready.

I took a deep breath. "Let me go take her temperature again." He didn't follow me, just settled into the chair and checked his phone while I let myself into Brooke's room as quietly as possible, so I wouldn't wake her if she'd actually managed to fall asleep.

"Who's out there with you?" she mumbled against her pillow.

I took a seat next to her and pressed the backs of my fingers to her forehead. It was still clammy and warm, so I grabbed the thermometer and tapped it against her chapped lips. "Open."

Brooke clamped her mouth shut around it, but lifted her eyebrows slightly at my non-answer.

"What if I said I was just watching TV?"

Yeah, right. I could read that clearly enough in her eyes. I laughed under my breath. "Cole knew you were sick, so he brought you some nourishment and me some wine for having to put up with your high-maintenance ass."

Her face softened, even through the miserable cloud of sickness.

I smiled when I pulled the thermometer out and held it up so I could see the readout. "One hundred point four, and it's been four hours since your last dose of medicine."

"Hallelujah," she said and shifted on the bed. "Still feel like shit, but at least we're going in the right direction."

"Need anything?"

Her eyes closed while she thought, like they were too heavy to stay up. "What kind of nourishment?"

"Soup, crackers, Gatorade, 7-Up. Pick your poison."

"What a suck up." She opened her eyes and stared up at me. "You can tell him I said that too."

"I will," I said around a smile.

"Don't tell him that I think he should be cloned for the betterment of females all around the globe. That, we can keep between us."

I laughed. "Deal."

"Soup sounds good, I think."

"Okay. Drink some more before I come back with it." I smoothed her hair off her forehead and she gave me a weak smile. "He got your closing scheduled for next week Friday. Inspection went great."

"Man is good at his job."

"Seems so," I agreed with a quiet swell of pride. "I'll be right back with your soup."

When I walked back into the other room, Cole was already opening a can for me.

"You don't have to do that," I told him.

He looked at me over his shoulder with an easy smile. "I know I don't. Figured it's the least I can do for the woman who wants to clone me for the betterment of females all over the world."

I shook my head, handed him a spoon out of the silverware drawer. "Not allowed."

"Why's that?"

Walking up to him while he still faced away from me, I wrapped my arms around his waist and pressed a kiss to the soft material of his t-shirt, right between his shoulder blades. "Because then I'd have to share you."

It felt impossibly selfish to say it out loud, when there was so much I still wasn't giving him, but it was also true. That was something that I could give him, my truth as I felt it. Cole laid his hands over mine where they were clasped against his stomach. Underneath my hands, I could feel the hard strength of his muscles, the warmth of them clearing his shirt like it wasn't there.

Cole's warmth hit all the places inside of me that had been left cold in his absence. Every time I was around him, touched him, kissed him, that warmth spread through me slowly and deliberately. It was just like him, something that he would have consciously done if he was capable. Chip away at the ice when it didn't melt fast enough for his liking. Another day with him like the one we spent at his house, and I'd be engulfed in flames.

He didn't answer me, simply lifted my hands up to his mouth and pressed a kiss against both of my palms. Together, we fixed a small meal for Brooke without exchanging another word. The silence didn't bother me, but I wasn't sure he felt the same. When I met his eyes, he smiled, but looked away first.

Throughout the entire course of our relationship, he was the one who understood and accepted his emotions far faster than I had ever been able to. His processing abilities were at warp speed compared to my own, something that apparently hadn't changed over the years. While my own head and heart would search for the name to what I felt, found the appropriate spot for it in my life, Cole was almost always sprinting ahead, reveling in the assuredness of his emotions.

Of course, that had been its own kind of steadying force. He was the first to say "I love you", only two weeks after our first date. It took me another two weeks to be able to say it back and mean it. But in his eyes, I saw how much more it meant to him, because he knew that I truly meant it. There were no pacifying generalizations between him and me. Nothing said with flippancy or shallow intentions.

It was as much our strength as our downfall, because the words we said in anger and frustration cut even deeper because we both knew they were true. So as much as I wanted to grab his face in my hands and tell him I loved him too, that I was all in, it still felt like too tenuous of a connection.

If Cole and I got remarried tomorrow, what would happen when the inevitable conversation about kids came up? We were young enough to try again, but just the thought of it exhausted me to my core. That conversation felt like eons away from us, from what we were ready to tackle.

So after I gave Brooke her soup and helped her use the bathroom, I curled up next to Cole on the couch, let him play with the ends of my hair while we watched a movie, and didn't ask him what was next for us. He didn't ask me either. For now, it could be okay. Tonight was one thing, one tiny step closer to whatever our new normal might be.

And that was enough for me.

CHAPTER NINETEEN

JULIA

"Oh yeah," Brooke groaned from her perch on a kitchen chair. With a beatific smile on her face, she took a long sip from her iced tea. "This is the best way to move. I can't believe I ever thought bed rest was a bad thing."

From behind the box that Cole was lifting, filled with her clothes, he snorted. I rolled my eyes, since she'd been saying it every day for the last seven, while she watched me pack and sort her things in preparation for moving day. As the house was empty, she was allowed to take possession upon closing, which went just as easily as Cole said it would. By the time we finally got to the title office, Brooke was well past her bout with the flu, and practically floating since she was normally only out of the house for doctor's appointments.

Sitting at a long conference table and signing the massive stack of papers that Cole diligently handed her, Brooke commented more than once that it was the greatest day of her life. And despite her flair for the drama, I knew she was probably being serious.

I remembered vividly, despite the fact that my divorce was the reason I was finally buying a house for the first time, how I felt when I walked through the front door of my quaint little bungalow house on March Street in the southern tip of Connecticut. The original wood floors were scuffed and needed to be re-varnished, but they were *mine*.

"You always have been gifted with the most incredible adaptability," I muttered around the sharpie cap in my mouth.

"So where are these movers you promised?" Brooke asked Cole.

He set the wardrobe box down next to the door, one of many lining the impossibly small space of the apartment. "Should be here any minute. Dylan and Tristan are the ones with the trucks, so between Julia's car and those two vehicles, we should be able to do this in only a few trips." He glanced around the space, the stacks of boxes that were set and ready to go and lifted his dark eyebrows. "I hope so, at least."

"Amazing how much was crammed in this limited space, isn't it?"

"Uh, yeah," he said and winked at Brooke when she scoffed.

"Will you miss this place at all?" I asked her when she sobered and looked around the room.

She let out a sigh. "It's weird to think so, but yeah, I think I might."

"Why is that weird?"

"Well, Kevin left me after we'd been together for so long. I should hate this place. But I don't. It was the first place where I truly felt like an adult. Like I was capable of making my own decisions, even if they sucked a big one." She shook her head. "So even though he turned out to be a royal douchebag, I can't regret the time we spent here, or the time that I was with him."

Regret was a funny thing. While I thought on Brooke's words, I couldn't help but roll around the list of my own regrets. One single decision can change the course of your life, and no matter how much you might wish that you hadn't made that particular decision, you can never know that it was truly the wrong one.

What if Cole hadn't gone back to return my dress to the dry cleaner until later?

If I'd never talked to him, or danced with him that first weekend, if I'd never said yes when he asked to see me again, my life might have followed a completely different path. Who might I have met instead?

Changing those initial decisions would never feel like a regret, no matter what came later for us. While I looked across the room at Cole, so strong and loyal, so sure in what he felt for me and for us, and I knew that he'd never, ever be a regret for me.

"That makes sense," I said quietly. I reached over and rubbed a hand over her belly, which was growing by the day it seemed. "Plus, you got these two out of the bargain."

Brooke set her hand over top of mine and squeezed. "Yes I did. And thanks to them, I get to sit in this very lovely chair and direct everyone, including my hypothetically hot movers."

I laughed and pushed myself up off the floor. "I'm sure Cole wouldn't lie to you about that."

There was a knock on the door and Brooke and I exchanged a glance. Cole was just shaking his head when he went to open it up. Three tall, very tall, very strong-looking, and holy hell hot guys walked through the door, shrinking the space immediately. Michael I recognized, but I can't even lie, I straight up gaped at the other two. When I risked a glance at Brooke, she was doing the same.

"Hi," she said weakly.

Michael gave her a charming grin, all white teeth and dimples. "Little sister, you are just as gorgeous as Julia promised. And just as pregnant."

Brooke raised an eyebrow at me and I gave her a small, apologetic smile. "I see your looks aren't the only impressive thing about you. You're quite the observant one, aren't you?"

The guy with dark hair and bright blue eyes coughed behind his hand and then stepped toward me. "Dylan. It's a pleasure to meet you."

I shook his hand and smiled. "Same here. I so appreciate you guys taking your day to help us. It really means a lot to me and Brooke."

"My girlfriend is going to join us later," Dylan said. "She's a vet tech and had to go in for some emergency something that I can't pronounce."

"Oh great," I told him, feeling the sudden weight of everyone's eyes on me. The third guy, just as tall as Michael, a bit broader in the shoulders and with a much more serious look on his face was assessing me openly. He had long hair that was pulled back into a low ponytail, and I found myself meeting that look head-on. Yes, I'm the ex-wife, I wanted to say. And yes, I'm the one who he's choosing to trust again.

I'd never thought about the fact that some of his friends might not actually be happy to meet me. Sudden nerves pitched my stomach and I broke eye contact.

"Tristan," the third guy said with a brief nod of his head at Brooke. "Where should we start?"

"Uhhh," Brooke stammered, blinking rapidly at the wall of testosterone facing her with expectant looks on all their faces. "With the boxes?"

Michael choked on a laugh and Tristan elbowed him in the stomach.

I stepped past the couch and pointed at the boxes that held all the kitchen stuff. "Those boxes should go over first, followed by the pile in the bedroom. Kitchen stuff will take the longest to unpack and organize, but she'll need it soon. Same with the bedroom. Then we can at least have beds made up tonight for sleeping."

Tristan nodded and clapped Dylan on the back, and they went to work on the already-packed kitchen boxes. Once they got into a rhythm, the apartment emptied out fairly quickly. Filling my car resembled a game of Tetris, and it took Cole and Michael a few configurations to fill it the most efficiently.

The trucks came and went, once and then twice. Through it all, the easy laughter and camaraderie of the men made for a remarkably pleasant experience. Cole seemed lighter, happier, with them around. Not that he was sad when they weren't, but seeing that side of him was a balm to the guilt that always hovered around the edges of my heart when it came to him.

He'd had love, brothers who made him laugh and supported him while I was gone. Not that friends could always replace the intimacy of a spouse, but it was so clear that these men loved each other. Personally, I'd never had friends who came even close. Brooke was always my best friend, and the women I got to know through work were perfectly nice, would occasionally meet me after work for a cocktail, but nothing that fed my soul, nobody to step up and offer to shoulder whatever emotional burden I might be carrying.

Dylan shoved Tristan on his way out the door with one piece of the sectional couch, drawing a tiny smile from the clearly very serious man. Throughout the first part of the day, Tristan was the only one who didn't really interact with me. He was perfectly polite, very kind to Brooke, and made his friends laugh often with a few quietly uttered sentences.

Brooke was taking a brief rest on the bed before they moved that over, which left me and Tristan in the living room. He glanced at me when I stepped around him in the kitchen, but didn't smile.

"Can I ask you a question?"

He froze, but nodded, turning just enough that he could see my face. There was no irritation in his eyes, but there was wariness.

"This isn't a trap either, I promise."

Tristan briefly lifted his eyebrows. "You do realize that when someone says that, you instantly prepare for a trap, right?"

His voice was low, like it came from somewhere deep within him, and so deliberate that it was almost impossible to imagine that he'd speak rashly or impulsively. I carefully folded a towel around Brooke's blue vase and set it on top of an almost-full box.

I chose not to acknowledge what he'd said. "You don't like me very much, do you?"

Tristan's eyes narrowed almost imperceptibly. "What makes you say that?"

A question for a question. Not a denial, but not agreement either.

Without meeting his eyes, I zipped the packing tape over the top of the box and pushed it across the floor next to the others that were ready to go. "You're quiet, I can tell. But you've been very thoughtful with my sister. Making sure her drink was refilled so she didn't have to get off the chair. How you treat your friends. You respect them, even if you're different than they are."

His face didn't change in the slightest while I talked, nothing registering in his eyes. I faced him fully and crossed my arms over my chest. "But you actively avoid me. I'm the only person in the room that you've only said one word to. One. And that was your name. I'm good at reading people, Tristan, even people I don't know very well. It's okay if you don't like me, I don't have a problem proving to you that I'm not whatever you might think I am."

His thumb tapped against the side of his leg a few times while he watched me. After a few awkward beats of silence, his chest expanded on a deep breath that he let go out through his nose. "I don't talk much to anyone, really. So what I'm about to say will probably be more words than any of those guys out there have heard me string together at a time." Tristan tilted his chin down to his chest so he could hold my eyes more fully, and swear to high heaven, I struggled not to fidget. "I don't dislike you, Julia. But I don't particularly like you, either. Cole is one of my best friends, and the kind of loyalty that he's shown to you since I've met him is almost unheard of in men our age. I understand loyalty, and I understand loving someone who—whether it's because of distance or ignorance—doesn't see that love. So while I'm ambivalent to you as a person, I am certainly going to keep my eye on you."

I exhaled roughly. "Are you threatening me?"

"No," he said simply. "Just stating a fact. You hurt him once, and it affected him so deeply that he was never truly able to move on. That's the kind of hurt that changes a man. It's a wonder Cole didn't lose himself when you left, and I'll be damned if you do that to him again. Because if you do, if you hurt him again, I don't think he'll survive it."

My eyes burned with unshed tears and I willed them to stay back.

"Do you really think I need you to remind me of how much I hurt him? I live with that knowledge every single day."

"Good."

His curt reply didn't bother me, because I understood enough about him after those few honestly spoken statements that he'd probably never soften his delivery for someone like me, someone he didn't trust with his friend's heart.

But when I gave him a small smile, he frowned. "Tristan, you may not believe me when I say this, but I'm really glad Cole has a friend like you. Who would risk pissing me off the first time you met me in order to stand up for him. We both know he doesn't need you to do it, because he's a grown man, but you're doing it anyway, simply because he's important to you." I took a deep breath, feeling some weight fall off my shoulders. "So thank you. Knowing he has someone like you in his life means a lot to me."

From the minute changes in his face, I could tell I'd surprised him. It was in the way his jaw slackened just enough that his mouth opened. In the way that he blinked a few times. But he couldn't answer because Cole walked back in.

He slid a hand up my back and kissed my hair. "I think that's the last of it besides the mattress, bed frame and these few boxes."

I smiled up at him. "Thanks. I'll go wake up Sleeping Beauty." When I walked past Tristan on the way to Brooke's room, I felt his eyes on my back, speculative and heavy. But it was a weight I would bear gladly. Cole didn't have parents to test my return in his life, question my motives. In truth, I could've hugged Tristan for his mini-Inquisition, but he probably would've hated it.

Brooke was a little groggy when I woke her, but the prospect of getting to her house was far too exciting for her not to shake that off quickly. The last few items were loaded into the trucks quickly, since there were eight strong hands doing all the work. With my arm wrapped around her waist, she locked the apartment for the last time and stared at the gray metal door for a minute before nodding once.

"Let's do it."

"Let's," I said with a smile.

She dropped the keys off to the landlord and we walked together to my car. The guys were waiting by the loaded trucks, all giving varying degrees of a smile at the way Brooke waddled across the parking lot.

"I feel like a freak show," she whispered.

"You're beautiful," I told her. "That's all they're looking at."

"It's true," Michael piped up. "You're probably the hottest mom I've ever met in my life."

Tristan closed his eyes, shaking his head slightly.

"They really let you out into public with lines that cheesy?" Brooke asked.

Michael nodded gravely. "They make me practice on them first, but yes."

"Come on," she sighed. "Let's just get my pregnant ass to my awesome new house."

We piled into our respective cars, and mine led the way to Brooke's place. My place too, I guessed. It was hard to imagine that it would be my home for the foreseeable future. Before Cole and I spent the night at his house, and the incredibly non-existent alone time that we'd had since then, it was easy to see my place in Brooke's home.

Everything was murky now. Even if Cole had never said it to me, I knew he was frustrated with the fact that I still hadn't told Brooke that we were … dating, trying again, whatever it was currently labeled. And even the sleeping together had only happened the once, much to both of our frustrations. Brooke's sickness abated only to be met with the task of packing up her home, which fell completely to me. Sneaking out to find time with Cole simply hadn't happened.

We'd find time, I promised myself while I stared in the rear view mirror to where he was sitting in Dylan's truck. I missed him. Being in the same place as him all day, and I missed him. Finding time wasn't good enough. It felt passive and weak. I'd *make* time.

When I pulled up to the house, Brooke bouncing in the passenger seat, I saw two new cars in the driveway.

"Who's that and why is my house the most adorable thing I've ever seen?" Brooke asked, practically squealing.

"It really is adorable." I pointed to the front porch. "I think we should sit right there tonight and have some iced tea, mine will be spiked, of course."

She sighed and took in the front of the house. "It's perfect."

"You haven't even seen the inside." I tilted my head. "Although, it'll be complete chaos in there with the things they've moved over so far."

"Don't even care, Julia. Don't even care." Brooke turned to grab the door handle, but Michael beat her to it, pulling the door open and holding out a hand for her.

"May I be of assistance?"

"Did you smoke crack on the way over?" Brooke asked.

"I try to keep that to Fridays only." He shook his head. "Come on, my attempt at amends for shoveling stupid pickup lines your way when you're clearly more evolved than the typical woman."

"Clearly," she mumbled under her breath while she took his hand. With a grunt, she stood from the car. I caught Michael's eye over the hood of the car and gave him a warning look. He returned it with a wink.

Still playing the role of perfect gentleman, Michael held her hand while she walked up the steps to the porch and through the front door. When I came in after, I couldn't even pay attention to her exclamations of all the things she loved, because I was too focused on the complete lack of chaos in the house. Of course, boxes were still piled everywhere, but the couch was put together and pushed against the long wall in the family room, the large framed picture that Brooke had hanging behind it at her apartment was already hung on the wall.

It wasn't much, but it still looked like a home was slowly beginning to form. Rory came through the arch that led into the kitchen, hair in a high, sleek ponytail and face covered with a wide grin.

"Surprise," she said and gave me a quick air kiss next to my face.

"I'll say. How long have you been here?"

She smoothed a hand over her hair and nodded back to the kitchen. "Kat and I met the guys here on one of their earlier deliveries. I hope it's okay we kinda started unloading the kitchen."

"Are you kidding? That's incredible." I leaned forward and wrapped my arms around her. "Thank you so much."

Rory patted my back with a laugh. "You're welcome."

A short, smiling woman came from the kitchen with messy, shoulder-length blond hair and she nudged her shoulder against Rory. "Don't let her take the credit. This was completely my idea." She stuck her hand out to me. "I'm Kat. Pleasure to meet you."

"Julia. Same." I pressed a hand to my forehead. "Sorry, I feel a little overwhelmed with the niceness. I showed up thinking that I would be unpacking all night."

Kat laughed, a tinkling little sound that matched her compact body. "I overwhelm people often, don't even worry about it. Go, show your sister her house, we'll keep working."

But when I turned, Brooke was holding Michael's elbow and walking through the slider into the backyard, completely oblivious to my presence. I thought about joining them, but Brooke was a big girl. She didn't need me to label the rooms for her.

No one was looking, so I snuck down the hall to what would be Brooke's room and sat down on the mattress that the guys had already unloaded from Tristan's truck. I let out a slow breath and listened to the sounds of all the people in the house. Cole's people. Not my people. And they just showed up because they knew it was important to him.

Like my thoughts conjured him, his head popped around the door frame. And he smiled, so happy to see me, that it did nothing to impede the panicky thoughts running through my head. Tristan's warnings, Kat and Rory's unbelievable generosity.

He blinked when I didn't smile back. "You okay?"

COLE

"I don't know," I told him honestly. "It's just a lot, you know? The house, how amazing your friends are, we're only like six weeks from when Brooke could have the babies. I guess it all just ... hit me."

Cole paused in the doorway before sitting next to me on the bed. "Maybe I shouldn't ask this in a house full with people, but, I haven't really had the chance to ask before now." He gave me a look out of the corner of his eyes and I swallowed. Definitely needed to make time for him, for us. "Was it hard when you found out Brooke was pregnant?"

I exhaled roughly, the question was about as unexpected as a baseball bat to the gut. Rory laughed from the kitchen, and I stood up to go shut the door. I leaned against it and stared at Cole. No one had ever asked me that question. Brooke was probably afraid to, my parents probably didn't want to know. But of course he would.

"I cried when she told me. I cried for her, because she waited to tell me until after Kevin left, so I was sad that she had to do it alone. And I cried for me." I swallowed. "But it didn't wreck me, not like it might have before."

"What do you mean?"

"If I'd still been with you," I held his eyes while I spoke, hating that I even had to put it into words, "I think it would've felt like she was ripping my soul right out of my body. But without you there, it lessened the pain, I think." A tear hit my cheek before I even knew I was crying. Cole looked miserable, and he stood to come to me when we heard Brooke's voice in the hallway. I blinked and took a deep breath. This wasn't the place, definitely wasn't the time to bring this up. So I opened the door and gave him a sad smile before I left the room.

I followed Brooke into the other two bedrooms, and when we walked back down the hallway, Cole was still sitting on the bed, staring at the wall.

CHAPTER TWENTY

COLE

The wave of irritation took me by surprise. It was slight, and dissipated quickly, but it was there nonetheless. Just a flash of a light bulb that you weren't expecting. The light may have turned off, but you could still see the remnants in the edges of your vision afterward, blurring and distorting your vision.

I knew, logically, that part of it stemmed from the fact that I wanted to show her affection whenever I was around her, and I wasn't allowed to. Not when Brooke was around. Part of me wanted to press the issue, grab her by the shoulders and plant a kiss on her when Brooke was in the room.

But Julia would be pissed, and for good reason. Despite knowing she'd have every reason to didn't stem the desire to creep up on the line that she'd drawn. One thing at a time. In my head, I could tick through a list as to why she laid that mantle over our relationship, but it didn't make it easier to abide by.

As evidenced by my blurted-out question that made Julia look like every ounce of blood was sucked from her face. I was well aware of how people tiptoed around couples who struggled with infertility. They announced pregnancies and births at a quieter level, with a guarded kind of propriety that was masked as thoughtfulness, but could easily be confused with self-preservation.

In my head, I'd worked out that no one had ever asked Julia how she felt about Brooke's pregnancy. Brooke rarely erred on the side of serious, so I didn't think she'd broach that subject with Julia. Which wasn't Brooke's fault. It was a difficult thing to ask someone. But it was me. And her. We'd crept past worse subjects than that one.

My timing could have been better. My approach. But it was done now, and I sat on that mattress for far longer than was appropriate considering how hard everyone else was working at Brooke's house.

But I wanted the irritation to pass, wanted to make sure my thoughts were steady enough to go back to smiling and joking with my friends, not seem like a complete ass because of what she and I were dealing with off-stage. That was the crux of it, wasn't it?

Off-stage. More than anything, I wanted to put our relationship front and center, before anything else in my life, but she was, as usual, moving at a slightly slower pace. I pushed off the bed and went back to work. Rory turned on some music, and over the next couple hours, we made good headway on unpacking a lot of the big stuff.

The family room was sparse, but Brooke would be able to add in more furniture. Rory and Kat got the kitchen almost completely put together, only arguing once about which cupboard the glasses should go in before Julia stepped in and said that clearly, they should be to the right of the sink. Rory smirked and Kat grumbled about tall woman discriminatory practices.

Tristan ordered pizza to be delivered, which surprised everyone, but most of all Julia. She stared at the delivery guy for a solid minute before Tristan gently moved her aside and paid. By the time the sun was setting and the air cooling outside, there wasn't much reason for all of us to stay.

Kat and Dylan said goodbye first, and Kat gave tight hugs to both

Brooke and Julia before they went home. Tristan and Michael left next, with Michael giving Brooke an exaggerated slug to the shoulder so that Julia wouldn't kick his ass for hitting on her little sister.

When the door shut behind the brothers, Rory sank back against the couch and patted her stomach. "I think I gained ten pounds from that pizza."

"Oh please, toothpick," Brooke snorted from the other side of the couch. She pointed at her belly and Rory laughed. "I gain ten pounds from breathing."

Julia stood from the couch and gathered plates. I did the same and followed her into the kitchen while Rory and Brooke chatted easily.

"I wish you could come home with me tonight," I whispered while she stuffed paper plates into the already full garbage bag.

She held the bag open for me while I put my handful in, but didn't look up at me until I was done. "I know. I do too."

"What if you told Brooke that you wanted to, I don't know, give her some privacy since it's her first night in her house?"

Julia smiled and wrapped her arms around my waist. I breathed into her hair, every muscle in my body relaxing instantly at the feel of her against me.

"You know I can't." She rolled her forehead against my chest. "Besides, I still need to make up our beds and do some unpacking in the bathrooms."

I hooked a finger under her chin and pressed my lips against hers. The softness of her mouth made my head spin, and I cupped the sides of her face so I could sweep my tongue against hers. Julia melted, sliding her hands up my back and pushing up on tip-toe so she could kiss me more fully.

When we were like this, everything felt perfect. Like there was no obstacle that we couldn't hurdle over with ease. It was the other stuff, families and future, that tripped us up when we were apart. Not even apart, just not able to be honest about what we were. My frustration turned the kiss fierce, and I bit at her lower lip. She whimpered softly, but the noise was enough to make her push back from me.

"Not here," she whispered. "Please."

I breathed deeply for a few moments, attempted to get my bearings. Rory and Brooke were still talking, so it was unlikely that they heard us. I wish they'd had, I thought instantly. Like a reflex I couldn't control, I felt the irritation again.

But I nodded and ran my hand down her hair before touching her mouth with my thumb. "Unless you guys need any more help, I'm gonna head home."

Julia covered her hand with mine and turned them so she could press a kiss to my palm. "No, I think we're good. Thank you. For your friends and the trucks and just ... everything."

"You're welcome," I said gruffly, feeling a weird twinge at her gratitude. I didn't want her to feel like she had to thank me for doing things that I didn't even have to question. It was Julia. Brooke, too. I'd do anything to help them, and she knew that. It felt like something she'd say to a stranger, or a friendly acquaintance.

I went and said my goodbyes to Brooke and Rory and drove home with a strange knot in my stomach. It didn't leave when I walked into my dark house, or while I watched *SportsCenter* before heading to bed. The knot was Julia, of course. It was always her.

By the time I did crawl in between the cold sheets of my bed, it took me a long time to fall into a fitful sleep. And for the first time in weeks, Julia haunted my sleep again, the past jumbled with the present, our first fight melding with things that had never happened while I tossed and turned.

"You'll never have to do this and feel alone, Julia," I promised, trying to grab her shoulders before she whirled away from me.

"But I am alone," she said wearily. "I just want to take this one thing at a time, one step at a time, one day at a time, can't you just let me?"

A calendar stretched out before me, an endless length of paper, and I frantically tried to find the end of it. One day at a time became months, years, of hiding and lying. Of never sleeping next to her at night. Evaded questions and empty answers.

"Julia, please." I grabbed her shoulders and she hissed like I'd burned her. I held my hands up and they were covered in coals. Every time my emotions flared, my body heated, and when I touched her, I seared them over her skin.

"It's too much, Cole." Julia cried and cried, started clutching at her chest. "I don't know how to find it."

I knelt down next to her. "Find what?"

"My heart, Cole. Where is it?" Her chest cracked open, the same yawning, bloody hole that I normally had. Her eyes flashed. "Don't you have it?"

I looked down at my hands, my burning, empty hands. "I don't."

"If you don't have it, where is it?" she shrieked, her tears lapping at my legs now. "If you don't have it, where is it?"

"I don't know," I yelled, powerlessness pushing me further and further into the water surrounding me. "God, Julia, I don't know."

When my head slipped under the surface, I gasped awake and bolted up in bed. My chest heaved while I struggled to calm myself. It felt like if I tried hard enough, I could still feel the water over my face, in my ears, in my mouth. The warped images of Julia's empty chest made me shudder, my eyes burn.

I pressed the heel of my hands into my eyes and took a few deep breaths until my heart slowed to a more manageable pace. The clock on my nightstand showed 12:32 a.m. and I took a chance by picking up my phone and sending Julia a text.

Me: Are you sleeping?

Julia: Not yet. What's up?

Me: Bad dream.

As soon as the text went through, my phone starting vibrating with an incoming call. With a smile, I swiped my thumb across the screen and brought the phone up to my ear. "Hey."

"You okay?" she asked quietly. Her voice was hushed and tired, and I could tell she was in bed. I had to close my eyes against the wave of longing.

"Better. Just freaked me out a little bit, wanted to make sure you were okay."

"Your dream was about me?"

I stared up at the ceiling and thought about how honestly I should answer her. "They're always about you, Julia."

In the background, I could hear her shift around. "Knowing it was a bad dream, I don't know how I should take that," she said lightly, but I could hear the concern in her voice.

"Don't take it as anything bad. It just means I think about you as much in my sleep as I do when I'm awake."

"I guess."

We were silent for a little bit, just listening to each other breathe.

"Cole, can I come over?" she said on a rushed exhale.

The selfish part of me wanted to scream yes. The protective part of me held it back. "It's so late. I don't want you driving if you're too tired."

She scoffed. "I'm thirty-four, not sixteen. I'll be fine."

I smiled. "Then who am I to say no?"

"I'll see you in fifteen minutes."

Seventeen minutes later, I was pacing by the front window of my house, still only in my boxers, when her headlights swept through the blinds. I opened the door for her, and laughed. Her legs were bare, her body covered by a black wool coat, and on her feet were another pair of fuzzy slippers.

"Nice outfit."

She walked past me into the house. "Once I'm in pajamas, I'm not changing again until it's morning."

After I locked the door, I hooked an arm around her neck and hugged her to me. The front of her coat was chilled from the air and I rubbed a hand down her back to help warm her up.

"I feel like I'm a booty call or something right now," I said into the top of her head.

Julia laughed into my chest. "As long as you only feel like that with me."

The last of my dream ebbed away from the feel of her in my arms. Real flesh and bone, not a misty, symbolic version of her.

I rested my chin on the top of her head and took a deep breath. "I'm glad you came over."

She kissed the skin over my heart. "Me too. I've missed you since the last time we were here."

My eyes pinched shut, relief sweeping through me at hearing her say it. "Missing you before was different, when I hadn't seen you in years. It was this dull ache that I just lived with, you know? But knowing you're here, knowing what it feels like to touch you again, sometimes I feel like I need to see your face again in order to keep breathing."

Julia looked up at me, so much sadness and regret in her eyes. "I know."

When she pulled back and started unbuttoning her coat, I had a moment of pause. We should talk, I thought in my head. Briefly. Oh so briefly. Under her coat were impossibly small sleep shorts, pink and soft-looking against her legs. The shirt she wore had straps that barely seemed substantial enough to hold it up over her shoulders.

She dropped her coat on the floor and then we crashed against each other, mouths fused and tongues sweeping together. I wrapped my arms under her ass and boosted her up so that her legs wrapped around my waist.

I groaned into her mouth when she raked her hands along my scalp.

"Bed or wall," I said in between biting, wet kisses. "Your choice."

"Bed," she said immediately. "I need to feel your weight on top of me." She pulled back and met my eyes. "I've never felt safer in my life than when I'm wrapped up in you, Cole. Never."

Julia leaned forward and kissed my bottom lip, then my top. Our foreheads pressed together and we held like that for a moment.

"When you say things like that to me," I whispered against her mouth. I had to close my eyes. Everything felt so big, like it would burst from my skin.

"I know. I know, Cole. It's almost too much, isn't it?"

I didn't answer, simply walked us back to the bed and fell on top of her. Her clothes came off easily, my boxers did too. She hitched her legs up around my hips and whimpered into my shoulder when I made her wait. I wanted to rush, I wanted to savor. Every brush of her fingers against my skin set me on fire, sped my heart to dangerous rhythms.

When I leaned my head to trace the curve of her breast with my lips, she arched up, impatient and greedy.

"I love you," I whispered into her jaw when I pushed inside.

CHAPTER TWENTY-ONE

JULIA

It was almost too much. The way he clutched at my skin. The words I whispered into his. The way we moved together, seamless and smooth. Cole filled me so perfectly, just like he always had, the same lover that grew up with me, in all the ways that counted when we were like this.

He knew me innately, just like I knew him. My skin prickled when he bit down on the edge of my earlobe. He moved faster when I drew my fingernails in sharp lines down his back.

Too much, too big, too intense to be contained into one mortal body. The overwhelming feeling of him and me, what we'd been, what we were now, pushed a tear down the side of my face. I would give him anything, I knew with a sudden, stunning clarity as I slid into a warm, slow roll of pleasure that made me gasp.

He did the same, gripping me to him in a tight, brutal hug while we caught our breath. We laid like that for a few minutes, simply breathing into each other's sweat-glossed skin. Cole rolled on his back and brought me up against him in a smooth motion that we'd done a hundred times, maybe a thousand. So many small habits that couldn't be counted because of how innate they were to our relationship.

Then I laughed, because he lifted an arm to hand me a box of tissues to clean myself up. Married habits die hard, apparently. His answering smile was slow and content, peaceful in how long it lingered on his face. My hand reached up to trace the lines of it. Like I could absorb it into my skin if I tried hard enough to capture its shape. This was happiness. I could feel it lining my skin, filling my heart with a warmth that I'd tried to capture every single day while I was away from him. I'd failed, of course, because I knew now that he was the truest form of happiness that I'd ever know.

And I'd made him wait for the smallest snippet of what was in my heart.

I turned my face into his chest and sighed. It should have been easy, effortless and perfectly simple to open my mouth and whisper against his body. But there was a kindling of nerves in the pit of my belly with every deep breath that I took before opening my mouth.

"I love you, Cole." And I kissed his skin, pulling in a deep breath, filling my lungs with him.

His entire body froze for a beat, but then he pulled back and stared at me. Then he smiled. After he smiled, he started laughing. I sat up and looked down at him, thoroughly bemused and slightly embarrassed. He laid back on the bed and his entire frame shook with laughter.

"Is that so funny?" I asked, poking his chest.

Cole grabbed my hand and kissed it before he sat up and faced me. "You can't be *that* surprised at my reaction."

"I can't?" I tucked my hair behind my ears and smiled at him, even though my cheeks were flushed and hot. "I don't think you've ever laughed at me when I've said those particular words before."

He tilted his head to the side when it must have registered that I was embarrassed. "Julia, come on. I'm not laughing *at* you. I'm ... well, I'm really relieved. I've felt pretty alone in my feelings for a very long time. It's nice to know you're still here with me."

I blinked a few times, something slightly colder replacing the bashfulness. Frustration and irritation warred inside of me. "Still here with you? I've been here with you since the day we kissed."

"Have you?" he asked lightly, but I heard the edge in his voice.

Too much, too big, too intense to be contained by one mortal body. But this felt like it wasn't *supposed* to be inside of me, but I couldn't get rid of it by sheer force of will. "You couldn't tell how I felt about you? At all?"

He lifted his hands up, a pacifying gesture that made me feel the slightest prickle of defensiveness, even before he said a word. "Why do I suddenly feel like we should have clothes on for this conversation?"

"Cole, you know me. You cannot honestly tell me that you thought I'd get this far with you and not feel love or commitment or even a desire for a future. That you'd think I would jerk you around like that."

Cole stood from the bed and pulled his boxers up, but I stayed right where I was. The only concession I gave was pulling the sheet up to cover my chest. He didn't get right back into bed, just propped his hands on his hips and stared at me for a few seconds.

"I didn't know where you were for seven years, Julia," he said in a low voice, words deliberate and clipped. "Seven years."

"I *know* that." I swallowed, pinching the sheets underneath my arms and tugging it even higher, the flimsiest armor I could possibly have, but at least it was something. "You didn't answer my question."

"For *seven years*, I had to replay every single thing that went wrong in our marriage and ask myself why it was that you chose to run instead of stand there and fight with me, fight with me for our relationship, fight with me over our future. So yes, Julia, I have often thought over the years that I knew you inside and out, but the fact that I could never answer that question proved to me that I didn't know you as well as I thought."

I closed my eyes, the sweep of guilt and mortification turning my skin hot in an instant. This was something I couldn't argue with him, no matter how much I wanted to. Slowly, I reached over the side of the bed and picked up my pajamas. I spoke softly, pleading with him when I opened my eyes again. "Cole, please, all I have asked for is to be patient. To take things one thing-"

"-at a time," he interjected, face hardening as he spoke. "We were *married*, Julia. For crying out loud, how slow do you expect us to be able to go?"

Annoyance made me pull my clothes on with jerky, harsh movements. "I am *not* asking for too much here. Okay? What we're attempting is so big, Cole. It's more than most people could probably even wrap their head around, so I don't think it's stupid for us to go slowly."

"Slowly?" he asked quietly. "We slept together after the first legitimate conversation we had. You think that's doing things slowly?"

I let out a hiss of a breath. "And somehow, that's now become a weapon that you can use against me? I didn't expect that of you, Cole."

He hung his head and took in a few deep breaths. "I don't mean it as a weapon."

"Why is it so hard for you to believe that I've loved you this whole time? You know that it's harder for me to put a name to how I feel, to say it out loud. That's always been the case with me." My voice grew in volume, irrationality spreading its dark veins through my body.

"People have to grow and change as they get older. We can't sit back and say, hey, this is how I've always done it, so it must be okay."

I huffed out a breath, the tears lodged in my throat made the sound full and heavy. "Wow."

When I got out of the bed, he rounded the end of it and held his hands out. "Hear me out, because I think I've been pretty understanding up until now."

My jaw clenched tightly, and the pressure against my teeth kept me from screaming. Every inch of my body was burning to flee, to get out into the cold night air so I could purge all these feelings from inside of me. But he was right. He had been understanding, so I stayed.

Cole bent his knees and lowered his head, so I was forced to meet his eyes. His face was blurry from tears, but I didn't blink. "Love means accepting someone, flaws and all. And I accept all of the worst parts of you, Julia. You know that I do, but if I stand back and let you bolt at the slightest roadblock again, then it's like I'm saying it's okay that you do it. It's not okay."

I pointed a finger at him, anger igniting a fire in my belly. "The slightest roadblock? I would've left a couple months into our marriage if that was the truth, and you damn well know it." I speared my hands in my hair and paced next to the bed. "I cannot believe we're doing this right now."

"We have to do it eventually," he threw back at me. "It was inevitable."

Helplessness at how I was, how I'd always been, made the tears fall. "All I'm asking for is for you to be patient with me, I don't understand what's so hard about that."

Cole shook his head. "You think I haven't been patient?"

"No, that's not what I meant," I said quickly, "I mean, I don't *know* what I meant. Come on, Cole, it's crazy that me telling you that I love you turned into this. Why can't you just accept it for what it is?" I sucked in a breath, and kept right on rolling, and I saw the warning flash in his eyes. "Not everyone moves at the same warp speed that you do, you know? Our entire relationship, I felt like there was something wrong with me because you were always so sure, always accepted exactly how you felt and didn't question it."

His mouth fell open. "I never made you feel like there was something wrong with you because of that."

"You're doing it right now," I cried. "And I don't understand *why*."

"Because I don't *trust* you," he yelled.

I fell back, a hand pressed against my stomach. My ears rang as if he'd slapped me. "What?" I whispered. "Are you serious right now?"

Cole blinked rapidly, like he couldn't believe he said it either. He swiped a hand over his mouth and stared at me for a second. "I think

I am, yeah."

"What am I supposed to say to that?"

He spoke quietly, firmly, after he took a moment to think about that. "Julia, I understand that this is how you've always done things. But I don't trust that you won't tuck tail and run across the country where I can't find you again. You hid from our marriage because we disagreed and I don't know how to stop worrying that you'll do it again."

He walked forward and cupped my face, wiped at the cold tears with his thumbs. My whole body was trembling. From shock. From the cold. From how much I couldn't blame him for feeling it.

Too much. Too big. Too intense to be contained in one mortal body.

Cole touched his forehead to mine, his voice heavy and weighted with emotion. "The way I feel right now, it's like I'd be chasing you the rest of my life. And not the good kind. Not the kind of chasing that a husband *should* do. Where I get to woo you, flirt with you, date you for the rest of our lives. But the soul-crushing, heart-shredding kind of chase. Where you're always just out of reach. If I make one wrong move, if I say one wrong thing, I don't trust that we won't end up right back where we started."

I cried softly, gripped his wrists where he still held my face. His pulse underneath my fingers was fast and steady, and I knew it probably matched my own. My heart was cracked in two, knowing that even now, I still wanted to flee from what we were doing, from the words that neither of us could take back.

There were no words trying to combat what he was saying, my tongue wouldn't form them, even though I knew that I should.

"I'm walking on eggshells," he whispered. "And I can't sustain that forever. When I don't know what's going on in your head, I feel like I'm one wrong comment away from losing you for the second time. That's not something I can handle going through again, Julia. You are my heart, and I don't want to live without you, but I can't keep feeling like this."

I sobbed and pulled out of his grasp. His eyes were red like he was fighting tears.

"I thought you forgave me." My voice wavered and he looked like he wanted to reach for me again, but he didn't.

"I did," he said roughly. "And I meant it. But I don't know what the balance is between forgiveness and trust. Whether they can stand separately within a relationship. I need to know, *you* need to know, that we can move forward, trust that we won't put each other through what we did before. Have tough conversations about our future without fear of annihilating what we've built."

The knot in my stomach grew and grew, thinking about the path we'd already traveled, and how far we still had to go. My breaths came faster and faster, and I pressed a hand to my chest, like I could slow my heart rate just by touching the skin encasing it.

"I have to go," I whispered.

His eyes narrowed, he shook his head and took a step back from me. "Don't."

I stepped toward him and tried to lay my hands on his chest but he turned his back to me and walked out of the bedroom. "Cole, wait."

He made a sharp pivot to face me, fire in his eyes and color high on his cheeks. "I am begging you not to run away right now."

"I need to think," I told him in a pleading voice, but annoyance surged hot and bright that I even felt like I needed to plead. "And I can't think, I don't even feel like I can *breathe* when you look at me like that."

"Like what?"

I snapped my chin up and straightened to my full height. "Like it's a fucking crime to need to take a step back and process everything you just said to me. Come on, Cole. Give me a break."

He held a hand out to the hallway. "Apparently that's what you're taking, whether I want you to or not. So please, don't let me stop you."

Swallowing roughly, I stared at him for a beat before I brushed through the doorway. My coat was still in a crumpled heap on the floor and I dashed a tear off my face after I slipped it on. Nothing good would come from me standing there, with him pissed and me feeling cornered.

I pulled my purse over my shoulder and looked at him before I walked out the door. His eyes made my stomach quiver, my heart pulse violently. The intensity in his eyes shook me, tightened my chest like it was in a vise.

But I still walked out the door.

I held everything in while I drove, while I crept quietly through the house and into my room. When I curled into a ball on my bed, I turned into my pillow and finally wept.

CHAPTER TWENTY-TWO

JULIA

My head felt like a bowling ball, my eyes were scratchy and raw, and they'd probably feel nicer if I'd taken sandpaper to them to dry them out. But I didn't realize just how bad I looked until I came into the kitchen the next morning and caught a glimpse of Brooke's face.

"Oh ... my ... word," she whispered. "What happened to you?"

I sat in a chair across the table from her. She stared, open-mouthed, at whatever horror that was my face and hair. "Why are you out of bed?"

"Good Lord, Julia, you sound like you smoked a pack of cigarettes last night." She blinked. "And I can handle walking down the hall to get some tea. We've got my thirty-two-week ultrasound today, remember?"

With my elbows propped on the table, I leaned forward until my head was held up by my hands. "Sorry. I did forget."

"No worries, we've got plenty of time. Now, do you want to tell me why you look like someone punched you in the face with a bag of hormones?"

I laughed under my breath. "Nice, thanks."

"Don't stall."

Why couldn't my parents have given me a brother? He'd never have badgered me like that. But, I realized with a sharp pang, without Brooke's meddling, I probably never would have seen Cole again after the grocery store. And I hid behind her as an excuse not to rush my relationship with Cole.

"I'm such a bitch," I whispered.

Brooke leaned forward and tapped my arm. I lifted my head up and she gave me a sad smile. "It can't be that bad."

"I lied to you," I said in a rush. "I slept with Cole the day we met for coffee, and I did it again last night after you were in bed. I told him I didn't want to tell you that we were ... I don't know, dating or whatever, because you'd put so much pressure on me about it and I wasn't ready for that. And last night we got in a huge fight. Like, really huge. So I cried myself to sleep. Hence the," I waved my hand in front of my face.

Her mug was suspended mid-drink, and her dark eyes widened where she was staring at me over the rim. Slowly, she lowered it, holding my eyes until it hit the table with a soft click. Very calmly, more calmly than I thought she was capable of, Brooke took a deep breath and folded her hands in front of her on the table.

"Let's address things one at a time." She cleared her throat. "First, I'm not stupid, and the walls of my apartment were more useless than cardboard. When you came home from *coffee*," she held up her fingers like air quotes, "you looked like Rachel McAdams after that one scene in *The Notebook*."

My face flushed and I traced the seam of the table. "Why didn't you say anything?"

Brooke snorted. "Look, I'm bored out of my skull, it's fun to watch you pretend like you're keeping some big secret from me. It's like my own private soap opera. Every time you thought I wasn't paying attention, you totally stared at his ass while they were moving boxes yesterday."

I laughed briefly and then sobered. Cole's words ran endlessly in my head, and I was unable to pull the film off track.

"What did you two fight about?"

I glanced up at her. "I'm going to give you the short version, because I really don't want to cry again. I feel like I've cried more in the last month than in the last five years combined."

She smiled at me. "You really have been a massive crybaby."

"I can't even argue," I said glumly. I took a deep breath. "He doesn't trust me, and I can't blame him."

Her eyes narrowed slightly. "Explain."

"How is he supposed to trust that I won't bolt again?"

"Do you want to?" she asked gently.

"No," I answered slowly. "But even after all of this, there's still things we haven't talked about. And I can't imagine they'll be any easier than the previous conversation." I pointed to my face. "We can all see how well that turned out."

"What things?"

"Family things," I exhaled. "Baby things. Adoption things." I glanced quickly at her ever-growing stomach and smiled. "I still want kids, Brooke. I'm sure he does too. *How* are we supposed to start over?"

"You're not starting over, Julia. You're starting fresh. You're both older, hopefully wiser, with a hell of a lot more life experience under your belt. If you and Cole decide that you're going to try this again, it's not a continuation of your previous relationship. It's a new one."

I dragged the tip of my fingernail across the pad of my thumb. "That's easier said than done."

"Yeah," she said easily. "I know that. And look, I'm the one who said you were a chicken shit when it came to Cole. While I could have probably used a little bit more tact than that, it's still true. You're sitting here giving me all the things that will get in your way, but the reality is that *you* are the only thing getting in your way."

Staring at my little sister while she said so many horribly honest, incredibly wise, mildly insulting things, my heart hammered in my chest and my tongue fairly itched to argue with her.

But I couldn't.

Brooke grabbed my hand and looped her fingers through mine. "Tell him what you're afraid of. Don't spend so much time digging in your own head, second guessing things that don't need to be second guessed."

We sat in silence after that. Brooke finished her tea and let me be. When my little sister became the harbinger of the best kind of life-changing advice, I didn't know.

"When is your appointment again?"

She smiled at my change of my subject. "Ten. We'll get another ultrasound today."

"Good. Something to look forward to." I stood from my chair and went to press a kiss to the top of her head. "I'm going to hop in the shower. Need help getting back to your room?"

Brooke shook her head. "Go. I can manage."

The entire walk from the kitchen to my bedroom, and on the drive to her OB, her earlier words rang through my head, delivered with a hefty boom every single time. She was right, I was the only thing getting in our way.

Now, what to do about it?

Two hours later, we sat around the table again, dissecting the orange and white blobby photos from the ultrasound.

"She looks like an alien," Brooke said and turned the photo to the side.

I smacked her arm. "She does not. She's perfect. And look, she's totally got your nose."

She smiled and traced the edge of her little button nose. "Look how he's trying to touch her, but that damn sac is in the way. And doesn't it look like he's smiling?"

"It does," I agreed, reaching forward to touch the shot in awe. "They're pretty amazing."

"They are," she said softly.

The ultrasound tech had printed off four shots for Brooke, the rest going on a CD that I tucked into my purse for her. They were growing well, Baby Girl was around three pounds and Baby Boy was about three and a half. Their heart rates were strong, and Dr. Robinson advised continued bed rest, much to Brooke's chagrin.

I squeezed her shoulders. "Keep bakin' em, momma. You're doing good."

Brooke groaned dramatically. "But they're so big. I feel like I'm going to explode." She rubbed at her sternum. "And my chest is on fire. All the time. I will never not have heartburn."

"Still no names picked out?"

She groaned again, even deeper and more dramatically than a few seconds earlier, and I laughed. Very carefully, she folded up the pictures and set them in the middle of the table, staring at the top one for a while. "I have some ideas. It's weird though. Like, even though I can feel them rolling around inside of me, they're still kind of abstract."

I swallowed roughly and busied myself with pouring us both some water. "I bet." When I set the glass in front of her, she was staring up at me, and it took me a second to meet her eyes.

"You wanna know the strangest thing though?"

I pulled the chair away from the table and sat in it. "Sure."

"I'm not even really pissed at Kevin anymore for leaving, because he doesn't deserve a shot with these kids if he's not man enough to stick around, but..." she paused and took a sip of water, "sometimes I wonder what he'd want to name them. Or whether one of them will remind me of him. Like, will Baby Boy laugh the way he did? Will it hurt me to hear it? Will they hurt someday because they weren't enough for him to stay around for?"

This time when I swallowed, it wasn't a stall tactic against my own emotions. Suddenly, my fears about Cole felt petty and insignificant. As if I'd used my own hand to whip them into a manic frenzy that they'd never been to begin with. My fears had been valid once, and maybe they still were, but hearing my normally happy and optimistic sister put voice to her own fears sobered me, humbled me.

Hers had no choice but to be faced and conquered, because she was choosing to be brave enough to do it. Kevin hadn't been that brave, and neither had I, with Cole.

"I think," I started slowly, "that you will love them so fiercely that they'll want for nothing. You are already such a good mother, Brooke. Better than anything you and I ever experienced."

She blinked at me with eyes bright with tears and nodded quickly. "And they'll have you, too. Coolest aunt in the continental U.S."

I laughed, watery and tremulous. "Don't sell me short. Coolest aunt in the whole world."

Brooke nodded again, wiped at a stray tear that fell down her cheek. Unbearably moved, I got up and moved around the table to where she sat and got down on my knees. I cupped her stomach and pressed my forehead to it.

"Do you hear me?" I whispered. "You two are so loved. There is nothing in this entire world that will ever change that." Brooke sniffed and I did the same, pressing a kiss to my fingertips and pressing it against the hard edge of someone's foot. Or elbow.

By the time I stood up, Brooke had tears streaming down her face. "Lordy, I'm too hormonal for shit like this."

"Well, I'm not done yet." I brushed her hair off her face and made sure she was looking at me. "You are one of the bravest women I have ever known in my life. I think I want to be Brooke Rossi when I grow up."

"Yeah?"

I nodded. "Yeah."

She clasped my hand. "All you need to do is get out of your own way. It's normal to be afraid of something, in any relationship, but I can guarantee that whatever you're afraid of is not bigger or scarier than how amazing it could be with you and Cole if you just give it a chance. You just have to show him that you'll face every single one down, and you'll do it with him by your side."

Brooke's phone started ringing on the kitchen counter, effectively snapping the heavy moment. When I saw who it was, I laughed under my breath. "Guess who?"

Her lip curled up a little. "I swear, Dad must have written down my appointments in his calendar. It's freaky."

I took a deep breath. "Actually, do you mind if I take this in my room first? I need to talk to them about something. I'll pass the phone along to you when I'm done."

She grinned. "Go get 'em, tiger."

Even though I rolled my eyes when I left the room, I was smiling when I answered the call. "Hi, Dad."

"How's Brooke?" he boomed on the other line, his Italian accent heavier now that they were in Capua. I could hear my mom in the background asking something, but he shushed her. "She had an ultrasound this morning, didn't she?"

"She did. Everything looks great." I turned into my room, or what would be the guest room after I moved out, and shut the door quietly before sitting on the edge of the mattress. "I can pass the phone to Brooke in a minute, but I actually wanted to talk to you and Mom about something."

"What's wrong?" my mom piped in, sounding tinny once my dad put me on speaker.

"Nothing," I told her. "Can we actually switch to FaceTime for a second? I want to see you both when I say this."

They both started talking, obviously both reaching to hit the right buttons and their phone clattered to the ground so loudly that I had to pull my own away from my ear. My mom tsked at my dad, and then the chime in that they were starting a FaceTime call with me. I accepted it, and found myself staring the wall of their villa.

"Mom, turn the camera the other way," I said patiently.

"You look terrible," she said on a gasp.

"Mom."

She mumbled under her breath, and my dad replied in Italian. *Donne testarde* was all I caught. Something about stubborn women. The camera swiveled the other way, and I could see half of both of their faces. They were both tanner than when I'd last seen them in person, and my dad had the puffy skin around his eyes that meant he was drinking a lot of wine, which was typical of his visits to Italy.

"What's the matter?" my dad asked with a slight frown.

"I just wanted to let you know something." I took a deep breath and tilted the camera so that I knew they could both fully see my face, see how serious I was. "I'm not going to get into details of how we reconnected, but I've been seeing Cole again since I've been back in Denver."

Immediately, my father started cursing under his breath, my mom gave him a hard side-eye and he quieted down. I held up a hand.

"I'm not joking, if you interrupt me while I'm saying this, I'm done. I'm not saying it again." They both nodded, my dad still looking wildly unhappy. My mom gave us the east coast blood of eastern European descent, so masking her emotions was practically a family heirloom.

When I knew they were going to stay quiet, I took a deep breath. "Thank you. I'm not going to blame the two of you for the fact that I left him, but if we're all honest with ourselves, you can admit that you heavily influenced me. But I did always love him. And by some miracle, I have a second chance. But I need to convince him that I'm not going to run again, and I have no intention of doing that. He has loved me in a way that defies any kind of logic, and even if he never chose to speak to me again, Cole is the love of my life. I don't know if we'll get married again, or how we might choose to start a family, but he is it for me. I will not entertain a single slight against him, so if you have something to say about him, don't say it to me." I held their eyes, barely blinked the entire time I spoke, but my knees were bouncing wildly, my heart doing something similar. "Okay?"

My mom lifted her eyebrows briefly, looked at my dad before turning the camera to her. "Okay. Thank you for letting us know."

It wasn't the happy family conversation, but that wasn't my relationship with them. If they'd answered with smiles and proclamations of encouragement, I'd question whether they were high or not, so her evenly spoken answer didn't really phase me.

"Thank you for listening," I said to her. "Do you want to talk to Brooke?"

She nodded, and I calmly walked the phone to my sister, who took it from me with a quizzical expression. I didn't stay for their conversation, simply went back into my room that was still filled with boxes and stared at the wall for a while.

Maybe there were things I could find on Pinterest for grand gestures to win over an ex-husband who didn't dare hope that I was here to stay for the long haul. Trust was precarious. Something you had to earn by showing up for someone over and over again. Even someone you'd never met before needed to earn your trust, no matter what another person in your life might think of them. An idea hit me, and I called Rory.

"Hey," I said as soon as she picked up. "Are you by Garrett right now?"

"I am," she replied cautiously. "What's up?"

"I need a phone number from you."

We hung up and she promised she'd text it to me. Once it came through, I fought a massive case of butterflies and clicked on the number, waited for the ringing to come through in my ear. Not surprisingly, since he wouldn't recognize my number, voicemail picked up after a few rings.

"Hi, this is Julia. I know this is going to sound crazy, but I'm wondering if you can help me with something kind of urgent. Please call me back as soon as you get this." I paused and took a deep breath. "I know you have no reason to trust me yet, but this is important, and I'd really appreciate it if you didn't say anything to Cole. Thanks."

I hung up and flopped back on the bed, cursing the fact that I could do nothing except wait. Not for long, apparently. My phone vibrated in my hand, and I bolted upright.

"Hi, Tristan," I said when I answered.

"What's urgent?" His voice was clipped, but not rude. Clearly, he was just someone who didn't like to waste time with unnecessary syllables.

"Well, I was kind of wondering if I could borrow you and your truck again."

The silence on the other end of the phone was loud, so, so loud in my ears. It took about ten seconds for him to answer, and I swear my heart beat three times faster than normal.

He heaved a sigh. "Depends on why."

I told him in an excited rush, and three minutes later, we had a date for the next morning.

CHAPTER TWENTY-THREE

COLE

Every time another minute ticked passed on the clock in my office, I felt it somewhere deep in my stomach. My empty stomach that didn't feel empty. I'd barely eaten in two days, but it felt bloated and sick, filled with sharp-edged rocks and a heaviness that I couldn't get rid of. Because every minute that passed was another minute that I was standing my ground and not reaching out to Julia. This time was different. When she walked out the door, I knew where she was staying, I knew exactly how to reach her. I knew that I could probably bang on the door to Brooke's house and ask to speak to her, but this time, I decided to wait. Decided to give her space.

I rubbed at my bleary eyes, gritty from lack of sleep and staring at my computer for too long in a dark office. But I didn't have much desire to go home. Even as I reflected on them now, I didn't regret the things that I'd said to Julia. They were necessary, unearthed in the moment from some part of me that I hadn't even realized existed until it burst out of me.

All the other things that we might need to face were truly secondary to the fact that I didn't know how to trust that she'd stay. With a weary sigh, one of thousands that I'd let go of in the last forty-eight hours, I closed my laptop case and unplugged the cord, putting everything I might need the next day into my bag. The office was quiet when I walked through, cubicles empty and offices closed up for the night.

My drive home was quiet, no radio to muffle the static in my mind or the heaviness in my heart. I didn't want to mute it, didn't want to water it down. It was completely possible that what I'd said to her would push her away from me. If that was the case, I wasn't even sure what I'd do about it.

There was no doubt in my mind that my heart would always be shackled to hers, especially after the last few weeks of having her back in my life. I didn't want to change that. Couldn't have changed it even if I did. The pervasive heaviness inside got worse as I took the last curve to my house, empty and dark, just like I'd left it.

But when I pulled past my neighbor's house, there was a light on.

I narrowed my eyes while I pulled my car into the garage, which was empty, just as I'd left it, and didn't see anything through the large front window. The guys had no idea what had happened with Julia, so they'd have no cause to pitch some pointless intervention for my moping. Since it was probably one of them, I took my time turning off my car and exiting, loosening the tie from around my neck, slinging my laptop bag over my shoulder.

The door leading from the garage into the back entryway was unlocked as I'd left it, and when I pushed it open, the first thing that I saw were two large cardboard boxes in the hallway leading to the kitchen.

"What the hell?" I muttered and slammed the door shut behind me. If Garrett was behind this, and the boxes were filled with sex toys or something, I'd slash the tires on his shiny black car. But when I turned the corner into the bright kitchen, it was not Garrett.

It was Julia.

My heart slammed into my ribs and the laptop bag slid off my shoulder, falling to the floor loudly.

"Hi," she said quietly. She stood slowly from the chair she'd been sitting in and knit her fingers together in front of her.

The rapid swell of excitement was overwhelming and almost took my legs out from under me, but I swallowed it down. Next to the table was another few boxes, and by the couch, there were more.

"Brooke kick you out?" I asked, just to test my suddenly weak vocal chords. Julia gave me a slight smile, and my eyes inhaled every inch of her. She was dressed simply, her hair loose around her shoulders and her face pale and perfect. She licked her lips, one of her rarely shown nervous gestures.

"No, she didn't." Julia took a deep breath and walked toward me. When she came close enough that I could've touched her, my hands started to shake with the need to reach out, but I held still. Her eyes were so clear, each vivid bit of hazel, browns and golds and greens, I could've tried to count each different color if I wasn't trying not to pass out. Julia's hands slid up the lapels of my jacket and smoothed the fabric. "And I won't let you kick me out either."

I let out a low laugh, incredulous and impatient. "Care to explain?"

Her hands moved again, up the sides of my neck until she cupped my face. "I will wear down every single fear between the two of us, Cole. I know you have them, and I do too." She pulled my head down until our mouths brushed together. Her breath was sweet, and I couldn't not touch her anymore. I gripped the back of her neck, underneath the heavy fall of her hair, swept the other down the length of her back when she started speaking again. "I've run from my fears my entire life. And I never felt shame in that until you, because you are my deepest, truest love."

I had to pinch my eyes shut to fight the burn that I felt, especially when her voice thickened with every word that she said. "Julia."

She swept her fingers gently across my lips, and I pressed a kiss there before she pulled them away. "I will never run from you again, Cole. Never. Every single day, I will choose you, choose us, no matter how scary it might be, because I'd rather be side by side with you fighting against those fears than be alone."

Happiness streaked through me through, hot and bright, a lightning bolt to my blood, but it cooled before I could act on it. My words to Julia about not trusting her—a surprise to me even as they'd come out of my mouth—tempered that happiness with reality.

I closed my eyes briefly, staring at the stack of boxes after I opened them. Once I felt like I had the tightest possible rein on my emotions, I finally met her eyes, so full of hope and determination that I almost folded.

"You *left*, Julia. The other night, right as we were breaking through some really ugly shit, stuff that we needed to break though, you walked out."

"I know," she said quietly. "Crutches are hard to get rid of when you've never really tried to walk without them before. But they are gone now, I promise."

I lifted a finger and traced the edge of her lips like she'd done to me. My heart thumped heavily, undignified in my visceral response to her, simply from the feel of her mouth against my skin. Julia closed her eyes and pressed a kiss to my fingertip.

"It's probably crazy that when you're saying the exact thing that you *should* be saying, I'm the one hesitating," I admitted quietly. "I want to believe you."

"It's no crazier than the fact that we're even here." Her eyes searched mine, and the heat of her body was inviting, a temptation and promise that was almost impossible not to sink into. "No crazier than meeting at nineteen, no crazier than you and I never being able to move on from each other after so many years. Cole, we don't need to compare our love story with anyone else's. I don't care how crazy it is, if it brings us back to each other."

Hope prickled my skin, and I shook my head while her smile spread. "Why are you smiling like that? I haven't said anything."

She closed her eyes with a laugh. When she opened them again, there was a fiery determination in them that almost took my breath away. This was the Julia I'd met so many years ago, when I didn't even know what it meant to be a man.

"Because even if you aren't ready to believe me, I will prove it to you, every single day. Because I am not going anywhere, Cole Andrew Mallinson. You are it for me. I'll tell you every single day until you believe it."

Emotion choked my ribs, pressed them tight and I had to breathe through the sublime pressure. I lifted her in my arms and laughed. Her arms wrapped around my neck in a tight hold, and our mouths met in a fierce, sweet kiss. Julia folded her long legs around my waist when I boosted her up.

I broke away and buried my forehead into the curve of her neck. She smoothed her fingers through my hair and sighed contentedly. When I felt like I could look at her face and not cry incredibly unmanly tears, I lifted my head and caught her eyes.

"I love you."

Her fingers traced my eyebrows and down the bridge of my nose while I held her. She smiled and it felt like the sun broke open inside of me. "I love you, too." Her fingers curved underneath my eyes, and I knew I had dark circles there from how little sleep I'd gotten the last two days. "You look terrible."

I laughed and kissed her. This one was slower and gentler. A reunion and a promise, and we'd have a million more just like it. Her legs fell from around me, and she lowered herself until her feet touched the floor again. If she thought that meant I was going to stop touching her, she'd lost her mind. Her hair was silky and smooth under the palm of my hand when I curved it around the back of her head.

"I didn't sleep much."

"I didn't either the first night."

My eyebrows lifted. "Just one?"

Her smile was mischievous, and she lifted her chin at the boxes behind me. "I was too busy packing all the stuff I'd just unpacked in order to move into your house uninvited."

I slid my hands around the curve of her hips and pulled her into me. "Our house."

"Our house," she repeated.

"How did you move all this in here?"

Julia laughed. "I called Tristan."

"What now?"

With deliberate movements, she pushed my suit jacket off my shoulders and we both let it fall to the floor. Her fingers plucked at the buttons on my shirt until it was open, and my body tensed at the feel of her fingers against my skin. "I needed a truck, and I knew he was wary of me being around you again. Figured I could prove myself to him at the same time I proved myself to you."

Rational thought became harder and harder as she undid the cuffs of my shirt, since the front was completely opened. "Tristan is wary of everyone, I'm sure you're no different."

She leaned forward and kissed the center of my chest. "Do you want to keep talking about your friend?"

Her eyes were luminous as she looked up at me, and I took her face in my hands. "No."

We kissed until both of us had to pull away to breathe, and her eyes were shining.

"Good tears this time?" I asked quietly.

She nodded.

"Can I take you to bed now?"

She nodded again, a smile creeping across her face.

The only words we spoke for the next hour were *please*, and *I love you*. Over and over, until sweat covered my body and she was shaking and spent in my arms. And even then, we never stopped touching each other. Every inch of my body was felt by her fingers and palms, every inch of hers by mine. We spent time in spots that I might have overlooked, like the small notch of bone at the top of her spine when she rolled onto her stomach. Julia counted the freckles on my back, kissing each one that she found. Sleep pulled at both of us, and though the heavy drag of rest was welcome after the last few days, I withheld, finding something new on her that I'd never noticed before. The delicate furl of her belly button, or the way the skin underneath her ear felt like silk.

She talked about her life in Connecticut, and I spoke of mine during the time we were apart. Her eyelids started falling sometime around two a.m. and I watched her fight sleep. I rolled to my side and gathered her in my arms, fitting her head underneath my chin while our legs stayed intertwined. Her breathing evened out despite the tangle that our bodies were in, and all I could do was lay there and breathe her in, the sweet scent of nothing but happiness, contentedness that I never thought I'd feel.

Loving her was something I knew I'd do for the rest of my life, but feeling her in my arms again, knowing she was truly mine, was almost too much to wrap my mind around.

"I can feel you thinking," she muttered into my chest.

I smiled and nuzzled the side of her head. "Go back to sleep."

Julia pulled her head back so she could see me, and she was so adorably rumpled, so thoroughly loved by me over the last few hours that my heart expanded yet again. "What are you thinking about?"

"What a woman thing to ask," I teased and then yelped when she pinched my nipple. "Ouch."

"Don't be an ass."

My laughter came from the very edge of my soul, the part that only ever belonged to her. I sobered quickly and placed a light kiss on her lips. "I'm thinking that I love you."

She smiled up at me. "Don't you want to know what I'm thinking too?"

"Always," I murmured after another soft kiss.

"I'm thinking loving you is the greatest thing I've ever had the privilege of doing, and every single day, I cannot wait to show you."

Her arms wrapped more tightly around my back, and that's exactly how we finally fell asleep.

CHAPTER TWENTY-FOUR

JULIA

One week later

Cole watched me from the bathroom, his toothbrush still on its two-minute cycle and his lips covered with toothpaste. I pointed a finger at him when I saw the judgment in his eyes. "Don't you look at me like that. I'll find it eventually."

His brush turned off and he spit into the sink. "You could always unpack the rest of your boxes. Maybe you'd find your noisemaker."

"I wouldn't need my noisemaker if your ceiling fan didn't make that annoying clicking noise that keeps me up." So maybe I passive aggressively mumbled that while I dug into my third box that morning. Hence the reason I didn't hear Cole sneak up behind me and lay a toothpaste-filled kiss on my cheek. I laughed and pushed him away. "Gross! Go wipe your mouth."

He smacked my ass before he walked back into the bathroom. "Your wish is my command."

"Ick." I wiped the last of the toothpaste off my cheek, but couldn't wipe the smile off my face. Happiness felt like a stupidly insufficient word for our life since I'd stormed his house and moved my stuff in. I still spent the bulk of my days with Brooke while he was at work, but every night we ate dinner together, watched a movie or played a game before spending hours in bed before any sleep was had.

Yeah. *Hours.*

All those *Cosmopolitan* articles that talked about sexual prime being in the mid-thirties were so freaking right. Unpacking came far, far down the list of ways that I wanted to spend my time now that I was back with Cole. We were existing on this insanity-filled plane of bliss that I didn't even know was possible prior to the past seven days.

Except for one thing. The subject of kids still hadn't exactly come up.

Birth control was never a topic for us. Accidental pregnancy was too wildly optimistic, and I mean, we'd only ever slept with each other. But it's not like we needed to watch out for anything. And neither of us had broached it yet.

My phone rang from the kitchen, and I stood up with groan. Stupid inner thighs had been sore allllll week.

Cole winked at me from the bathroom when he saw me wince. I rolled my eyes. Men.

"Hey," I said to Brooke when I answered.

"So umm, remember when I told you that you didn't need to hurry over this morning?"

"Yeah." I wedged the phone in between my shoulder and my ear so I could pour myself some coffee.

"I'm officially retracting that."

I set the coffee pot down when I finally registered the sharp edge of panic in her voice. "Brooke?"

"My water totally just broke," she cried.

"Oh shit," I yelled and slammed my mug on the counter. "Okay! I'm coming. Are you having contractions?"

Cole came from the bathroom with a worried look on his face. I waved him off and ran to get my purse.

"A few, but they're irregular," she answered tightly. "Like, now, ow, ow, ow. But it's been about seven minutes since the last one."

I pulled my keys out and ignored Cole when he yelled my name. "Brooke's in labor," I yelled over my shoulder and yanked open the door into the garage. He ran after me and snatched my elbow. "*What?*"

"You're not wearing pants," he said with a soft smile.

Dazedly, I looked down and oh yup, sure enough, no pants. Just a t-shirt and hot pink socks. "Brooke, I'll leave here in thirty seconds. Do you think you can wait for me to pick you up or do you want to call an ambulance?"

She hissed out a breath while I yanked some yoga pants on and slipped some shoes on my feet. Thank the Lord I had a bra on already. Cole shoved my keys in my hand and dropped a kiss on my head when I ran past him and into the garage.

"Drive safe," he yelled. "Call me when you know anything."

I darted back through the garage door and pulled the phone away from my ear. "I love you."

He smiled. "I love you too."

"Oh, vomit," Brooke said in my ear, voice tight with pain. "Can you just *get* here already?"

The normally fifteen-minute drive took me eleven with some seriously questionable driving, and I was completely out of breath by the time I got to her bedroom and helped her out of bed, snatched the hospital bag that hallelujah, she'd had the foresight of putting together after her ultrasound last week. Apparently passing the thirty-two-week mark was some of sort of magic when it came to the whole gestation thing.

Brooke sat in the passenger seat and then looked up at me with horror. "Should we put a towel down?"

"*What?*"

"Do *you* know how to get amniotic fluid stains out of upholstery? It cannot be easy."

I slammed her door shut and ran around the front of my car. She yelled something about the front door and I looked back in exasperation. Sure enough, the front door was still standing wide open. I locked it from the inside and jogged back to the car.

"Oh my word, I'm out of shape," I wheezed while I threw the car in reverse and peeled down the driveway.

"You shouldn't be, with all the make-up sex you're having," Brooke said on a laugh.

"Shut up. Shouldn't you be panting through your pain or something?"

Her breathing picked up, and she gave me a panicked look when we got a red light. "Oh holy shit, Julia. I don't have a room ready! Where the hell am I going to put them?"

I reached out to pat her leg. "It's okay. We've got plenty of time. Plenty of time."

She looked at me with something akin to horror, and then we both burst out laughing.

Everything for the next couple hours was a complete blur. Triage was a bustle of measurements and monitors and them shoving an IV up Brooke's hand while she cursed so vilely that my ears actually blistered. The labor and delivery room that they wheeled her up to was larger than I expected, and in short order, she was moaning and writhing on the narrow bed, hooked up to more wires than I thought possible.

I kept her forehead covered with a damp cloth and generally tried not to piss her off.

"Oh my hell on earth," she gasped while I watched the little chart thingy that tracked her contractions. "I can't do this."

"Yes, you can," I said firmly. "The nurse is going to check in five minutes, and if you're past five centimeters, you can have the epidural if you want it."

As the words came out of my mouth, the smiling nurse came in and Brooke practically levitated off the bed. "Please, please, please for the love of all things holy, send the drug man in here."

There were veins popping in her forehead and I watched with wide-eyed wonder as the nurse went about her duties, completely unruffled by the possessed woman crunching my hand to tiny little bits. Luckily for Brooke, she was able to get the epidural, and twenty minutes later, after the very nice woman with the very big needle left the room, my sister was actually smiling again.

"I feel like I'm on vacation right now," she said with a blissed-out smile.

I looked up from my phone after sending Cole and Mom an update. "Good." My mom responded quickly, and I read it out loud to Brooke. "Looking at flights now, tell Brooke we'll get there as soon as we can."

She rolled her eyes. "Is it bad that I'm totally fine with the fact that it will take them at least twenty-four hours to get here?"

After tucking my phone back in my pocket, I lifted her cup of ice chips back up to her, and she waved them off. "Nope. I can understand that."

"Can I ask you something now that I'm feeling human again?"

"Of course."

Brooke watched the heart rate monitor for a moment and then glanced at me. "I meant to ask you this after the ultrasound last week, but it got too sappy too fast." She swallowed and ran her hands over her belly. Her huge, huge belly. "Will you be their godmother?"

"Oh, Brooke," I leaned forward and laid my hands over hers. "Of course I will."

"I can't think of anyone else that I'd trust with my kids if something were to happen to me." She blinked rapidly when a tear streaked down her temple and into her hairline. "I'm going to change my will next week, if you're okay with that. Make sure everything is in writing."

I could see her heart rate increase as she said it and I made a soothing noise before I stood and kissed her forehead. "You're going to outlive me by a long, long time. But you know that you don't even have to ask, right?"

She nodded and her eyes cleared. "Thanks, sis."

I kept one hand on her belly while her attention turned toward the TV on the opposite end of the room and I wondered at the little humans still inside of her. They weren't mine. How would I feel about them once I could hold them, kiss them, feel their little fingers curve around mine?

It made me feel inexplicably nervous. But I shouldn't have been.

Two hours later, and coming into the world one minute apart, I held my sisters' hand while we both sobbed as they laid the two most perfect little goop-covered lumps on her chest. The babies were whisked away almost immediately by nurses who washed them, weighed them, listened to their hearts and wrapped them into tight little bundles. Brooke wept in the bed, and I tried to wipe the tears off both of our faces.

"Did you see them?"

"I did," I whispered. "They are perfect. Just like I told you they would be."

"Here you go, momma. Can you handle them both for a minute?" one of the nurses asked.

Brooke nodded frantically, and I backed up so I could take a picture. In each arm, Brooke held an impossibly small bundle. I could barely see their faces above the blankets, and Brooke wept softly while she stared down at them.

"I don't know which is which," she cried and we all laughed.

"Blue hat is probably the boy," I said quietly.

"Oh yeah." Brooke sniffed and looked between them again. She gently lifted the arm that held the little pink hat. "Do you want to meet your niece?"

My heart pounded frantically in my chest while I put my phone away and then slipped my hands oh-so-carefully underneath the tiny little body. I cradled her against my chest and caught my first glimpse of her face.

And I was dead.

Poof. Just like that.

This was love at first sight. My heart exploded in a messy burst, and she was only half of the duo that I got to love now.

"Hello, beautiful girl," I whispered, staring in awe at the perfect curve of her lips, exactly like Brooke's. "Did your momma give you a name yet?"

"Piper Julia," Brooke said and I snapped my head up to stare at her.

"Really?" I asked, completely overcome. Oh, I'd be covered in snot for the next twenty-four hours at this rate.

She nodded and then smiled down at the other. "And this is Jacob Marcus."

I smiled at her nod to Dad, but also at her break from tradition. "Perfect."

The nurses took the babies for some more tests to make sure that everything was as it should be, and in a daze, I wandered down the hallways so that Brooke could get some sleep. I found myself heading toward the glass-lined wall of the nursery when I saw a wonderfully familiar tall, broad-shouldered frame staring in at the babies.

"Hey," I said softly.

He turned with a smile, wrapped me in his arms, and I cried at how happy I was.

"Is that them?"

I pulled back and wiped at my face, pointed at the two nurses in the back of the room that were checking out the twins. "Piper Julia and Jacob Marcus. Not even a combined eight pounds between the two of them."

"Amazing," he answered in a hushed, reverent tone. Cole wrapped an arm around my shoulder and drew me against him. "How's Brooke?"

"Good," I said absently and watched the women laugh and coo over my two new precious bundles. They better have washed their hands. Oh my word, I was losing it. "Do you know what terrifies me?"

"What?"

"I'd already kill for them."

Cole laughed, but quickly sobered when he saw my face. "Baby, what's wrong?"

I hiccupped out a sob. "I'm not even joking. Like, if someone tried to hurt them, I think I'd commit murder. And I've only known them for like fifteen minutes."

I collapsed in his arms, and he held me wordlessly while my mind raced. He didn't ask me what was wrong, just held me while I cried and when I finally pulled back, he wiped the tears off my face with a small smile. "Okay?"

Even though talking did not seem wise considering my current mental state, I took a deep breath and said the first thing that came into my head. "I think I was afraid I couldn't really love a baby if it wasn't ours."

Cole's mouth dropped open, and he looked beyond my shoulder before steering us to a small couch in an alcove. "Julia, what are you talking about?"

I sniffled, wiping under my nose with the back of my hand. Sobs caught in my chest and I had to actively try to breathe around them. "I ... I don't think I ever realized it before, but ... but I think I was afraid that if we adopted a child, I'd," I pressed a hand to my chest to make sure I wasn't dying, and then looked up at him again. His eyes were so soft, so full of love, that even more tears fell. My insides were cracking, everything from the last few hours spilling out of me in uncontrollable waves. "What if we'd gone through with everything and they put this perfect little baby in my arms and I didn't feel love for it? I would've *hated* myself, Cole. I think ... I think I was so afraid of that happening, of what would happen to us if it did, that ... that," I hiccupped and he tucked me into his chest without hearing another word out of me.

"Shhh," he whispered into my head while I cried myself out into his shirt. "It's okay. I'm right here."

His hand on my back moved in soothing circles, never ceasing, never slowing. He didn't pry, and he didn't push. There was no judgment in his eyes when I pulled back and attempted an embarrassed smile. "Sorry, I don't really know where that came from."

"Hey," he cupped my chin and gave me a soft kiss. "Don't apologize for something like that. I think we needed that to happen, yeah?"

I shrugged my shoulders, feeling like I had a bowling ball strapped to my head from all the crying, all the emotion. "When I saw her, saw Piper..." I trailed off and shook my head. "I loved her so much, I almost felt like I could *die* from it." I looked up at him. "I don't know why, but it took me by surprise, I think. At how much I did."

"Good," he said. "It doesn't surprise me though. You love so easily, Julia. But if that's not a path that you're ready to go down, then we won't. Simple as that. I love you, and with Brooke's babies and your crazy-ass parents coming back, we have plenty to keep us busy. Whatever you want to do."

"Really?" I sniffled and wiped under my eyes.

"Really." He cupped the side of my face. "We can do this whatever way we want, but all that matters at the end of the day is that we have each other. That's all I need to be happy."

"Right now, I think that's all I need too." I sighed and leaned my forehead into his chest. "You're too good to me."

"I know," he agreed.

I pinched the skin on his side and he laughed.

He nodded to where the nurses were wheeling the twins back down the hallway. "Want to follow them? I'd like to meet these little people who made my wife into a crazy person."

I laughed and then drew back. "Your wife? Getting a little ahead of yourself, aren't you?"

He kissed me again and then whispered against my lips, "You're my soul, Julia. My *wife*. You'll never not be a part of me."

The same thing he said to me the day we got married. The first time. We walked back to Brooke's room hand in hand, and I had a strong suspicion that we might not be able to wait much longer to get back to that courthouse.

I didn't care if we had a big wedding, or just the two of us in front of the same judge as last time.

All that mattered was that we had each other. Everything else was just details.

EPILOGUE

JULIA

Six weeks later

"You think it's enough?" I asked Brooke, turning and looking over my shoulder in the mirror. The simple ivory dress fit snugly against my body, the deep V in the back showing almost my entire spine.

She looked up from where she was nursing Piper on a couch in the family restroom at the courthouse. "I think it's sexy as hell, Julia. Hottest bride I've ever seen." She paused and raised her eyebrows. "Again."

My hair was swept up in a complicated twist of braids and curls that Brooke had slaved over that morning. This time around, Cole went full-on traditions. I'd spent the night at Brooke's and hadn't seen him since the day before. Outside of the restroom where Brooke and I finished getting ready, Cole was waiting with Dylan and Kat, Tristan and Michael. Garrett and Rory were out there too, the newly married Mr. And Mrs. Calder. They went in a similar route when it came to tying the knot, a simple ceremony in front of a handful of people.

There was a knock on the door, and Brooke called out that it was occupied.

"It's Rory."

I leaned over and unlocked the heavy wooden door, and she popped her head in. "You're almost up. Only one couple in front of you guys."

"Thanks, Rory," I said. She winked and shut the door.

"Nervous?" Brooke asked while she wrapped a sleeping Piper back into her muslin blanket and laid her in the front seat of the double stroller that took about half of the room.

I smiled at Piper and Jacob, both sleeping soundly. "Not in the slightest."

She hugged me after she stood up. "Good. Let's go do this."

After one last look in the mirror, I smiled and held the door open for Brooke. Maneuvering the stroller deftly, I saw her smile widen when she looked into the hallway.

The swarm of butterflies took flight, and suddenly, all I wanted to do was run to Cole, who I couldn't even see yet. Brooke looked back at me and gave me a comically wide-eyed look. *He looks hot*, she mouthed.

My small bouquet of bright blue forget-me-nots was still sitting on the bathroom counter, tied with a simple white ribbon. The door had swung closed again, and I knew Cole was waiting for me, but I took a moment of quiet to reflect on the magnitude of what we were about to do.

There would be no tears today, I'd spent all of those in the days and weeks leading up to the moment he proposed to me again, which really was the same quiet, reverent mood that we were invoking today. He found my ring in a box while he was helping me unpack, and while I was sleeping, he woke me up by sliding the ring back on my finger.

Those were the last tears I shed, while I kissed him, whispered yes against his mouth, even though it was a mere formality for us at that point. I picked up the small bundle of flowers and pressed them to my face, the fragrance of the vibrant flowers filling my heart with the sweetest sense of peace.

Our future wasn't something that scared me anymore. The unknowns were things that we were going to face head-on, by each other's side. Our family would be complete someday. We agreed to one more round of IUI, then we were going to try our hand fostering a newborn, no matter what the outcome of the procedure was. I'd already printed out the information we needed to get the process going, and the prospect excited me unbearably.

Another knock came from the other side of the door, and this time, I knew it was Cole.

Instead of calling him in, I took a deep breath and opened the door. Except it wasn't Cole, it was Michael, nervously tugging at his tie.

"Hi," I said with a confused smile. "Can I help you?"

"Cole is waiting in the courtroom."

He looked so uncomfortable, that I reached out and grabbed his hand. "You okay?"

"No," he said and rolled his broad shoulders. "Do you need someone to give you away?"

My mouth fell open and I laughed under my breath. "What?"

Michael squinted past me at the door and then finally met my eyes. "I heard Brooke tell Rory that your parents aren't here. And I didn't want you to feel like shit if you didn't have anyone to walk you down the aisle. Or whatever it's called in a courtroom." He took a deep breath and held out his arm for me. "So, I'd be honored to give you away if that's something that's important to you."

Warmth settled whatever nervous anticipation had sprung up during my quiet moment in the bathroom. I smiled at him and hooked my hand through his elbow. "Michael, that is probably the sweetest gift you could give me today."

I leaned up and kissed him on the cheek. His face flamed and he cleared his throat uncomfortably.

"You'll make someone very happy someday," I told him, unbearably touched by his gesture, even though I would have been fine if he hadn't made it.

"Well, whatever you do, don't go spreading that around."

I laughed and he finally seemed to breathe easier.

"Shall we?" he asked, and I nodded quickly.

We walked into the courtroom, the stiff material of Michael's suit clutched underneath my fingers like a lifeline. As soon as we turned the corner, and I saw *him* waiting for me with a wide smile on his handsome face, my fingers relaxed, my heart sped up, and it took everything in me not to sprint directly to Cole.

His gray suit, white shirt and bright red tie only got the barest of glances, because I couldn't look away from his face, his eyes that glowed with so much happiness, I knew I'd cry before everything was said and done.

But I didn't.

We said our simple vows, part prayer of thanks, part lifelong promise, every word coming straight from our hearts. And when Cole wrapped me in his arm and sealed it with a deep kiss that I felt into my toes, I knew that there wasn't a single thing that we couldn't get through, if we were together.

Cole kissed the skin underneath my ear while our friends clapped and whistled, and then he whispered against my hair, "I'd wait another hundred years just to be able to be standing here right now."

I pulled back and cupped the side of his face, and smiled. "If you live another hundred years, then you're spending it with me."

"I wouldn't have it any other way."

We held hands and left the courtroom, ready to start our lives together.

Again.

The End

ACKNOWLEDGEMENTS

You'd think that on book six, these would get easier, but they just really don't. You either forget someone, or fail to put into words just how much a single person impacted your book-writing process, and it sucks. So … if I forgot to mention you, I promise that I'll want to kick my own ass about a week after the book gets printed and I realize it.

My husband truly had no idea what he was getting into when I first mentioned that I wanted to try my hand at this author thing. Support from a spouse isn't a given in this industry (in any industry, really), and I certainly don't take it for granted that I have it in spades. Almost four years into this crazy endeavor, he doesn't bat an eye at having hour long discussions with me about what a character might or might not do. Cole's intensity of emotion is something that reminds me of my husband, the way he speaks, the friendships he forms, and we spent more time talking about this character than just about any other one that I've written.

My parents, sister (and sisters-in-law!) and friends who read every single word. I can't fathom doing this without your unwavering support.

Another thing I don't take for granted is the group of women that I've been fortunate to be side by side with in the last handful of years. A tribe may be a trendy word to throw around, but I'm still claiming it in this instance. They don't live by me, which stinks a whole bunch, but it allows for some amazing weekends around the country in order to see them.

Whitney Barbetti and Jena Campbell (the only person who read Cole as I wrote him and helped shape the book into what it is now), my favorite people in the world to room with and text the day away. Katrina Kirkpatrick, Stephanie Reid (beat sheet and plot QUEEN who can never leave me as a beta reader) and Brenda Rothert who've been there since day one, and never fail to make me laugh. Chicago next spring needs to be a go. Just sayin. Staci Brillhart for being talented and funny and supportive. Every single one of these women (and more, who I'm so fortunate to know) make me a better writer, a better person, and I know they'll never judge me when I pour a glass of wine and lock myself in the bathroom because my kids are trying to kill my sanity.

My group of beta readers, Jena, Whitney, Stephanie, Amy Daws and Caitlin Terpstra. I wish I was someone who could write a book without feedback, but I just can't. Sorry, you're stuck with me.

Jade Eby for, yet again, making this book so gorgeous on the inside, and petting my hair when I worried about the opening.

Najla Qamber and Lauren Perry for creating the most gorgeous cover everrrrrrrrrr.

Alexis Durbin, Ginelle Blanch and Amanda Yeakel for catching my MANY errors.

J.R. Rogue for writing the most perfect poem for Cole. It makes my heart hurt when I read it, and that's how I know it's right.

Southern Belle Book Blog for my promotion, and for legit organizing the best signings I've ever attended.

My readers!! I love my reader group and how much they understand my love affair with wine and Outlander. Especially Christina Harris, who got lots of voice messages asking questions on Brooke's behalf.

Julia and Cole's struggle with infertility was a difficult tightrope for me to walk, and I hope that if this is something that's personal to you, you feel that I've done it justice. I know a handful of women that have been firmly entrenched in that war, and I have marveled endlessly at the grace, strength and determination that they show. Adoption is something personal to me, to my family, because we've been twice blessed by it. But I know that journey is not for everyone. Particular help to me in writing this book, and writing Julia, were my sister Renee and my beta reader Amy, for her unflinching honesty and insight. Thank you.

Hope deferred makes the heart sick, but a longing fulfilled is a tree of life.
Proverbs 13:12

OTHER BOOKS BY KARLA SORENSEN

The Three Little Words Series

By Your Side
Light Me Up
Tell Them Lies

The Bachelors of the Ridge Series

Dylan

Garrett

Coming soon

Michael (book four) will release in July 2017, and *Tristan* (book five) in October 2017.
And, in June 2017, a dark romantic comedy co-written with Whitney Barbetti, author of *Ten Below Zero*.

For exclusive teasers, content and giveaways, join Karla's Facebook reader group, The Sorensen Sorority
(facebook.com/groups/thesorensensorority)

ABOUT THE AUTHOR

Karla Sorensen has been an avid reader her entire life, preferring stories with a happily-ever-after over just about any other kind. And considering she has an entire line item in her budget for books, she realized it might just be cheaper to write her own stories. It doesn't take much to keep her happy…a book, a really big glass of wine, and at least thirty minutes of complete silence every day. She still keeps her toes in the world of health care marketing, where she made her living pre-babies. Now she stays home, writing and mommy-ing full time (this translates to almost every day being a 'pajama day' at the Sorensen household…don't judge). She lives in West Michigan with her husband and two exceptionally adorable sons.